LOVE BURNS

CALLAHAN CLAN, BOOK ONE

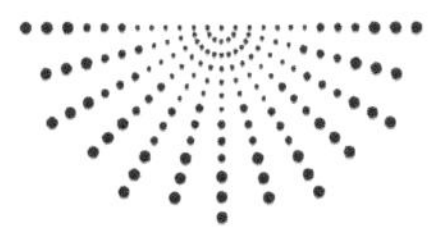

GREENLEIGH ADAMS

Cover by Wicked by Design

Published by Greenleigh Adams
www.GreenleighAdams.com

*To B.T.: You are my one and only. You are the best partner I could
have ever hoped for.*

1

CHARLIE

The grocery store can be a very dangerous place when you go in without a list. I should have made a list. I seriously thought I needed everything in every aisle.

Why in the world is the freezer section and refrigerated section on opposite sides of the store? Shouldn't they be near each other? When my only plan was to fill my cart with nonperishable items first, I had to shop the middle of the store and then head to the north and south poles for refrigerated and freezer items.

After that realization, I moved into the cereal aisle. When I turned into the row of breakfast junk food, planning to fill my cart with several boxes of cereal and oatmeal, I saw him. Surely my eyes were playing a cruel joke on me. *What the hell is he even doing here?* I held up a box of Froot Loops cereal to shield my face. *Hopefully, he won't see me.* Maybe I could just casually turn around and retreat down the aisle.

"Charlie?"

I heard *his* voice. The voice of my twin brother's lifetime best friend. The last time I had seen him, we were only eighteen years old—he was still a boy. It only took that quick

1

moment for me to see and hear him for me to discover that he was definitely a man now. He had seen me, so running now was out of the question, and continuing to hide behind the cereal box was completely ridiculous.

Even though I hadn't seen him in over five years, rather than act surprised—because I truly was—I decided to play it casually. "Hey, Louis," I said in my best monotone voice as I tossed the cereal box into my cart. Considering I didn't even like Froot Loops, it didn't really make sense for me to do that. But Louis didn't know that.

"Eating that kind of sugar first thing in the morning is bad for you."

I wondered what his feelings were regarding seeing me again after so many years had passed, but his blue eyes didn't give me any information at all. His expression completely lacked emotion, which completely annoyed me. *How dare he criticize my cereal choice?*

"What are you doing in town? I'm sure it's not to ridicule my breakfast preferences." Grasping the handle firmly, causing my knuckles to turn white, I pushed my cart past him and proceeded to examine the oatmeal section. I expected him to follow, but there were no sounds of movement behind me. So I peered over my shoulder, noticing that he wasn't looking in my direction. He was observing the protein bar choices.

I eyed him up and down without changing my position in front of the oatmeal. He was tall. *Is it possible that he's grown a few inches since high school?* His blond hair was cut short, and he had filled out well. His shoulders were broader, his T-shirt clung to his chest from his muscular physique, and his jeans hung low on his trim waist.

"See something you like, Callahan?" He didn't turn toward me. He continued to stare at the protein bars. But he noticed me staring. How embarrassing!

I had no choice but to pretend I wasn't drinking in the sight of him. "As a matter of fact, I did." I marched toward him and snatched a box of oatmeal off the shelf near him. "Apples and cinnamon." I waved the box in front of him and dropped it into my shopping cart.

He actually laughed at me. "You're still as feisty as I remember."

This time when I observed his facial features, I noticed his lips tugging up in the corners, and the most spectacular pair of blue eyes shone in my direction. They were two pools of cobalt-colored swirling water, and I could see my reflection in the sparkling spheres. I was about to say something to him, but for the life of me, I couldn't remember what. I was at a loss for words.

Has he always been this smoking hot? Surely not.

Abandoning the distraction of his good looks and spectacular physique, I was forced to address the heaviness weighing in my chest; and I remembered I was angry with him. He walked away from me all those years ago without even a goodbye. That memory left a tarnished spot on my heart and an emptiness within my soul. He didn't bother to contact me at all in the years that passed. I'd even called and texted him without a response. My cheeks felt flushed, and I was confused whether it was due to anger, heartbreak, or both.

"You still didn't tell me why you're here."

"I don't need to tell you anything." Redness flashed over the skin of his face, and he spun away with such intensity that his sneakers screeched against the sleek linoleum surface.

"Fine then," I retorted and shoved my cart from in front of the oatmeal section toward the pancake mix. As I dropped a box of pancake mix with a bottle of maple syrup into my cart, a hollow thud resounded behind me.

When I swung around to acknowledge the noise, I spotted an older man on the ground near the Pop-Tarts. Louis and I scrambled on our feet and approached the man.

"Sir! Are you okay?" My voice was loud and harsh as I stooped down on the smooth floor.

He didn't respond. He remained on the ground, motionless.

"He's not breathing," Louis said coolly as he lowered himself down next to me.

I placed two fingers on the old man's neck and attempted to locate a pounding blood vessel. "I don't feel a pulse." Before I finished pushing the words out of my mouth, Louis was already performing chest compressions. Knowing time was of the essence, I snatched the phone from my pocket and dialed 911. Holding the phone tightly in my grasp and bracing it against the side of my face, I was forced to endure the sounds of several elongated rings pulsating against my eardrum. *How can 911 not pick up on the first ring?* Although a mere few seconds ticked by, I decided it was taking too long for the dispatcher to respond, and the old man's life was at stake.

"We need an AED!" I yelled, scanning the aisle of the breakfast foods as if the life-saving automated external defibrillator would be located there. The sooner we could restart the man's heart, the better chance he had for recovery.

Still pumping away at the old man's chest, Louis tilted his head back and narrowed his eyes. "I saw one by the front entrance."

With desperation fueling my instincts as I continued to await the voice of assistance from emergency personnel, I accepted his direction with a nod and rushed toward the front of the store. Thankfully, a lot of businesses have automated external defibrillators available for laypeople to use when they witness a cardiac arrest. Years ago, a cardiac arrest victim had to wait for paramedics to arrive before having his heart essentially restarted with a jolt of electricity.

While running to retrieve the device, I finally spoke to the 911 dispatcher and reported the description of our location and what we had witnessed. I was away no longer than one or two minutes before returning to the cereal aisle, where a crowd surrounded Louis and the old man.

I forcefully pushed through the throng of people who were in my way and resumed my position next to Louis as I turned on the machine. "Apply pads to patient's bare chest," the machine directed. I did as instructed and interrupted Louis's compressions long enough to unbutton the man's shirt and applied the sticky pads to his chest.

"Plug in pad's connector," the machine ordered next. I followed the prompt as directed by the automated device and awaited the next step. "Analyzing heart rhythm. Stay clear of patient."

Louis removed his interlocked, overlapping hands from the man's breastbone and leaned back on his haunches. The man on the ground developed a blue hue around his lips that was spreading to his cheeks and still wasn't breathing. Louis, however, had heavy, labored breathing.

"Shock advised. Stay clear of patient," the machine stated. "Charging." The device sure did say a lot. "Depress orange button."

I surveyed the patient to assure that no one was near him and depressed the button on the device. The man jerked as a jolt of electricity dispersed through his chest.

"Shock delivered. Resume CPR." I guess the instructions needed to be super detailed for non-healthcare personnel.

In the briefness of a moment, I decided to take over chest compressions. I placed one hand on top of the other, interlocked my fingers, and pumped against the man's sternum as fast and as hard as I could.

"I can do that." The smugness of Louis's voice indicated to me that he obviously didn't have confidence in my ability.

"You pumped while I called 911 and retrieved the AED. Now it's my turn," I said, becoming breathless quickly. "The AED will let us know when it's time to switch."

"I'm a paramedic." *When had he become so arrogant?*

"So?" Two could play at this game. "I'm an ER nurse."

"But I'm a man."

Lord, he's become chauvinistic.

"And I'm a woman." The physical excursion of compression delivery was causing me to grow tired after only a few cycles, but I certainly didn't want to let him know that.

When the two minutes finally elapsed for the machine to analyze the man's heart rhythm again, and I could relieve my arms from the unexpected exercise they endured today, the commotion of the EMS providers arriving caught my attention. Louis spoke to them and aided in switching the patient from the store's AED to the ambulance unit's defibrillator. Meanwhile, I shifted my seated position, hoping to fade into the background.

Louis and my twin brother, Cameron, had been volunteer firefighters in a cadet program for our town's fire department when they were in high school, so it was no surprise that he knew one of the EMS providers. Using the commotion as a cover, I discreetly stood up from the floor where I had been kneeling next to the old man and tiptoed over to my shopping cart.

The man still hadn't regained consciousness, and I didn't feel the need to continue to gawk at him like all the onlookers from the store. Having only been an emergency room nurse for less than a year, I was certainly still considered new to my position. I lived these kinds of scenarios every shift I worked, but today was a day off for me.

The situation was obviously being handled, and the man

would soon be transported to the hospital, so I took the opportunity to resume my shopping. Clearly, I would need to revisit the cereal aisle once the ruckus dispersed.

As I roamed up and down each aisle, I continued to think that maybe I'd see Louis again. I scanned everywhere while still having a purpose behind traveling up and down the aisles. Once I approached the checkout lanes, I resumed my surveillance. I didn't see him anywhere. I guess I wasn't going to. I couldn't help but feel disappointment...and resentment.

He wasn't just my brother's best friend. He used to be my best friend too, and I felt like he had abandoned me after high school. I missed him. I didn't miss him the way you miss your friend who goes away to college. My heart missed him. I tried not to think about him anymore because the anguish was too difficult to bear. Fortunately, my efficient brain suppressed my thoughts regarding Louis for the last five years in order to protect my heart.

After putting away my groceries, the emotional toll from the day created an overwhelming need to clear my head, so I decided to take a run. Due to the addition of the physical toll that I suffered, I figured a short run was in order, not a ten-mile-long run like I sometimes indulged in. Four or five miles was long enough to clear my head but not long enough to completely wipe me out.

The month of June on the eastern shore of Maryland always starts out pretty mild. Since it was now close to three o'clock in the afternoon, I appreciated the mild temperature during my run. In the later summer months, I only ran early in the morning before the scorching temperatures reached their peak of the day.

I began my jog along my usual path from my apartment building along the bicycle path toward the park. But I decided I would alter my usual route and began to head in the direction of my parents' house. They only lived a couple of miles from me, but I rarely ran in my old neighborhood. The old women who reside there worked in their gardens this time of year, and they would always wave me down, making me feel obligated to stop my run and speak with them.

However, today was different. I wasn't sure if I was looking to speak to the older women of my childhood neighborhood after seeing the older man suffer from a medical event earlier today or merely looking for the comfort and familiarity of where I grew up.

I jogged past my old house almost twenty minutes later. My parents were both at work, so I didn't stop. I didn't see any of the older women in their yards like I had anticipated, so I was able to run without interruption. As I continued my journey along the neighborhood streets, I made an unexpected turn onto the street where Louis used to live. I wasn't sure what I was thinking—maybe I would see him? *Do I even want to see him?*

My mind was made up for me in a matter of a few minutes. As I approached his old house, not only did I see Louis, but my twin brother, Cameron, was standing outside of his house waving me toward him. I made eye contact, so I couldn't pretend that I didn't see them.

2

LOUIS

I knew coming back home came with a risk of seeing Charlie. The rational side of my brain told me I would. But somehow, I didn't think it would be quite this soon. I only came back into town yesterday. Now, not only had I seen her, but I had also spoken to her *and* performed CPR with her on a random cardiac arrest victim in the grocery store.

I should never have texted Cameron. He was my best friend a long time ago. It felt like a lifetime had passed since we were together every day. I didn't just leave Charlie five years ago; I'd also left my best friend. However, talking with Cameron made it seem like no time had passed at all. I couldn't say the same about Charlie. She had grown into a beautiful woman. Now, as she jogged in my direction, I had to swallow the growing lump in my throat. *I was still angry with her, wasn't I?*

Even with wet hair plastered to her forehead, a flushed face, and a shirt that clung to her body from perspiration, she was beautiful. Her shiny, brown hair was pulled back into a ponytail, and her long, lean legs moved gracefully in an even stride. She had sun-kissed skin, most likely due to her running routine. *Did I not notice all these things about her when I saw her earlier today at the grocery store?*

"Hey, Lean Bean," Cameron called out to Charlie. I guess that nickname had stuck all these years.

She huffed heavy breaths as she approached my porch. "Hey, guys. What are you up to?" With her breathing still resonating air in and out loudly, she popped an earbud out and propped her hand on her hip when she spoke to us.

"I'm trying to talk Louis into coming out with us for a drink later." Cameron bounced a glare at me and then back to his sister. "I had asked him when he texted me, but he refused, so I figured I might be able to convince him if I showed up in person."

I wouldn't mind grabbing a beer with Cameron, but when he suggested the three of us go out together, I adamantly refused. "I'm pretty beat, Cam. Raincheck?"

"You two should go and catch up," Charlie said while still trying to catch her breath.

"The three of us should go. It would be like old times." Then he tossed that daunting glare between us and let out a forced sigh. "Well, before…you know…"

I was unable to stop the hard eye roll and hushed laugh that escaped while Charlie's posture stiffened, forcing her to shift her weight from one foot to the other.

"Come on. You two can't still be upset over some high school bullshit." He clenched his jaw, causing the muscles in his cheeks to twitch, and after a quick glance in our direction, he threw his forearms up in a frustrated gesture. "Seriously? It's been over five years. That just means it's even more important to talk this out, preferably over a few beers."

"Cam, I don't know. I've had a long day. Maybe some other time."

Evading the invitation due to her tired state was plausible, but her rigid body language implied there was another reason she didn't want to go. I figured her shifty gaze and deep sigh indicated she was uncomfortable and perhaps a little nervous.

"What are you both afraid of? Or are you embarrassed?" His questioning tone was emphasized as his eyebrows drew together and lines on his forehead deepened.

"I'm not afraid or embarrassed of anything," she curtly refuted her brother and then pulled her arms tightly across the front of her chest and jutted out her chin.

"Well, neither am I." I wasn't really sure what feelings I was having at that moment, but I didn't want either of them to think I was a wuss.

"Great! Then let's meet at Brady's Pub at eight." Cam clapped his hands together once and satisfaction swept across his face as his lips curled up.

"Great," she said, gritting her teeth together while she spoke and forced a fake smile on her face. I knew I hadn't seen her in a few years, but I could still tell when her smile was genuine and when the upward tug at the corners of her mouth was a cover for hidden resentment. *What does she have to be so angry about?*

"Great." I returned the same half-smile half-scowl in her direction. I didn't want her to think I was happy about hanging out with her, but somehow, I needed to convince my brain of that, too.

I pulled into the parking lot of the bar at five minutes after eight. I went along with meeting the twins, but I certainly didn't have to be on time. I didn't want to look eager about seeing Charlie again, even if I kind of was. I wasn't exactly sure when that happened. Initially, when I returned to town,

I was determined to avoid her or at least ignore her for as long as possible. I hadn't always felt that way. We were pretty inseparable early in life.

Cam and I became friends in kindergarten. We'd met on the school bus, and we were in the same class. Charlie had a different teacher that year, but during the time we attended elementary school, there were a few times that the three of us were in the same class. It really didn't matter, though. We were together all the time—before school, after school, during school, during summer vacation, and any other time possible.

Charlie was quite the tomboy, so she always followed us on any and all of our excursions. Living our whole lives around water meant that we weren't happy unless we had at least one foot in at all times. We would fish. She would bait her own hook, even though most girls didn't. We would swim in the lake, and a lot of girls thought the water wasn't clean enough. She didn't care. We would race in kayaks. She'd never win, but that didn't deter her from trying.

Sometime during high school, I began to notice her as more than just my best friend's sister. Puberty set in, and in my heightened hormonal state, I began to realize she was developing into a woman. I'd kept those feelings buried deep within me, trying my best to remain her friend, knowing that she wouldn't feel the same about me...until that night senior year.

That night, I'd spilled my guts to her, and she rejected me. I wished I had never told her how I felt. And now, all these years later, things were still awkward. We couldn't go back to just being friends again. Releasing those bottled-up feelings had somehow gotten her pissed off at me, and we didn't speak to each other again until today. She tried to call me a few times, but I couldn't bring myself to ever call her back. I didn't need to hear again that she didn't reciprocate my feelings.

I thought I had convinced myself that I didn't still have those feelings for her, but somehow, seeing her today—at my house, not at the grocery store—brought all those suppressed feelings to the surface. And again, it was apparent that she didn't feel the same. When she crushed me five years ago, I swore to myself that she would *not* be able to do that again. I assured myself that I would never let her have that much control over my heart again. I figured it was probably better that things ended before they could begin. If we started dating back then, she would've broken my heart at some point, far worse than what I'd truly experienced that night.

Deciding that I would no longer be affected by feelings I had years ago, I stepped out of my car and shut the door before slipping inside the pub. I scanned the tavern, and it only took a moment to locate Cam, who was waving at me from a high-top table near the bar.

Charlie wasn't at his table. Maybe she wouldn't show. It would be great if that were the case. I could spend time with my childhood best friend and not have to live through more torture of seeing his sister again. So I let myself relax and took the seat next to Cam. Within a moment of my butt hitting the wooden chair, a waitress was next to me, ready to take my drink order. I liked that my beer order was taken so quickly.

"Will my beer land at the table as quickly as the waitress appeared when I sat?" I asked Cam while looking over my shoulder at the waitress walking away. She sashayed toward the bar, successfully grabbing my attention.

"I like it here." Cam displayed a wide grin and raised his eyebrows up and down after glancing at the tight skirt clinging to the backside of our waitress. "Charlie will be here soon. She texted me that she was running a little late."

How can he switch from admiring our sexy waitress to talking about his sister?

Great. Just when I thought tonight wouldn't be that bad after all, he managed to conjure up the image of Charlie, and that picture completely invaded my mind. I couldn't even think or look at our waitress anymore.

I still managed to enjoy the time Cam and I had before she arrived. I caught him up on my life over the last five years, and he told me about his. I soon regretted that I hadn't kept in touch, but spending time with him tonight was like no time had passed. After we engaged in at least twenty minutes or more of good conversation and a couple of beers, he rose to his feet and waved in the direction of the door.

I swiveled on my stool to look at who he was summoning, and I found my eyes drawn to her for the third time today. She had her hair down in loose brown curls that hung below her shoulders, and she wore a purple T-shirt that dipped into a V and fit snugly to her torso, exposing just enough cleavage to cause an abrupt inhale from me. I think my new favorite color is purple. It only took that brief encounter for me to realize how difficult it would be to stay angry with her if the mere sight of her caused such a strong reaction from me. But I forced myself to remember that night, and I firmly decided to remain detached.

Watching her white jeans cling to her long, lean legs was difficult to ignore as she approached our table.

"Hey, Cameron." After a quick glance at her brother and a brief nod in my direction, she sat alongside Cam and me. "Louis."

"Charlene," I retorted.

Heat visibly rose in her cheeks and the warmth reddened across her face. Whenever I called her Charlene when we were younger, she would punch me in the shoulder. She did *not* like to be called by her given name. I guess it still bothered her.

Thankfully, the waitress appeared before our reintroduction became any more awkward. Charlie ordered a beer, which intrigued me. I guess she was still one of the guys... even though she didn't look like it.

"So can we talk about the elephant in the room?" Cam turned his head between both of us, expecting one of us to speak up.

Charlie sighed and broke the silence from the standoff that had held on for over a minute. "I don't know what to say." She stared at the beer that was delivered and set in front of her on the table.

"I don't, either." I honestly didn't know how to tell her that I felt like a fool for admitting my feelings for her all those years ago, then walking away from our friendship. Losing her as a friend hurt me more than the embarrassment of knowing she didn't feel the same way about me that I did about her.

"We used to be the three musketeers," Cam reminded us. "We were best friends—the three of us. Then you told Charlie you loved her, and she didn't feel the same way." His eyes stared at me while he nudged his sister with his elbow. "You both have moved on, so it's time we forget about the high school drama and become friends again."

I may have moved on as far as dating other women, but I never shared my heart with any of them, even if sometimes I shared my bed with them. He must be referring to Charlie in regard to moving on. She moved on the night after I confessed my love to her.

"I still don't know what to say." A nervous giggle released from Charlie no louder than a whisper beneath her breath before she pressed her bottle against her lips and took a long swallow of her beer.

"Can't you both just forget the whole thing?" Cam's pleading voice was drawn out as he continued his attempt to smooth things over between the two of us.

"That's fine with me." Offering no more than a shrug to my friend, I glanced over my shoulder at the waitress who brought my first beer. Once our eyes met, I pointed to my bottle. She acknowledged my gesture with a nod and headed to the bar, hopefully to retrieve me another bottle. I would need more alcohol if I was going to be able to forget *the whole thing*.

"I'm good with that. I can try to forget the whole thing, too." Charlie continued to focus on her beer as her fingertips picked at the label before indulging in another long swallow. I watched her throat move up and down, and as she did, a hint of scarlet spread along her neck and face again. In contrast to the warmth on her exterior, her chilly disposition had me no longer thinking she was nervous or embarrassed. As her cold stare darted at me, I was pretty confident she was angry with me. *Why the hell is she mad at me?*

"Great!" Cam slapped his hands together and practically jumped off the barstool. "I'm going to run to the john, and then let's play some pool when I get back."

Charlie's piercing gray eyes only grabbed my attention for a moment before she and I both found something else to look at instead of each other. *This is ridiculous.* I wished that night had never happened.

"I wish that night never happened." A quick rush of warm air blew into our close space with her contemplative sigh.

I whipped my head back around toward her. She just said what I was thinking. *Can she read my mind?* "As do I."

"We ruined everything." Her eyebrows scrunched together while coldness rolled off her shoulders as those wintery eyes bore into me.

"You mean *I* ruined everything." I was fully aware of the

role I'd played in the exchange that night. I didn't need the accusation she was throwing at me with her silent actions to feel guilty. I already accepted the blame.

"Are we really going to do this here?" She waved her hand around, emphasizing we were in the presence of a bar full of people.

"I thought we were going to *forget the whole thing*." After all, that was the agreement we had just made with her brother.

"I know what we said to Cameron, but it wouldn't be the first time we told him one thing and did something else." I saw her lips turn up ever so slightly, as if she was trying not to smile. "How about all the times we played hide and seek in the woods without him?"

She was trying. I'd give her that. If she could smile, then maybe I could bend a little. "Or go fishing without him?"

It only took that one comment for a smile to sweep across her face. I hadn't seen her smile in years. I hadn't seen *her* in years. We used to be friends. I used to know everything about her, and she knew everything about me. Now I was looking across the small cocktail table at the smile of a girl I used to know, and the beautiful woman that I didn't know at all. And she was truly beautiful.

"It hurt when you left, you know."

Her bright smile faded when her teeth hid behind her lips as they pressed together into a thin line.

"I had to get away." A deep inspiration forced me to look up. Then with an extended exhale, I tilted my head back down as I forced air out through my nose. The conversation was beginning to get a little too deep, and Cam would be coming back from the bathroom at any moment.

"If I knew I was going to lose my best friend, maybe I would have considered your proposal." A glossy sheen coated her gray eyes as water covered her steel-colored orbs.

"Proposal?" I scoffed. I had to lighten the mood. "I asked you to prom, not to marry me."

Her clenched fist connected with my upper arm, and I flinched. *She truly punched me in the shoulder.* Nostalgia struck me, and I was overcome with memories of similar interactions between us during our friendship. "I told you I wasn't interested in you that way…" Her voice wavered, and I wasn't sure if that meant she was going to cry or yell. "…because I didn't want to lose you as my friend." And then the collection of water held by the rims of her eyes broke out of their confinement and flowed down her face in two rivers of tears. "But I lost my friend anyway."

And now *I* really didn't know what to say.

3

CHARLIE

How do I go from being angry at Louis to crying because of him? That revelation was enough to make me angry by itself. *And why did those words come out of my mouth?* I never had any intention of telling him the truth. Since that confession left my lips, he sat silently staring at me.

Thankfully, Cam showed back up before the full-out sobbing I felt rising in my chest was ready to pour out. "Hey, why don't we grab a pool table..." My brother's voice trailed off as soon as he observed the tears streaking down my face. "Actually, I left my phone in the car. I'm just going to grab it, and I'll be right back." And then he left. He walked out of the bar. My brother fucking left me crying on a barstool.

"He's so subtle," Louis mumbled beneath his breath. The swishing sound of the beer in his bottle from him swirling it around was louder than his declaration.

But even as soft as his comment resonated, it drew a chuckle out of me. My brother was certainly anything *but* subtle. I wiped the tears off my face, raised the glass bottle to my lips, and chugged my beer. "I really should be going." Once the amber liquid finished its descent down my throat, I slammed the empty bottle back down on the wooden table, creating a vibrating clang.

With a quick exit in mind, I began my descent from the barstool, but before my shoes could meet the floor, a warm hand clasped around my wrist. "Please don't go." I had my gaze focused on the door, so I wasn't facing him when his throaty, husky whisper sent a delightful shiver through me. *Has his voice always been this incredibly sexy?*

With salty tears still stinging my eyes, I stopped myself from moving away from him and turned to meet his stare. "I feel like a fool. I want to ease away from here with a little dignity." But I made no attempt to pull my wrist out of his hold. Now with my feet firmly in place, I just stood in that spot and admired his beautiful face. Those amazing blue eyes held me captive, and I couldn't walk away. It was like he had a magnetic hold on me that I couldn't escape. His chiseled jaw made him so ruggedly handsome, and the way his short blond hair was styled in that just-out-of-bed look had me completely mesmerized. "I am completely embarrassed." I was surprised that I could even squeak out whispered words by that point.

"Don't be embarrassed."

I knew he was trying to reassure me, but I just wanted to run away from the situation. That was if I wasn't completely frozen in place, of course.

"Come on, Charlie. Sit down." The stool screeched across the smooth tile as he pulled it out and patted the seat.

Once he released his grip on my wrist, my butt fell onto the stool with a loud plop. *That was unquestionably not grace-ful. What's happening to me?*

"I miss our friendship, too. It would be nice if we could go back to being friends." His gaze remained fixed on my eyes as the comforting sound of his voice provided me with the reassurance I desperately sought. Maybe he didn't hate me for what I did to him. At least maybe he didn't hate me anymore.

A buzzing sensation erupted from the back pocket on my jeans as my phone vibrated in response to an incoming text message. I pulled the device out of my denim-clad pouch, not because I was really interested in the text message, but it allowed me to pry my eyes away from his piercing gaze. The text was from Cam. **Text or call if you need me. I rolled out. You two looked like you needed to work things out… just the two of you.**

"Cam isn't coming back." I sniffed back another sob at the declaration of my brother's permanent departure.

"You knew that as soon as he walked out the door." He cocked his head at me as if it was completely obvious that my brother had ditched us.

"Yeah, he's really uncomfortable in front of crying women." I shrugged knowingly. "That's how I always got my way."

Louis flashed his megawatt smile in my direction, and somehow the comfort I briefly felt envelope me was replaced with an overwhelming feeling of emptiness. I had really missed him. I missed us. The waitress arrived with the beer he requested with his silent gesture. "She'll take another, too." He bounced his pointed finger from me to the empty bottle sitting on the table, causing the waitress to throw a dramatic eye roll before she walked back toward the bar. Louis gave her a brief glance but quickly returned his gaze to me. "She was a lot more attentive before there was a girl sitting at this table."

"I could go." I knew he didn't want me to go, but I needed to mess with him a little, so I stood up from my stool again.

"You never were very good at playing games, Charlene." Irritation rang through his clipped words. I knew he was annoyed with me, and he retaliated by throwing out my birth name. Calling me by my full name was always a surefire way to irk my nerves.

As childish as it sounds, I regressed to pulling my arms in a crisscross pattern over my chest and stomped my foot against the floor. Then his laughter rang out loudly. His amusement was not expressed with a lighthearted snicker. It was a full-out belly laugh.

Only a few seconds lapsed before snorts escaped his nostrils, and he grasped at his sides while attempting to maintain his balance on the barstool. I found the combination of hilarity from his display of merriment mixed with the tickling echoes of his wails contagious. So before I even realized what was happening, I was laughing too, complete with my own snorting and side-splitting pain. Somehow a calming presence once again washed over me, and I plopped onto the barstool next to him. It felt good to laugh that hard. My very soul was ecstatic to be with Louis after so many years of being without him.

Our fit of laughter eventually subsided, and we exchanged several long, cleansing breaths before he managed to be the first to speak between us. "I've missed you." There was that sexy voice. Even with the tail end of a laughing fit, his voice was low and husky.

"I really hope we can be friends now." I could sense my loneliness lifting and feel the emptiness in my heart filling with love for him. All the pent-up anger that I had been holding on to for the last five years was finally disappearing. There was no longer a place inside me for the resentment. As cliché as it sounds, I truly felt like there was a huge weight lifted off my shoulders. "So, how long are you going to be in town?" I wasn't ready for him to leave already. I needed to know I would be able to see him more before he left.

"I hadn't determined that yet. I have off work for a couple

of weeks." The intensity of his stare drew me back in, causing me to attentively regard every one of his movements.

As he lifted his beer bottle toward his mouth, I watched it touch his lips, and when he swallowed, I examined his Adam's apple as it moved up and down. *What's wrong with me?* "Why do you have off from work?" It occurred to me he told me he was a paramedic when we were in the grocery store earlier today.

"Just a minor injury. But protocol is protocol." He didn't look injured to me. The way his chest tightly stretched out a T-shirt and the definition of the corded muscles of his arms certainly gave me the appearance that he was fit enough to do anything he physically wanted.

"Well, I'm glad it isn't anything serious." If he could give chest compressions to that old man for endless minutes, it couldn't be that bad. "So, *friend*"—I emphasized for him— "what have you been up to the last five years?"

A sullen expression promptly crept across his face as his eyes narrowed and those lines expressing delight across his forehead disappeared. I wasn't sure how my question caused such a reaction. *Did I ask something I shouldn't have?*

"I mean, you told me you were a paramedic…" I stammered and sputtered my speech, trying to retract anything offensive I might have said, even though I wasn't exactly sure what that was.

Thankfully, his stern expression softened as he cut off my words with his own. "Yes, I am. I've been working as a career firefighter and paramedic for the last three years." In between sips from his beer, he explained that he'd gone to a community college to become a paramedic, and then he went to the University of Maryland to acquire a bachelor's degree in fire science. Currently, he was working for Anne Arundel County Fire Department. *He had only lived one and a half, maybe two hours away from me for the last five years. We* could've seen each other if we had wanted to. Sweltering, all-consuming sadness and sorrow developed deep within my core on account of that realization.

"How about you?" I wasn't sure how I was going to respond as the scorching heat from stomach acid ascended. "Emergency room nurse, right?"

Somehow, I managed to push the lump crawling up my throat back down and nearly coughed out my response. "Yeah, I went to Sandy Cove University." He had been at my house when I opened my acceptance letter. I guess he remembered my career aspirations and dreams. "Got a degree in nursing and went to work at the hospital in town after graduation."

"I'm sure the ER suits you. You were always looking for adventure when we were kids. I know that kind of job offers that to you on a regular basis." It was true. I'd always been an adrenaline junkie. I loved that rush of excitement that came along with saving a life. Even though he had been gone so long, he still knew me so well.

After leaving the bar, I made sure to text my brother that I was fine and heading home. Of course he asked if things had been rectified with Louis. I assured him that we managed to smooth things over. Cam responded with several smiley faces. I swear, he was such a girl sometimes.

I was scheduled to work the next day. Even though it was a Saturday, the ER remained open every day of the week. And since I'd only been a nurse for a little over a year, I was still working the night shift. In a way, it was a good thing I didn't have to go to the hospital in the morning, because after an hour of lying in bed and staring at the ceiling, I couldn't manage to fall asleep. My mind refused to rest.

Nagging memories about Louis haunted me every time I tried to close my eyes.

Talking about that night helped alleviate some of the current simmering tension, but I still didn't know what his thoughts were back then. *Why did he leave so abruptly? Where did he go? Why did he end up at a community college?* He had been accepted to Florida State, so I knew he would leave after the summer, but he left a hot second after graduation without even saying goodbye. In fact, he didn't say anything to me after that night.

The three of us were sitting in the basement of my parents' house watching TV. I was sitting on the couch with my legs folded up underneath me, and Cam was sitting on the opposite end. Louis sat in the armchair that'd been deemed "Lou's chair" as it seemed to be his spot. That was where he always sat when he came over to our house, which was every day. If he didn't come over to our house, then he was either sick or on vacation with his family.

We spent the entire day fishing on the lake in our canoe. I caught a small bass. The boys didn't catch anything. But we had a great time. We always did. My brother and Louis were my best friends. I always found girls to be a little too...well, girly. They didn't like to swim in the lake or go fishing. They never wanted to get their hands dirty, and most of them were so busy chasing boys. Honestly, I thought girls were kind of boring.

It's not like I was never around girls. My sister Claudette was very much a girly girl. She is three years older than us, so she used to tell us we were juvenile with our outdoor antics. She repeatedly told us one day we would grow up and realize farts weren't funny anymore. And for the record, I could armpit fart better than Cam or Louis.

I laughed to myself about that recollection. *We were exhausted after our day on the boat in the sun, so we came back to the house to eat dinner and relax. It was a Friday evening, so like every Friday evening, my parents had ordered pizza. We each* grabbed a few slices and retreated to the family room downstairs to eat and relax in front of the television. We drank soda and had a belching contest. I could belch the loudest, but Cam could belch for the longest duration. Louis could pretty much belch on command without needing the effervescence of the soda bubbles.

So we were curled up in each of our own satiety, and Cam began to doze off. After the third or fourth drop of his head, he told us he was going to bed. Louis and I each said good night to him. I stretched my legs out on the couch once my brother retired for the night, and Louis stood up from "his chair" and sat next to me, sinking into the cushions. Anywhere else, it would not have been strange for him to sit next to me, but it felt weird at my house where he had his own favorite spot.

He lifted my legs gently and slid beneath them so that they rested across his lap. I don't remember what was on television, probably because I was focused on his unusual behavior. Once his fingertips touched my leg and massaged circles into the muscles of my thigh, I blurted out, "What the hell are you doing?"

He withdrew the pressure from his fingertips on my leg immediately but turned his torso toward me rather than facing the television as we had been. "I need to tell you something." His sweet innocence displayed in his facial features and I was convinced he was going to tell me bad news.

"What's wrong?" Worry and concern grappled in my belly. I left my legs on top of his, but panic was hastily rushing through me—like I might need to get up and run away at a moment's notice.

"Nothing's wrong." His blue eyes danced around in circles like magical swimming pools reflecting back at me. "I just need to talk to you." I nodded for him to proceed, and I remained frozen in my spot with my calves still sitting on top of his thighs. "I've... started to develop feelings for you other than friendship."

Crap. That's not even remotely close to anything I thought he would ever say to me. I didn't know what to do or what to say, so I just sat there motionless while he continued.

"I want to be your boyfriend." Absolute shock pulled a lurid gasp from within me. "I want to take you to prom." As his head drooped forward, a whooshing sigh left him and his shoulders fell from their usual proud position. "I want us to be together."

Then he raised his head up and with the slightest of lateral movement, his piercing gaze searched my eyes. I'm not sure what my eyes said, I just know my mouth didn't say anything. Apparently, whatever my eyes told him, gave him an indication the best thing to do at that moment was to drag my legs off his lap and drape his body over me. Then, while hovering a few inches from my face, he leaned in further and gently brushed his mouth against mine.

I remember thinking how soft his lips were, but it only took half a second before I started thinking, what the hell is happening? This is Louis! *Since my mind wasn't working clearly, my lack of resistance encouraged him to deepen the kiss. I felt like he was stealing my breath away, but at the same time, he provided me much-needed oxygen. If I didn't keep kissing him, I wasn't sure if I would be able to breathe again. So when his tongue swept across the seam of my lips, I willingly parted them and allowed him access to the inside of my mouth.*

He tasted like pizza and cola, which were two of my favorite things. He was one of my favorites, too. His tongue was warm, and the surging heat began to dissipate throughout my entire body. Our breathing increased, as did my heart rate.

The kiss deepened, and soon, we were kissing each other with passion and desire neither of us had ever known in our eighteen years on Earth. I could hear a heart beating fast and loud. I didn't know if it was mine or his, but there was likely a bomb ready to detonate. My brain decided to work again because with that realization came a moment of clarity.

I had made out with boys before, but no one had made me feel this way. And this was my brother's best friend. This was my *best friend. I didn't want to lose him as my friend. I didn't want some passionate necking to be the reason we couldn't be friends. I didn't want him to be my* boyfriend. *I wanted him to be my friend. I had a couple of boyfriends during high school, but both of those relationships ended. I didn't want my relationship with Louis to end, so I did probably the hardest thing I ever had to do. I pushed him away. With flames licking and sparks flying during our teenage make-out session, I halted the fire.*

After I successfully shoved him off me, Louis fell back, away from me, and the noises of heavy panting pierced the silence as his chest rose and fell dramatically with his erratic breathing.

I tried to normalize my own breathing because I needed to tell him how I felt. But his fingertips stroked across my face, and I thought I would melt into a puddle right there on my parents' couch.

"I love you, Charlie," he managed to force out through his labored breathing. Then he drew me into his chest in the most tender embrace I had ever experienced. He rested his head on my chest for several, unmoving moments. My chest continued to rise and fall rapidly, but he made no attempt to move his head.

"I'm sorry, Louis, but I don't feel the same way." I would have never had the nerve to say those words if those blue eyes of his had been boring into me. Even still, tears emerged from the depths of my eyes. I didn't want to hurt him, but I didn't want to hurt us *more.*

Only a brief glimpse of time lapsed before his head jerked away from my galloping heart, and he lured me into an entrancing state with those cobalt-colored spheres. I knew he was peering right into my soul. Because of our tethered connection at that moment, I thought he would see right past my words and know that I loved him, too. But instead, sadness fell across his face. The corner of his eyes sagged, and his demeanor wilted. I swear his mournful expression made me feel like I had just told him his dog died. His slouched posture uttered devastation and heartbreak, and I was all too aware that I had done that to him.

With a sluggish movement, he flopped his dejected body off the couch. No words were said by him as he shuffled his feet along the hardwood floor and stomped up the stairs. The squeaky hinge on the side door screeched as it opened, followed by a soft thud as it shut. The basement was cold and empty...much like the broken heart tumbling against my breastbone.

I figured I would see Louis the next night at prom, but he didn't show. I briefly saw him at graduation one week later, but we didn't speak to each other. I found out he left town shortly after that. I wasn't sure when he departed exactly because he didn't say good-bye. He didn't say anything actually.

At that point, I knew I had probably made a bad choice, but I was only eighteen. *How could I have known that things would turn out the way they did?* Now, at twenty-three, I not only realized I made a bad choice, but I also realized I needed to make things right again.

Before today, his last words to me were, "I love you, Charlie." Maybe I couldn't make him love me again, but I could at least make him *like* me again. He said he was going to be around for a couple of weeks. I prayed that it was an adequate amount of time for him to forgive me. I didn't want him to leave again without saying goodbye. If I was completely honest with myself, I would admit that I didn't want him to leave ever.

4

LOUIS

Well, today was a lot more exciting than I had anticipated. Had I known that returning to my hometown would've been like this, I doubt I would've done it. Or maybe I would have done it sooner. Aside from the unexpected CPR, seeing my best friend again had gone better than expected. Cameron didn't question why I hadn't seen him in five years. He didn't ask what had taken me so long to come home. He just inquired about what had been going on in my life. I filled him in, and we went right back to where our friendship was.

I wish I could say the same about seeing Charlie again. She had been my friend during the majority of my childhood years. I should have thought more about how telling her that I wanted to be her boyfriend would impact our relationship. But when you're young and foolish, you don't necessarily think before you act. I'd just needed to tell her. I'd had to get that elephant off my chest before I left for college.

However, being young and foolish came with great heartache as well. The impulsiveness that went along with being young and foolish yielded great anguish. That anguish became less and less the older I got, because I'd created fewer opportunities to make myself vulnerable. I'd decided there would be no more heartache for me after I left home. I'd decided that I would never put myself in that situation again. A human being could not possibly have his heart crushed beyond repair more than once in a lifetime and continue to live.

I sound like a sap, but being young and foolish also meant that I didn't have much life experience to deal with the anguish and heartache. I just knew I had to get away. So that's what I did.

I'd called my cousin Drew and explained that I needed to get out of town for a while. He was only five years older than me, but he owned a landscaping company. My uncle had turned over the company to him, but not before he went to college. My uncle wanted Drew to learn how to run a business, not just the art of landscaping. So Drew had gone to college and graduated with a degree in business. Then he was essentially handed a company to run.

Drew offered me a job working for him the summer after my senior year of high school, but he lived near Washington, D.C. It was almost a two-hour drive from the town I grew up in. I didn't care at the time. He also offered me a free room in his house where I could stay. Desperate to get away, I accepted his offer of a job and a place to live.

I'd joined a local firehouse near my cousin's house as a volunteer during that summer, and it didn't take long to decide that attending Florida State in pursuit of a degree with an undecided major no longer appealed to me. I liked being an EMT, and I liked being a firefighter, so I'd made the decision to become a paramedic. The certification program yielded a two-year degree, and I was able to attend school while keeping my job at my cousin's landscaping company. My volunteer firehouse set me up with a program that paid for my paramedic degree, so I also had the luxury of attending college without going into debt.

After I graduated and passed the registry for a paramedic, I was promptly hired by the Anne Arundel County Fire Department. Training school was tough. It was physically and mentally challenging, but I survived. I was only twenty at the time. I wasn't old enough to buy beer, but I had a career and a two-year college degree. The benefits for health insurance, dental, and vision were impressive, but a twenty-year-old doesn't really care about those things. However, finding out that the organization would pay for my education did pique my interest.

So I continued college and graduated with a degree in fire science from the University of Maryland. I didn't work for my cousin full time anymore, but I still worked most of my days off when the weather was warm. I only worked two days a week as a paramedic. Don't get me wrong, they were grueling days. Each shift was twenty-four hours long. But luckily, I had three days off in between each shift to recover.

I still belonged to a volunteer firehouse, but I found it more difficult to put in as many hours as I used to. I'd moved out of my cousin's house and into an apartment close to Annapolis once I landed my paramedic job. Although I had lived my life and had good experiences, I didn't realize how much I'd missed my hometown until I returned yesterday.

I didn't realize how much I'd missed Cameron and Charlie until I saw them today. I guess I had been keeping myself so busy that I hadn't allowed myself any time to miss anything. I had heard that everything in life happens for a reason. Maybe my minor injury had happened so I could reconnect with my two friends again. Even with meeting various people and making new friends, Cameron continued to be the best friend I'd ever had. And Charlie, well...the verdict was still out.

As I lay in bed that night, I shifted uncomfortably from my back to my side, and I thought about her. I don't know why, but as I drifted off to sleep, I thought about why purple was my new favorite color.

❦

"Louis!" I could hear my mother yelling, but I was riddled with confusion as my brain tried to wake up from the sleepy fog. I guess I had forgotten I wasn't at my apartment again. *Is it morning already?*

"I'm going to work. Call if you need anything," she hollered again. This was the way it had always been. My mother didn't come upstairs and knock on my door. She would just yell it was time for dinner, or I had a visitor, or it was time for school. It was strange, because my mother was a librarian, so she told people to be quiet all day at work. I used to say she suppressed her natural urge to yell all day long at work so that by the time she got home, she needed to yell everything and anything.

"Okay. Thanks, Mom!" I yelled back. I had only been home for two days, but it already felt like I needed to get out. I liked being able to do my own thing without answering to anyone about what I was doing, where I was going, or forced to be pleasant to anyone if I didn't want to.

I heard the click of the door shut downstairs, and her car engine roar to life outside of my window. My bedroom over-looked the driveway on the side of the house. I rolled over and tried to go back to sleep. However, now that I was awake, my body wouldn't cooperate. My back was itchy and uncomfortable, and no matter how I shifted my weight from one side to the other, it pulled and burned. I even attempted turning onto my stomach, though that wasn't a comfortable position, either.

So I rolled out of bed and decided to go for a run to clear my mind. After I pulled on a T-shirt and mesh gym shorts, I jogged downstairs to locate my sneakers. As I tied my shoes, I took in the silence. My father must have already left for work. There was no sign of him left in the house. The suit jacket that he wore usually hung by the door, and his brief-case usually sat on the breakfast bar. Both items were gone. I whipped back the curtains and peered out the glass panes lining the living room and noticed his SUV was also gone. I hadn't had much of an opportunity to see him in the couple of days I'd been home. His ritual is to travel into his office early and return home late at night.

My mother's work schedule had always allowed her to work when I was in school and be home when I was home. So of course, I had seen her several times over the last couple of days. Plus, she would leave me notes. She left me a note that just said she was happy I was home, and she also left me a list of items to get at the grocery store. Running into Charlie was definitely not on her list, but I always had a knack for getting additional items not included on the shopping list.

Because of my mother's personality and work schedule, she and I had always been close. My dad was gone a lot. In fact, Cameron's dad, Mr. Callahan—or Mr. C. as I always called him—taught me how to hit a baseball and how to ride a bike while he was teaching his own kids. He also played soccer and basketball with us. I was always a little envious that Cam and Charlie had such an amazing dad. My father tried to be a good dad in his own way. He bought me what-ever I wanted. And being an only child, when I had his atten-tion, I had it all to myself. We went on family vacations once or twice a year when he could get time off work, but most of the time, he still brought his briefcase and laptop and had to do some work when we were on vacation, too.

My mother never complained about my dad's long hours or his lack of involvement in my upbringing. She never really said anything negative about him in my presence. They were never very affectionate with each other in my presence either, in contrast to the Callahans. Cam and Charlie's parents were always kissing and hugging each other. While I was growing up, I wasn't sure which extreme was normal. Now that I'm a little older, I've realized that every relationship is different. Finding the right person that fits with you is what is important. I hadn't met that person yet, but I was only twenty-three. I still had plenty of time to meet that person who understood me and accepted who I was without feeling the need to change me.

Tossing the memories swirling around in my head aside, I breathed in a long inhale and headed outside. The sun had taken refuge behind some clouds, so it was a good time to go for a run. And since it was still early, the temperature hadn't cranked up to the miserable status it would reach later in the day. There was a slight breeze, and given that it was a little overcast, the sun wasn't directly glaring on me. Once I trotted into a slow jog, I realized I should have brought my phone and some earbuds so I could listen to music during my run.

Being alone with your thoughts isn't a pleasant experience. You find yourself questioning choices you've made, things you wish you had done, and things you still need to do. As the adrenaline coursed through my veins, I progressed to sprinting mode. I willed myself to run faster and harder as I rounded the corner onto the road next to mine, a mile from my parents' house.

I successfully managed a ninety-degree rotation in the perpendicular road's direction when a beautiful brunette jogged toward me. Earbuds were seated in her ears, and a pair of long, lean legs propelled her along the pavement.

Even though I sprinted full force ahead in her direction, she didn't appear to notice me.

I stayed focused. I continued jogging straight toward her but adjusted my path so I would slip past her. An oblivious expression hung on her face while she held a steady pace. "Hey, Callahan!" I yelled as I steadily approached her. I performed an overexaggerated wave to her, but she didn't pay me any attention. *Geez. Maybe I need to literally run into her for her to see me.*

I decelerated into a slow jog, so I didn't pass her too quickly. I intently observed her gaze until it finally connected with mine. Her gray eyes widened, and her mouth quickly formed an O.

"I didn't think you would notice me," I said as I changed direction and took a position jogging alongside her.

Without breaking her stride, she popped out an earbud and shot me a quick smile. "I don't like to talk when I run."

"Okay. I'll just keep pace next to you in silence." I had no idea where she was running to, but I figured I would go along. If she wasn't going to speak to me, then she couldn't argue. I was happy I ran into her, even if she didn't want to talk. Although I was used to being alone at home in my new life, being alone in this town where my old life used to be was suffocating. I did not enjoy being alone with my thoughts. And I so rarely was ever alone when I lived here that being alone now seemed strange and unpleasant.

"Suit yourself." She placed her earbud back into her ear, and we jogged together for several miles. Maybe not several, but at least four. We ran without saying a word to each other, and even though there was only the sound of our sneakers hitting the pavement, the silence didn't feel awkward. I didn't feel like we needed to have a conversation. I felt comfortable and content with just having my friend by my side.

When we turned the corner to my street again, I merely

waved and ran toward my parents' house, and she waved back to me as I retreated. Once inside, I grabbed my phone on my way to the shower and saw I had a missed call from Cam. He also sent me a text message. **Fishing today?** He had sent the message at eight fifteen. It was eight twenty-five now. *Maybe he hasn't left yet.*

Sorry. Went for a jog. Fishing sounds good. I'm in.

He fired back a reply right away. **Great! Be by in fifteen to pick you up.**

I needed a quick shower and an even quicker bandage change to be ready in fifteen minutes. Thankfully, Cam didn't arrive for another twenty minutes, and I was just pulling on my T-shirt when his knuckles thumped on the door. I knew it was him. It felt strangely bizarre to hear him knocking, though. I realized that the reason the sound of his fist pounding against the wood seemed unusual was because I had always left the door unlocked when I was expecting someone. I guess I should have practiced the same routine I used when I lived here. Back in those days, Cam and Charlie would just let themselves in. I really missed those days.

Cam pulled up in his pickup with a canoe strapped into the bed of the truck. I couldn't help feeling a little excited about going fishing. I hadn't been in so long. The only times I made it out on the water, it wasn't the same as when I was a kid out on the canoe with my two favorite people. Today, I managed a jog with one of my favorite people, and now I got to spend the rest of the day fishing with my other favorite person. *Why did I stay away for so long? Why have I denied myself the happiness I have been feeling these last couple of days?*

We didn't say much while we fished. After all, fishing typically involved quiet for success. Between Charlie's no-talking-while-running rule, and the voiceless fishing excursion I was currently on, I would have thought the twins were giving me the silent treatment.

The tranquil lake hosted sounds of frogs and crickets and was surrounded by loblolly pine trees displaying a lush shade of green. The calm water revealed only the occasional small ripple from a fish or some other underwater creature.

We caught several bass and bluegill and released each one of them. We may have caught the same ones over and over. I didn't care. I had a great time doing something I loved as a kid. And fishing with my best friend was just how I remembered. It was peaceful yet exhilarating at the same time.

We sat on the lake in his canoe for hours until we were starving for lunch. The heat from the sun high in the sky caused my back to become uncomfortable from my perspiration collecting beneath the bandages. We rowed to the beach area and lifted the canoe out of the water to tote back to Cam's truck. After sliding it back into its position in the bed of his pickup, we decided to grab food from our favorite diner right off the highway.

The diner was exactly how I remembered it. It even smelled the same. When I entered, an instant wave of nostalgia flooded my senses reminiscent of their pot roast and mashed potatoes. The aroma of biscuits and gravy hit me first, followed by the sweet smell of cheese fries. I figured I would have to order each of those menu items to satisfy my drooling taste buds.

The quiet calm that existed on the lake didn't last once Cam and I were seated at a table at the diner. Cam spoke nonstop. We didn't talk about anything important, but we still talked about everything. By the time he dropped me back off at my house, I was happily exhausted.

With determined effort, I trudged up the stairs to my old room and collapsed onto the bed. I'm not sure what time it was when I fell onto my mattress, but I heard my mother yell "Dinner!" and I shot out of bed in that drowsy fog like I had done earlier that morning. I had napped long enough that I knew I would have a hard time sleeping that night.

❀

My mother retired to her room at ten, and my father still wasn't home from work. I retreated to my room and stretched out on my bed. I knew I wouldn't easily fall asleep, but I did feel a little tired. At eleven fifteen, my phone vibrated with a text message. When I saw Cameron's name across the screen, I figured I better open it. *He must need to tell me something important.* **You still awake?**

Yes. Everything okay? I immediately began slipping on my shoes. I already thought that I would need to go somewhere.

Was going to head to the hospital to bring some of the nurses coffee. Want to go with?

Seriously, Cam? But I couldn't sleep, so what the hell? Why not? **Sure. Where should we meet?**

His text arrived within seconds of my reply. **I'll be by in ten minutes.**

I waited outside for his arrival. I reminisced about my childhood when I would sit on my porch and wait for the twins to pick me up to go to the movies or out to eat or canoeing on the lake at night. Comfort and contentment washed over me from those recollections, and I really liked that feeling. I especially liked how easy all those feelings came back as if I'd never left.

Within a few moments, headlights shone in my driveway. When I realized it was Cam's pickup, and not my father's SUV, I practically leaped off the wicker chair on my porch and hopped into the cab of his truck.

We weren't in the vehicle long before picking up four coffees through the Dunkin' Donuts' drive-thru and heading toward the hospital. I guess this would add to the nighttime adventures of Cameron and Louis. It did feel a little odd not having Charlie around for the adventure, though. I had seen each of them separately during the day, but I felt like the three musketeers needed to be back together. At least for the next two weeks while I was still in town. That intrusive thought of my leaving made me nauseated. *Do I really want to leave again? My life's now located two hours away from here.*

"Thanks for coming along. This is kind of a weekly thing I do," Cam said as he pulled into a parking space near the ER entrance and pulled me away from my thoughts.

"Is it because you are crushing on some nurse?" I couldn't help but laugh at my own comment. Cam was always the flirt. He loved the attention of many women, and therefore, he could never limit his options to just one.

He shrugged, which I took as an agreement in my assessment of the situation. I watched him grab the cardboard tray of coffees as we stepped out of the truck. I figured there were more than four nurses working—at least that was what I was accustomed to at the big hospitals I transferred patients to during my shifts as a paramedic. So I figured he had four favorites he brought coffee. I envisioned his favorites as young blondes with big breasts. Having known Cam nearly my whole life, he absolutely had a type he preferred.

I followed along behind him as he walked through the double glass sliding doors. "Hey, Cameron!" The voice of the nurse bellowed from behind a glass window. She pointed toward a wooden door and it swung open. I figured she pressed a button to open it for him. He merely waved and motioned for me to follow.

As I walked into what I assumed was the emergency room, I realized I was definitely in a small town. There were probably only ten or eleven stretchers in the tiny rooms separated by curtains. It was the smallest emergency room I had ever remembered walking into. I was used to fifty-plus beds and tons of people around all the time. There would be people lined up in hallways, in patient rooms, and behind random screen dividers. ERs were always noisy and crowded in my experience. This place lacked the clamor and massiveness I was accustomed to. It was quaint and eerily quiet. It felt surreal to me—as if I traveled back in time.

"Hey, ladies." Cam smiled while distributing coffee-filled cups to the three women dressed in navy blue scrubs at the nurses' station.

"You are the sweetest man." The woman from the front entrance was now standing in the nurses' station with us.

"Who do you have with you tonight, Cameron?" a young, busty blonde inquired. She must've been the one Cam had his eyes on.

"This is my friend Louis," he stated while smiling in my direction.

Even though I was standing several feet away from the women encircling my friend, I felt each pair of eyes rake up and down my body. I didn't appreciate the attention he created toward me. I wasn't like him. Having several women gawk at me made me feel incredibly uncomfortable. Cam, of course, ate it up like the last slice of pizza.

"Charlie is in a room with a patient, but she should be out soon," the third woman in scrubs said.

Crap. I'm a total idiot. Charlie told me she was an emergency room nurse. Cam didn't tell me we were going to take coffee to *her. Why am I suddenly self-conscious about what I'm wearing?* I was in a T-shirt and mesh shorts. Luckily, I had showered again since my fishing excursion earlier.

Her stern voice rang out as she approached the counter that Cam was leaning against. "You didn't get me decaf again, did you? I know you swear you ordered regular, but that last drink was totally decaf. I'm still not convinced you didn't prank me. I barely made it through that shift." She had her back to me as she laid a smack against the flesh of her brother's arm. That slap resonated and drew me into another memory from my childhood. I could recall so many times she playfully hit him on his upper arm as far back as early elementary school.

I felt compelled to approach her as she held a light conversation with her brother. I didn't give a damn about the attention of those other women, but I wanted Charlie's attention. Cam shifted his arms off the high worktop surface, causing her gaze to shift. She quickly jerked her head as if she finally caught sight of me from her peripheral vision and needed to convince herself that I was really there.

When our eyes met, my mouth went dry, and my palms leaked perspiration. She was so much more beautiful than those other three nurses. Her shiny, brown hair was pulled into a braid, and she had something shiny applied to her lips. *Why am I staring at her lips?*

"Hey," I managed to croak softly and throw an awkward wave at her.

"I didn't expect to see you here." I didn't know if my being here was a happy surprise or not. Based on the mystified expression on her face, I couldn't be sure.

5

CHARLIE

My brother showed up at the hospital with coffee once a week. He had always been a good friend and a great brother, but I also happened to know that he liked the attention from the young ER nurses who were stuck on the night shift with me.

Supporting my caffeine habit by bringing me coffee was one thing but showing up with Louis unexpectedly had my heart racing and my senses more on edge than the outcome any hot beverage could deliver. I loved how his chest filled out his T-shirt and those gym shorts hung low on his waist and showcased his muscular legs. And judging by the reactions of my co-workers, they liked the way he looked, too. I was never jealous of girls admiring Louis when we were in high school, but I'd be lying to myself if I didn't admit I had a serious problem with the three of them eyeing his body up and down now.

They practically had their mouths hanging open and openly drooled over his good looks and how amazing he looked in casual wear. I didn't like it one bit, but I hoped my watchfulness wasn't suspicious to anyone. As my eyes

43

connected with his, we held our gaze for several seconds. *What is this pull that we have to each other?* Once we were locked into each other's stare, neither of us could look away. We weren't able to break the union we formed. It was as if our minds, bodies, and souls were held to each other through our gaze. The beeping from monitors and ringing of telephones dimmed and eventually faded, and the periphery of my vision softened but darkened as if there was only a tunnel leading me straight to him. The light surrounding him was still bright, and I should have moved toward him, but my feet remained glued in their position on the floor.

Cecilia, a young nurse colleague, crossed the path that separated the few feet between us and consequently disrupted our connection. "It was very sweet of you to come along with Cameron to bring us coffee." Although I couldn't see her expression, the image of her fluttering her long lashes at Louis had my face burning as anger rolled through me. She was a petite girl, around twenty-two years old, with long blond hair that she defiantly kept around her shoulders and not pulled up and away from her face. Being on night shift not only meant we were less experienced, but with less administration looking over our shoulders, we didn't always adhere as strictly to the rules as dayshift employees.

We weren't deliberate rule-breakers, but we did bend the ones we didn't agree with. For example, we ate at the nurse's station, which is a big no-no on dayshift. Because there were fewer of us working during nighttime hours, it was not very feasible to sit in the break room for a thirty-minute meal. Because there weren't any bigwigs working in the middle of the night, many nurses preferred to go with the no ponytail look. I wasn't one of those. I liked to have my hair out of my face. I preferred a high ponytail when I ran, a messy bun while lounging at home, and a long braid when at work. Really, the only time I wore my hair down was when I wasn't doing one of those things. Functionality had always been my priority. But again, as I have already established, I'd never been a girly girl. However, many of the nurses I worked with very much fit that typecast. I wasn't sure why they went to so much trouble to arrive at work with their hair styled perfectly and makeup applied to their faces.

My brother might've had something to do with their wanting to appear their best. He showed up once a week but never the same day, and never at the same time. He was an athletic trainer for our old high school. September to June kept him very busy with sports practices and games every day, but it worked well for his internal schedule. He never liked to wake up early, and he preferred to stay up past midnight every night. I never knew why he liked to stay up late, but that's how he'd always been.

When we were very little, he would stay up late and raid the refrigerator and freezer. He wasn't even quite tall enough to reach the freezer, so he would push a kitchen chair up to the appliance to retrieve frozen goodies late at night. Our mother would wake up the next day to find melted ice cream cartons or sometimes the freezer door still open.

I'd told him that if he cut out the nighttime feasting, he'd be able to fall asleep sooner, but he didn't listen. He would rather skip breakfast than his late-night snacks. Despite his poor eating habits, he maintained being physically fit. He didn't like to run outside as I did, so we didn't often exercise together. He preferred to be chained to a machine at the gym like a treadmill or stair machine to have a good cardio work-out. Then, of course, he lifted weights, which I despised. Lifting heavy things had never been fun to me. I always chose to run and go somewhere. I loved the wind on my face and the sights that I saw. I loved being outside, no matter what the temperature was.

We both enjoyed riding our bicycles, which was a

workout we could do together. Because my brother was in such great physical shape, he turned many girls' heads. So once a week, when he brought coffee, the women I worked with would line up to flip their hair and flash their smiles at him. If he didn't come with a caffeine offering, I'd have put a stop to the flirtatious shenanigans he engaged in with my fellow nurses a long time ago. I guess I chose to overlook the embarrassing ogling to support my caffeine addiction.

Even though I had become desensitized to his banter with my female colleagues, I would not be okay with that happening with Louis. He was completely off-limits. I wasn't sure why I felt so possessive over him, but I surely felt quite territorial. Maybe it was because I just got him back into my life, and I wanted him to myself for a little while.

"Don't you all have more important things to do than to gawk at my brother and his friend?" I felt the movement in my feet return, and I nudged forward, determined to terminate the lecherous stares from my co-workers surrounding Cam and Louis.

"No," they replied simultaneously. Shameless. They were all shameless.

Thankfully, Cameron and Louis only stayed for a few more minutes during my shift in the ER and then headed out after some friendly goodbyes. My brother smiled at each of my co-workers, promising to see them all again soon, then he gave me a brotherly hug.

Green had always been my favorite color, but seeing it on the women I worked alongside from jealousy over our embrace? Gross. They longed for any touch with my brother, whether it was innocent or not.

Louis approached me after Cameron for what I knew would be a similar hug, but I held my breath, nonetheless. As he pulled me into him, the smell of his soap and after-shave tickled my nose. That mixture of fresh pine and crisp linens was the best scent ever to stimulate my sense of smell. It was Louis. It was woodsy and masculine. As I inhaled in one long breath, his lips delivered a light kiss on my temple. The skin on the side of my head tingled from the brief contact.

"Let me know when our next run is." His lips turned up in a smile, exposing beautiful white teeth, but I didn't say anything. My vocal cords were frozen, much like the rest of me. "I promise all running and no talking." Without waiting for a response from me, he walked away with my brother toward the exit while I stood motionless for several more moments. And just like that, I had become just like my gawking co-workers, shamelessly eyeing the backside of the most magnificent male specimen I had ever known. Two weeks wasn't going to be long enough with him.

I was exhausted after that shift, but I lay restlessly in my bed. I rubbed the side of my head that had been touched by Louis's soft lips. I had released the braid from my hair before I had climbed into bed, but I could still feel his touch. This was ridiculous.

After climbing back out of bed and opting for a warm bath, I could finally relax enough for my fatigue to allow me the sleep my body craved. I only slept for five hours, but I figured it was sufficient since I wasn't working tonight.

Bike ride? I texted my brother. I didn't feel like being alone, and Cam was always up for whatever adventure I was. Some things never changed. He had been my best friend since forever, but especially these last five years.

Although we pursued different majors, it was nice to attend the same college together. Then, after graduation, we chose to live in our hometown. So I got to see him whenever

I needed him. Fortunately, he enjoyed hanging out with me, too.

Sounds good. Be there in fifteen.

He arrived in ten. It usually took longer than ten minutes just to load a bike onto the rack on his truck, but somehow, he managed to load his bike, grab a helmet, and drive to my apartment in a very short period of time. Although we lived in the same town, I lived in midtown near the park, and our parents and Cameron lived on the east side, close to the lake. We each had one-bedroom apartments, which suited us just fine. I know we could have saved on rent by sharing a two-bedroom apartment or condo, but after some discussion, we agreed that we were grown-ups and thought it was best to have our own places.

Besides, with as fast as my brother went through women, it would be awkward for the entrance to our apartment to become a revolving door of Cameron's female companions and latest conquests. There were some things a sister didn't need to see, hear, or know, for that matter. However, he still knew me better than anyone, even though we didn't live together. Maybe it was the twin thing.

He had always known when something was on my mind, and oftentimes, he even knew exactly what bothered me before I even verbalized it. I'd always assumed he was extremely perceptive for a male. I, on the other hand, never seemed to have a clue what anyone thought. Hence the whole fiasco with Louis five years ago. I *never* knew he had any feelings for me other than friendship. I'd felt completely blindsided at the time. But for some reason, now I couldn't stop thinking about how things might have turned out if I had given us a chance to explore a new kind of relationship.

I opened the door to my apartment when I saw Cam pull into the parking lot and approached him, rolling my bicycle with my helmet hanging on the handlebars. Living on the first floor made transporting my bike in and out easier than if I had stairs to negotiate.

"Hey, Lean Bean. What's up?" His voice remained casual as he unloaded his own bicycle from the rack attached to the hitch on his truck. It would certainly be easier for Cam to throw his bike in the bed of his pickup truck, but I must admit, my brother didn't often do things the easy way. He would call it doing things the right way. I would always argue that taking a shortcut here and there never hurt anything.

"It's a great day for a bike ride." I smiled at him while I buckled my helmet in place. I wore my ponytail at the base of my neck today to accommodate the helmet. The high pony-tail that I usually wore with my exercise endeavors would not allow the helmet to fit across my head properly, and being an emergency room nurse, I would never ride without a helmet. Nor would I let anyone I ride with go without the safety precaution in place.

"Who do you think you're fooling?" The perceptive brother voice came out as Cam leaned his bike against him and secured his own helmet in place. "What did you want to talk about?"

"You always think you know everything." I let out a slight huff of a laugh, trying to avoid how he obviously *did* know me too well. "We go bike riding together all the time. Just thought it would be nice today."

"Okay. Fine. You aren't ready to tell me right now, but I really don't feel like riding thirty miles today, so fill me in before then, please." I received his clipped message loud and clear as he mounted his bike and began riding toward the path near my apartment complex.

I jumped onto my own bike and pedaled quickly to draw near to him. "Are we going to ride together, or am I going to spend the whole time trying to catch up?"

He slowed his speed and positioned himself to my left on the paved path, riding right alongside me. "Is this about Louis?"

See? He always knew before I even had to say anything. I pressed my lips together tightly, so I could think before words came out of my mouth that I wasn't ready to hear.

"So it is." A huge grin stretched across his face, but he kept his face focused on moving forward and watching things ahead of him rather than looking at my reddened cheeks.

I was certain the warmth I felt flush through them wasn't from the sun or the wind. It was from the emotion that stirred within me every time I thought of Louis now. "What do you think?" I might as well hear what his thoughts were regarding the topic since he was always the perceptive one.

"I think you're crushing on him." His grin quickly faded as his lips turned down and the happy lines at the corners of his mouth disappeared. "But he's leaving soon, Lean Bean. I know things ended badly before, and I don't think it's a good idea for you to pursue anything with him. You'll only end up getting hurt."

"I completely agree with you. I'm *not* going to let him know I'm crushing on him. I had my chance five years ago, and I chose not to pursue things then. I have no right to try now." The realization that I would never be kissed by Louis again caused a tight twist within my belly. "Please don't tell him or *anyone* what I just told you, Cam."

"Have I ever given away your secrets?" He really never had. He was the best keeper of secrets of anyone I knew. My sister Claudette was always such a blabbermouth. I couldn't even believe I ever trusted her with any information I didn't want the whole world to know. But Cam, I could trust with anything. One would think that two sisters would be closer than a brother and sister. But Cam and I were thick as thieves. The truth of the matter is Claudette was probably envious of our relationship. She tried to never let it show, but she was so often the odd man out. If I had to pick between hanging out with her doing girly things or spending time with Cam doing whatever it was that he thought of on the fly, I one hundred percent of the time chose my twin.

"No, I suppose you haven't, and I trust you will continue to do so."

LOUIS

A few days after I saw Charlie in the emergency room, I wondered how it was possible after all these years that I still harbored the same feelings for her as I did when I was eighteen. I supposed I wasn't as uncomfortable as I once was because I was absolutely terrified the night that I had spilled my guts to her. Now I felt more at ease with us, and she seems more receptive to being around me lately. I figure if I continue to act confident when I'm with her, she won't feel so uncomfortable with me.

When I showed up to her job with Cam the other night, she was genuinely surprised and taken aback by my hug and friendly kiss. I think I rattled her a little bit, and I had to admit, it felt pretty good. I was probably flirting somewhat, just as I had been at the grocery store the other day. Maybe I wanted her to realize what she missed out on. Perhaps I wanted to know that she found me attractive, even though she hadn't five years ago. I guess my ego needed a pick-me-up. If I said that she had crushed me when we were eighteen, it would've been the world's biggest understatement. But now I was receiving my redemption, as the slightest hint of regret peeked out. Maybe I was a jackass, because her feelings of the regret made me feel better.

I spent the last five years wondering if she continued to think of me or if she wished she would have chosen a different course for our journey if she had the opportunity to do it all over. I don't know that I would ever trust her enough to not break my heart, but I was confident I could be friends with her again. At least I thought I could. I was older now and more in control of my emotions.

Run today? I changed the dressing on my back, pulled on my mesh gym shorts, and had my shoes on and tied when she barreled through the front door of my parents' house.

Her loud breathing and heavy respirations broke up her words when she spoke. "I was already out when you texted, so I figured I would just come by." When her gaze hit me, the sound of her breathing softened, and the heaving of her chest slowed.

I wasn't a fool. I knew when a woman liked what she saw, and as I stood before her without a shirt on, I could tell she was taking in the view. "Like what you see, Callahan?"

My comment caused her to jerk her head away forcefully. It was so fun to tease her. Of course I pestered her plenty when we were kids, so it felt completely natural to ruffle her feathers. "You sure are full of yourself." A mumble purred from under her breath.

"Oh, come on. If I didn't harass you every now and then, it wouldn't feel right."

Her eyes peered back in my direction then. "I suppose not."

"Besides, I already know you aren't interested, so I guess I have to stroke my ego occasionally around you." I accomplished what I had set out to do, so I turned away from her, grabbed my shirt, and pulled it over my head.

"Louis, what the hell did you do?" She must have seen the bandage on my back when I turned around.

"It's nothing really. Just a little burn." I shrugged off her concern. I really was fine. I was more annoyed that I had to miss work than I was physically hurt.

"How did that happen?" Her voice was laced with apprehension, and I certainly didn't want her to worry about me. However, telling her the story of how I acquired the burn wouldn't help with her trepidation.

"It's a story for another time. I thought we were going to run."

"Fine then." Her disconcerted expression told me she was going to let the topic go temporarily, but she would ask again. That was fine with me. Maybe next time I'd be ready to talk about it with her. Just not now.

So we took off for a long run. I wasn't even sure how long we ran for, but I was pretty sure it was the furthest I had ever run in my life. If I had to guess, I would say it was anywhere between eight and ten miles. Since Charlie had the no talking while running rule, I remembered to bring my earbuds so I could have music occupy my brain while my arms pumped and legs loped in long strides. When we rounded the corner on our return to my street, I didn't run back to my parents' house as I had before. Confusion regarding my unusual course prompted her to slow down and eventually come to a full stop. I did the same.

She popped out an earbud, and with erratic breathing, she managed to ask, "Why didn't you go home?"

"I'm having a good time with you. I wasn't ready to have it end." Even though my legs were in desperate need of ice and ibuprofen.

She managed to stifle a giggle in between her quick breaths. "Why don't we go to lunch after we go home and shower?"

"Okay, I'll follow you to your apartment so we can shower. It would be weird for us to shower together at my parents' house."

A pink hue flashed through her cheeks, and it was adorable. Then she slapped my arm as I expected her to. "Louis! You know what I meant! You go home and shower, and I'll go to my home and shower…separately. We can meet up again afterward."

"Fine. We can do it your way. But my way is more fun." I waggled my eyebrows at her, and she shook her head at me while letting out that same little laugh.

"Come pick me up when you're finished. I'll text you my address." Her hair was saturated with perspiration, and her shirt clung to her chest from the sweat and heat her body had produced during our run. I was only half kidding about the showering. I definitely would have jumped into a steaming hot spray of water without the slightest hint of hesitation if she had taken me up on my suggestion.

"I don't know, Charlie. That kind of sounds like a date. I'm not sure we're ready for that. You're moving a little too fast for me."

She knew I was being flippant, but it was still fun to mess with her. "You need to stop with all the inappropriate comments. We're only friends, remember?"

"Believe me. I remember." Even though I had been taunting her and playfully teasing her, that last comment stung. "See you in a little while," I said with clenched teeth before I turned on my heel and took off in a fast sprint toward my parents' house.

The shower helped to ease my annoyance. I tried my best to let the water wash away the hurtful comment she had made to me. *Why was I angry with her comment anyway?* It wasn't like we were more than friends, or we ever would be, for that matter. I guess it was wishful thinking on my part that things could ever be different between us. She was only stating what we had agreed to, yet the hope I had possibly let shine through was now replaced with a dark reality. I needed to get a grip.

She still had control over me. I wanted to deny it, and I certainly didn't want her to know that she could still hurt me. I needed to be able to get my emotions in check. I could continue to flirt and tease, but I needed to realize *nothing* more was going to happen. Maybe I just needed to get laid. Perhaps getting tangled under the sheets with another woman would take my mind off Charlie.

My thought was interrupted by a voice…a voice I recognized. "Louis."

I had heard that voice most of my life, and now I heard it in the bathroom with me.

The water still ran over me, and steam had filled the entire room. *Have I really been in the shower that long?* "I said I was going to pick you up." Maybe leaving the door unlocked to the house was a bad idea.

"I was worried you wouldn't show. I got the impression I had said something to piss you off."

I was glad I had the shield of the shower curtain to cover the look that must have displayed across my face at that point. "Not sure what you mean." I guess I hadn't covered my irritation very well when I left her and returned home.

"I just wanted to clear the air."

"Do you want to do this now, or wait until lunch?" I had to raise my own voice to overshadow the sound of the water.

"I'd rather talk now if that's okay…before lunch."

Um. Okay, if that's what she wants. Determined to give

her exactly what I figured she wanted, I abruptly turned off the spigot and opened the curtain.

When I pulled back the hanging fabric, I stood naked in front of Charlie for a moment before grabbing the towel I had on the hook by the tiled wall. "Okay. I'm all ears." I wrapped the towel around my waist and stepped out of the tub with water pebbling on my skin and streaming down my body.

She stared at me blankly for several moments. Maybe it hadn't been a good idea to reveal myself to her in that manner. But then again, she was insistent that we were only friends. Besides, what did she think was going to happen? She was bold enough to show up in a room where a man was naked after all.

"Well?" I could tell she was flustered, but I wanted to hear what she had to say.

A cough escaped her throat, and the sound scraped through the humid air. "I just wanted to say..." Then she shook her head. "I don't even remember what I was going to say."

"Look, you don't need to say anything. You've made it perfectly clear that you always have and continue to only want a friendship between us. I get it. Truly, I do."

"Okay. Can we go to lunch now?"

I sensed a hint of hesitation on her part with the reluctance she had in divulging whatever she had planned to tell me, but I figured if she was willing to interrupt my shower in order to see me, then I figured the least I could do was take her to lunch. "Should we invite Cam?"

"Nah. We can make plans with him for later." Her lips turned up in the slightest of a smile, and she was truly adorable standing in her T-shirt and jeans in my bathroom that was still full of steam. Her hair was curlier than usual.

Maybe the humidity in the small room tightened the brown ringlets of hair that framed her face.

"Are you going to watch me get dressed, or do you want to just meet me downstairs?"

"Louis!" She resorted to slapping me on my wet shoulder. I hoped that meant things were returning to some sense of normalcy. "I'll wait downstairs."

Hmmm. She appeared flustered again. Maybe it would be fun to tease her a little more. Even though she said she wanted to just be friends, she seemed to be physically attracted to me. I wondered if the physical attraction would overthrow the obvious psychological roadblock she had put up. *Then again, who am I kidding?* I wanted more than physical attraction could offer anyway.

Charlie and I had a great time at lunch. We laughed and talked about everything—not anything super important, but everything that two people who hadn't spent much time with each other in five years might.

Our conversation was disrupted by the vibration of my phone in my pocket. I pulled it out to see a text from Cam. **Night-time canoeing?** I glanced over at Charlie. "Cam wants to know if we want to go canoeing tonight."

"We haven't done that since we were kids." Her finger tapped against her chin as if pondering her decision. "Okay. Count me in." She directed her gaze back toward me, and her lips turned up in a smile that couldn't hold back her enthusiasm. Her excited grin reminded me that she was always willing to engage in an outlandish adventure. I missed having crazy friends like Cam and Charlie.

Charlie and I are in. Meet at your place at what time? I texted back to him.

He responded immediately. I had forgotten that about him. I guess he was still attached to his phone at all times. **So you're with Charlie now? Just the two of you?**

When I didn't respond immediately, he texted me again.

I'm not going to start being a third wheel now, am I? I guess Cam was becoming suspicious that something more was going on between Charlie and me than mere friendship.

No man. It's not like that. *Why was I even texting this conversation to my best friend?*

Okay. Meet at my place at 9 pm.

"He wants us to meet at his place at nine." Since she sat across from me in a booth at the restaurant, she couldn't see over my shoulder at the texts I had exchanged with her brother, thankfully.

"Sounds fun. Glad I'm off tonight."

I still wasn't ready to say goodbye to her even though I'd see her again later tonight. "Hey, do you want to go by the library and say hi to my mom with me?" It was the only thing I could come up with to maybe keep her around longer.

"It would be great to see your mom again."

I was glad she agreed. I signed the credit card slip the waitress had returned to me. Charlie tried to pay for her own lunch, but I insisted on paying. She did seem to give up rather easily, though. I expected her to argue a little with me.

"Hey, and then afterward, I can take you for ice cream since you paid for lunch."

I tried desperately to hold back the elation I felt, knowing that meant I'd get to spend even more time with her. Perhaps I could convince her to stay with me until we met her brother tonight.

"I like ice cream." I didn't eat it much anymore. I'm not a health nut by any stretch, but I tried to avoid sugary, high-fat foods as much as possible. Given that Charlie ate Froot Loops for breakfast, I would guess she still very much had a sweet tooth. Her running routine has kept her body in amazing form, though.

"I remember." Her words took me away from my own thoughts and back to our conversation. "Is mint chocolate chip still your favorite?"

I nodded at her while we stood and walked out of the restaurant toward my car. Part of me was happy that she remembered my favorite ice cream. It made me think that I *did* matter to her. That one comment made me realize that we did have a great relationship until I went and messed it up.

Don't get me wrong, I'd still love more than a friendship with her. But the memory of what we had made me crave to get back what we once were. Maybe I should halt with the friendly flirting and the suggestive banter. And perhaps I shouldn't let her see me naked again.

Okay, so that thought caused my shorts to become a little tight. If she were to see me naked again, it would only be because I was seeing her naked, too.

I'd have to think of something really unfavorable and disgusting to get the image of Charlie naked out of my head. Although I had never really seen her without clothes on, my imagination told me that I wouldn't be disappointed. Seeing her in the T-shirts she liked to wear that had a deep V exposing her cleavage most likely hid perfect breasts. The way she fit in tight jeans made me picture a perfect ass. And watching her in the running shorts that revealed her long, lean legs, had me thinking what perfection lay between those amazing thighs.

I needed to stop. Right. Now. I was pretty sure walking into a library with a huge boner would make me look like some kind of pervert. So I chewed on the inside of my cheek while we rode in my car to the library, and I forced myself to remember the last disgusting house I went into at work. *It was a small kitchen fire that was still confined to the stove. But the tenant of the home had been a hoarder. There were empty takeout containers everywhere with roaches and large bugs that I couldn't even identify scurrying across the entire living room.* Recalling the stench of that place alone was enough to make me wretch and almost lose the lunch I had just enjoyed. Okay. Maybe this would work. I could feel my shorts becoming looser by the second.

We arrived at the library a few minutes later. The large, historical building that I remembered as a child had rafters up in front of it covering part of the front exterior. I guess there were some restoration efforts in effect. The building was built in the 1800s, so it most likely was due for a facelift.

I climbed up the many steps outside the stone exterior with Charlie next to me. There was a handicap entrance installed years ago, but there was something magical about ascending those massive steps into a building that had gargoyles perched on columns out front that really got the adventure blood swimming through my veins faster.

Moving through the rotating glass door used to be a game for Charlie and me. We would hold on to the brass handles when no one was in the archway and run as fast as we could until our stomachs felt like they would purge their contents. As I saw the smirk cut across her face, I knew exactly what she was thinking. We both raced to the door and slid into the same space within the separation between two of the revolving doors.

I peered over my shoulder, and she looked in both directions. When we both realized there were no others within the door itself or waiting to enter or exit the building, we both pushed against the brass handle as fast as we could. We started slowly because the old door was heavy. But soon, the door offered less resistance, and we moved into a comfortable jog pushing the door in a steady rhythm. Once the sprinting began, I could see Charlie trying to halt her stride. She grasped the sides of her head and catapulted her body out of the confines of the door into the building as I continued around for one more rotation before I jumped out and joined her.

Her complexion had grown pale, and her face was glistening with perspiration. "Are you okay?" A sudden flush warmed my face as well.

"Just a little dizzy. Things became pretty blurry, and I thought I would lose the lunch you just bought me." Her head hung down, and her hands braced her weight against her upper legs while she spoke.

I reflexively reached for her hand and put my other arm around her shoulder. "I guess we aren't as young as we used to be." I brushed a quick kiss against her temple and held her close as I walked toward the bathroom located on the main level. I let go of her long enough to run into the men's room and wet some paper towels under the faucet. Then we lowered ourselves to the ground and as she leaned against the wall, I placed a wet stack of cool paper towels across her forehead. "I guess I made it go too fast for you to handle."

A closed fist struck my shoulder and the color returned to Charlie's cheeks. I was relieved to see her feeling better so quickly. "It was just too soon after we ate lunch, that's all." Her gray eyes swirled with uncertainty like thunderclouds before a storm.

"So next time, we should follow the swimming rule?" Her eyes narrowed, but I could still see their steel-gray color. "You know how you're supposed to wait an hour after you eat to go swimming? Well, we should probably wait an hour after we eat before running in circles full force in a revolving door." Sitting so close to her on that thin, contractor-grade carpet shouldn't have created the swirling emotions I had. But the smell of old books coupled with the nostalgia, and the heat emitting from the proximity of her body next to mine made me want to keep her near me and hold on to this moment for as long as I could.

I gently placed my lips against her temple, and when I pulled away, there was a pinkish hue to her cheeks. Not only had the color that drained from her face returned, but her facial features now held a warm, red tone. I didn't know why I had kissed her on the side of her head, or really, why I had kissed her at all. It just seemed right. I didn't mean for my lips to touch her, but for some reason, I couldn't stop myself. If I couldn't have my lips touch hers, then I would just have to use them to feel the pulse on the side of her head. It calmed me, but it also gave me the opportunity to get a quick sniff of her hair. She hadn't told me not to touch the side of her head with my lips, so I'd keep doing it as long as she wasn't resistant to my touch.

Any onlookers would have seen that quick peck to the side of her head and thought the kiss was completely inno-cent. I've seen the twins' mom kiss them both high up on their cheeks or the side of their heads. It wasn't truly a public display of affection, but rather a friendly gesture.

Too bad not everyone could come to the library and keep their affection brief and innocent. Several feet from where we sat was an older man and woman embraced in a rather passionate, inappropriate kiss to occur at the library. I knew the main level wasn't the children's area, but those two should have at least kept the necking PG-rated.

Charlie examined the spectacle I had been watching while I stood and helped pull her to her feet with my hands firmly within her grasp. The couple broke apart, and the woman peered up toward the man as he reached out to take her hands in his own. Realizing that we could safely walk by without disturbing their make-out session, the two of us headed in that direction to find my mother.

Her information desk sat nestled in a nook surrounded by tall bookshelves. As we continued several more steps on our route, the older woman turned slightly, revealing her profile. I recognized her.

I hadn't recognized the man when the couple was kissing. He was facing toward me, and the woman was facing the opposite direction.

Even though I recognized the woman as the caregiver I adored my whole life, I felt like I no longer knew her like I thought I had. That seemed to have happened with a lot of people I once thought I knew during my absence in the last five years. I thought maybe I would walk by without any sort of greeting, but anger began to fuel a fire within me that I couldn't seem to stop.

"Hey, Mom. Charlie and I thought we'd come say hi." The flash of embarrassment highlighted the fine lines on my mother's face. She must have known that I'd witnessed the show she had put on with the tall man in a suit next to her—who was *not* my father. I was sure the resentment and anger that ran rampant throughout my body were blazingly written across my face and seen in the stiffening of my stance.

Then I felt a soft, warm touch. The faintest of caresses tickled along the inside of my forearm. I felt my posture soften against that soothing contact from her fingertips. And I refocused my attention to Charlie while she continued the magical touch of trailing her fingers up and down my arm. I knew she had seen the same crazy shit that just happened. She was attempting to comfort me, and she had succeeded.

"Louis…" my mother began to say, but I held up my hand.

"I don't want to talk about this right now." The woman who gave birth to me appeared heartbroken when she studied me. I knew she wanted an opportunity to explain, and maybe I would give it to her at some point. But it wasn't going to be that moment. I had to get the hell out of there.

7

CHARLIE

I couldn't believe what I just saw. I mean, I don't think I had ever seen Louis's mom kiss his dad, and now I had seen her make out with some random man. "Give me your keys." I held out my hand as we stood next to his car.

"Why?" The hardened look across his face nearly broke my heart.

"Because I want to drive," I said plainly. "Please." I wasn't beyond begging. I didn't want him to drive while suffering the shock he was in. So I decided to be bold. I leaned toward him and reached into the front pocket of his khaki shorts to snake out the keys I knew resided within.

He initially flinched when I shoved my hand into the pocket. But then he relaxed and shifted slightly, allowing me better access to his keys. He remained silent but watched the movement in his pocket as I attempted to loop my finger around his key ring.

Just as I would hook a fish, I pulled the ring slowly out of the depths of the abyss of his pocket. Feeling gratified with my catch, I smiled and pushed him aside as I opened the driver's side door and climbed behind the wheel.

He shuffled his feet around to the other side of the car and allowed himself to get into the passenger seat. He flopped himself into the seat next to me, without a word being said. The car was silent except for the loud sigh that whooshed out of him when his shoulders slumped forward. I trailed my fingers along his arm for only a few strokes before starting the car. I couldn't take away his pain, but perhaps I could provide a distraction.

I pulled out of the parking lot and Louis never lifted his head. His sullen mood had my heart breaking for him. He was hurting, and I just wanted to comfort him. "Ice cream makes everyone feel better."

He lifted his chin and peered through the windshield at the town hand-dipped parlor. "I don't know, Charlie. I'm not much in the mood for ice cream now."

"So you're just going to watch while I inhale a scoop of strawberry cheesecake on a cone?" I reached across the console that separated us and laced my fingers in his. I knew it was an intimate touch, but it felt so incredibly right. So I made the decision to move the hand I held within mine toward my face, and I planted a quick kiss to the dorsal side. "Come on. I'm buying."

Dropping his hand quickly, I exited the vehicle and skipped to the passenger side. He sat within the confines of the car interior for a few moments before departing his side in slow, drawn-out movements. I grabbed his hand again and led him toward the front of the shop.

When we entered, I ordered strawberry cheesecake for myself and mint chocolate chip for Louis. He reluctantly took it from me when I offered it to him after I paid. We sat at a round table in the shop, and I began licking the delicious, creamy dessert. He stared at his until the green glob began dripping down the sides and he needed to lick up the melted liquid soon or he would end up with very sticky fingers. So I did the only thing I could do.

I grabbed his wrist with my free hand and licked the dripping ice cream with my tongue. I did see his lips tug up at the corner of his mouth after my gesture. "Are you going to make me eat both of these cones?" I said in between lapping up the ice cream he was holding and returning my attention to my own cone.

Then he did something I didn't expect. He grabbed on to my hand holding my half-devoured cone and bit into the crispy wafer pastry and licked some strawberry cheesecake-flavored heaven that tried to escape the boundaries my cone created. And when he smiled at me, I think I started to melt more than the ice cream. "You licked mine, so it was only fair for me to lick yours." Holy crap. He had gone from sulking and withdrawn to sexy as hell in ten seconds.

"Hey!" I snatched my cone from his grasp. "Eat your own." He was back to teasing me. That was a good sign.

"Fine. I will." While he licked his ice cream, I somehow managed to imagine what his tongue could do to me. Even though my ice cream was cold, the warmth that thought sent through me produced a heat that made my cheeks hot and my panties wet.

We continued consuming our sweet treats with only a few exchanges of words. I knew he didn't feel like talking, and he knew I was there and ready to listen if he did. I intertwined our fingers and walked out to the car with him. He seemed more relaxed within my grasp at that point, which helped to alleviate some of my worry.

I took Louis to the arcade next. The place hadn't changed much since we were kids. We played Skee-Ball and video games. He laughed several times and actually seemed like he enjoyed himself. But once we were back in his car, I wasn't sure where else to go. I drove back to my apartment in the hopes I could convince him to spend some more time with me before heading back home.

"Why don't you come in for a little while?" I asked while sliding his vehicle into a parking spot in my apartment complex lot.

"You've been very nice to me after what happened today, and although I appreciate it, I know you must be tired of me and my gloomy attitude by this point." I couldn't let him leave after I witnessed his sorrowful eyes and despondent expression.

"Don't be silly." With his car safely parked, I had two free hands. So I covered his hand with my own. Apparently, I needed to constantly feel the warmth of his palms and fingers. "I have never—and will never—get tired of you." I meant it, so I was certain he could see my comment was genuine.

"Well, okay then." He pushed his door open and followed me up to my apartment.

"Make yourself at home." I pointed to the couch in my living room once inside my apartment. "Do you want something to drink?"

"No thanks." He moved toward my couch and when he sat on the cushion, he leaned his head on the back of the sofa and closed his eyes.

I scurried across the room and plopped down next to him. Feeling the overwhelming need to hug him or lean myself into his chest, I lifted his arm and slid underneath so my ear could rest on his chest. While listening to his even breathing and rhythmic heartbeat, I found myself becoming tired.

I woke up still in the embrace I had created. Louis had fallen asleep, too. Had we always been so touchy-feely? I didn't remember ever holding hands before, or licking each other's ice cream cones, or having him kiss my temple, or falling asleep on him. But somehow it felt so natural. It felt like we had been this way with each other forever.

I thought he was still asleep until I felt him kiss the top of my head. I pulled my face away from his chest and tilted my chin up at him.

His vibrant blue eyes swirled contently as his eyebrows furrowed. Then I couldn't help myself. I inched my face toward him and touched his lips with mine. As I pressed my lips to his, he pulled me closer into him with the arm that was still draped around my shoulder. But when I tried to slip my tongue into his parting lips, he pushed me away. "Charlie, you don't have to kiss me to make me feel better." He swept the hair that had gone awry during my nap behind my ear. "I don't need the pity kiss. Just being with you makes me feel better."

Ouch. He thought I was giving him the *I-feel-sorry-for-you-so-I'm-going-to-kiss-you* kiss. "I was kissing you because I wanted to. It wasn't a sympathy kiss."

I resumed kissing him, and this time he didn't pull away from me. He opened his mouth and allowed me access to the inside of the warm cavity with my tongue. He nibbled on my lower lip, and I ran my tongue along his teeth. Then he cupped his hands around my face, and I felt my insides beginning to heat up. When I heard a moan escape my throat, he pushed away from me again.

"This isn't a good idea, Charlie." I heard his words, but I couldn't help but feel a sense of déjà vu, as if I had already experienced this before. So this was what rejection felt like.

"Do you not like kissing me?" I had very much enjoyed kissing him as evidenced by my erratic breathing and quickened pulse.

"Oh, I do." His lips drew upward into a smile, but his face didn't reveal the passion I expected to see. "I just don't think this is the right time."

Embarrassment burned a hole in my gut. I had practically thrown myself at him.

"You shouldn't be taking advantage of me while I'm this vulnerable." He was teasing me again. Maybe things could go back to normal again.

I slapped him on his arm and his smile widened. We had always been playful with each other, ever since we were kids. In fourth grade, Cam insisted I liked Louis because I slapped him all the time and that's what girls did if they liked a boy at that age. Well, I guess I never outgrew that. I did like him. A lot. Things between us were different now for sure, but some things were the same. Our relationship was comfortable and natural at times and heated and uncertain at other times.

It seemed that open-mouthed kissing was off the table, but light touches and gentle kisses to the head or hands were okay. And holding hands was acceptable, too. That was undoubtedly my favorite. If falling asleep on his chest was acceptable as well, I could probably stay happy for a while. I might as well stop lying to myself. I had heard it's easier to lie to other people than it is to lie to yourself, and that was certainly the case when it came to Louis.

I loved spending time with my old friend, but I had to admit that I loved the new level of intimacy we shared. We sat closer to each other, we touched each other, and we shared some amazing conversation. I felt as if I could talk to him about anything and everything. I had *never* felt this comfortable or elated about a relationship before.

I had a couple of boyfriends in high school and a few more in college. But I never shared a part of my soul with any of them. I shared my bed with a few, but never my heart. Yet somehow Louis seemed to have captured my heart in a matter of a few days. *I'm lying to myself again.* He has always had my heart. I was just as sure of that as I was that an EpiPen was used for an allergic reaction. I was stabbed through the heart by one of Cupid's arrows just as an EpiPen is deployed forcefully into the thigh of an allergic reaction victim.

Now that he was back in my life, I wasn't sure if I could bear to watch him leave. I didn't want him to go. I was the one who had chased him away in the first place, and now I would have to watch him leave and take my heart with him. I wasn't sure how I had lived without him for the last five years, and I didn't want to learn what it was like to live without him ever again. Being friends wasn't going to be enough to get him to stay, and being more wasn't something that I thought we could explore yet.

Maybe I could move to be closer to him. There are several hospitals in the metropolitan parts of Maryland, so I could certainly find a job as an emergency room nurse. *What the hell is wrong with me? We are* not *a couple. He only wants to be my friend. I can't chase after him like an adolescent girl with a teenage crush.*

For now, I just needed to enjoy the time we had together. I would take as much as I could get at this point. As we sat next to each other on my couch, he reached toward my hand and interlocked our fingers. He left his head leaning on the back cushions of my sofa and had his eyes closed. He located my palm without looking. Of course he did. He knew I was here for him, and I wasn't going anywhere.

I sat up straighter on the couch with my fingers still intertwined with his, but I figured *what the hell*? I leaned toward him again and rested my head on his shoulder. "Are you ready to talk about the bandages on your back now?" I asked with my eyes closed, enjoying the moment.

He let out a disagreeable half moan, half sigh. "I guess talking about that is better than talking about what we saw at the library."

8

LOUIS

I didn't intend to speak to anyone about my burn. But then again, I hadn't exactly planned to see Charlie and Cam when I returned home for a few weeks. Now the burn on my back was nothing compared to the burning my legs were going through after that treacherous run Charlie had me endure earlier today. My heartache was burning a hole in my chest as well. I wasn't ready to talk to my mom about what was going on with her at all.

It had really been a rough day, but somehow with Charlie leaning into me, I was able to relax. She had that profound effect on me. When my insides were in a twisted knot, she could unravel it with her touch. I wasn't sure if it had always been that way. I just knew I wouldn't be able to get through this without her.

Her head was cocked to the side and resting on my shoulder. Even though we were touching, I wanted her closer to me, so I kicked off the flip-flops I had stepped into after my shower earlier today and they landed on the floor by her coffee table. Then with one swift motion, I hoisted my legs up onto her couch and pulled her toward me, positioning her back against my chest and her ass nestled between my legs.

I couldn't explain why I thought kissing her was a bad idea, but having her ass rub against the front of my shorts I was okay with. I wrapped my arms around her, and she snuggled into me. I could smell the coconut shampoo she used on her hair. Coconut was now my new favorite smell.

"Are you going to tell me about what happened to your back?" I could still make out her whispered voice even though she was facing away from me.

"Yes. I was just getting comfortable." I kissed the back of her head and took a long smell of her scent before beginning to explain my reason for returning home. "I was at a training fire. We were going to do one last drill before letting it go. In other words, letting it burn to the ground and clear it. I was stoking the fire...you know, trying to build the fire back up for the next crew to come through. I began to walk out of the front door, but I was stopped by the instructor. He told me to go out the back door because they were getting ready to come in the front." I massaged small circles into her shoulders as I continued.

She sighed happily, and I couldn't remember hearing another sound I had ever enjoyed more.

"However, as I walked toward the back of the house, I saw that the back wall was totally engulfed in flames. So I was stuck in that room. I looked at the front door waiting for the crew to come through, but they were having an issue with getting the door pried open."

Her shoulders stiffened beneath my fingertips, and I did my best to try to loosen the tight muscles with my thumbs.

"The fire coming from the back of the house was getting really hot, so I had no choice but to eat the floor...meaning I had to lay down and hope the crew would be able to quickly put out the fire. I swear I had lain there for only about thirty seconds, but it felt like half a lifetime until they finally came in and knocked the fire down."

A gasp escaped her and vibrated against my chest before she turned over to face me. With her gray eyes wide with apprehension, she clenched my shirt as I continued.

"I scurried out the front door. My helmet was on fire, so the firefighters outside had to extinguish the flames. I quickly began to take off my gear, and I realized it was smoking and my back was burning. The paramedic looked me over and said I needed to go to the burn center to be evaluated. I was diagnosed with a second-degree burn and forced to take off work for two weeks. So I decided to come back to see my parents because being in my apartment at home only reminded me of not being able to go to work. The irony is that after what I saw today, I don't want to see my parents now, either."

"You will eventually *have* to see your parents again, Louis." She stared up at me and stroked my arm with the light touch of her fingers that sent an electric jolt of pleasure straight through to my soul.

"I will, but not today. Probably not tomorrow, either. I'm just going to ask Cam if I can crash at his place for a few days when we go out later."

"Why don't you just stay here? I'm off for two more days. We could go fishing or swimming or biking if you want." She didn't realize I was unsure of how much self-control I would need to spend the next forty-eight hours with her.

"Can't I still do all those things with you if I stay at Cam's place?" A look of disappointment washed across her face and nearly crushed me.

"I suppose." She jumped up from the couch then and picked up her cell phone. "I should text him now anyway and see if he wants to join us for dinner."

"Why?" I wasn't ready to share her yet.

"Why not?" She was challenging me. I had a feeling she wanted me to say I wanted to be with her. I knew from her previous look of disappointment that she was having a hard time dealing with my rejection from a few moments ago.

"Sure. That sounds good. Should we go somewhere or order takeout?" I wasn't going to admit to her what she was looking for. I wasn't even sure *what* I was looking for. I really just wanted to live in the moment, but she obviously wanted things on her terms or else she was going to push me away. I guess that's how it will always be with her.

She punched some buttons on her phone and then set it back on the counter. "Fine. I asked him." She could be so stubborn at times.

I shrugged and resumed my seated position on her couch. After grabbing the remote off the coffee table, I turned on the television. She huffed and turned her back to me. "You said to make myself at home." I stared at her back, willing her to turn and face me.

She stood next to the counter with a wall around her fortified with attitude. When her phone vibrated, she picked it up and appeared to look at the message on the screen. "Cam has a date, so he can't make it for dinner."

She kept her head down and still faced the opposite wall. I felt frozen on the couch—like I couldn't move toward her and yet I couldn't breathe if I didn't.

After a long sigh, she turned back around with her gaze held downward even though her body was facing my direction. It was difficult to know for sure, but I thought I saw the slightest hint of a watery sheen in her eyes. She was trying not to cry. That was all it took for me to climb off the couch and move toward her.

It took only a few strides to meet her. I pulled her toward me and encircled her waist with my arms. Her stiffened stance softened, and she melted into my embrace. I kissed the top of her head and took another long inhale of my new favorite coconut scent. "Charlie, what's going on?"

"I didn't realize how much I missed you until you came back." She pressed her cheek against my chest and my heart rate increased.

"I know what you mean." I rubbed her back with my hand over the cotton of her T-shirt. "I spent so much time trying to forget you." I let a quick breath escape my lips. "But I should have known that I could never forget you."

So maybe when I came back home, I had a whole speech planned of what I would say if or when I ran into her. I had wanted her to know that she hadn't affected me. I wanted her to know that I had finished college and had a career I loved. I wanted to tell her that my life had been great without her.

Of course, all those plans went out the window the moment I saw her in the cereal aisle at the grocery store. The feelings I had held at bay for so long began spilling over. I had tried my best to disguise my feelings with sarcasm and false confidence, but my heart skipped several beats when I laid eyes on her for the first time in all those years.

Now all I could think about was how I wanted to hold her and never, ever let her go. However, our embrace was torn apart by a knock at her door. She pulled her body away from me but reached her hand to mine and held on for another moment before peering through the peephole in the door. She smoothed out her shirt and wiped imaginary wrinkles out of her jeans before pulling the door open.

"Hey, guys!" Cameron, the man that had grown from the boy I spent my childhood with, strode into Charlie's apartment not realizing his best friend and twin sister had just been embracing each other a moment ago.

"Hey, man." I approached my friend and did the obligatory fist bump and barely touching man hug. "What are you doing here? I thought you had a date."

"Yeah, well…Charlie made it sound like it was important." I glanced in her direction and she gave me the I-don't-know-what-he's-talking-about expression.

"She said you were having a bad day." Cam walked into the kitchen and retrieved a bottle of water out of the fridge. "So I decided to ditch my date and hang out with the two of you. I was at the store picking up wine right around the corner when I received Charlie's text." He opened the plastic water bottle and took a long swig.

His gaze bounced from me to his sister. Charlie and I exchanged glances as well.

"Are either of you going to tell me what happened? Or are we going to all just stare at each other without speaking." Cam always had a way of getting straight to the point. He never had been one to beat around the bush.

"You aren't going to believe it. In fact, if I hadn't seen it firsthand, I wouldn't have believed it if someone told me." I couldn't help but shake my head in disbelief.

I recounted my day minus Charlie seeing me naked in the shower and kissing me on her couch. I told him about my long run and lunch with his sister. He raised his eyebrow when I spoke about our time together. Clearly he already suspected something was going on between us since he had texted me the third wheel comment.

"Then we went to see my mom at the library." Before I could begin the vivid details of seeing my mother in another man's arms, Charlie interrupted my thoughts.

"And we ran around the revolving door until I almost puked!" Her comment drew a chuckle from her brother. I knew what I said next would fade the humor quickly.

"And then we saw my mom…kissing a man that wasn't

my dad." Cam sat on the sofa next to Charlie, and I sat in her armchair while narrating the details I wished I could forget.

"Wow. That's crazy. I'm sorry, man." Cam's expression of disbelief was apparent as I watched his eyebrows draw together.

"So now I can't go home. I'm not ready to talk to my mom…or my dad, for that matter. Would it be all right for me to crash at your place for a couple of days?" I asked him the question, but rather than maintain eye contact with me, he glanced in Charlie's direction. *I know they're twins, but is he really sending her a telepathic message?*

I swung my eyes in Charlie's direction, she appeared emotionless, unaffected by the question I had asked. In fact, she didn't even bother to turn toward me at all. She was held in a weird hypnotizing stare with her brother until it broke, and she gazed down at her feet.

"Tonight is fine, but since I had to break my date with Tessa for this evening, I'll need to make it up to her tomorrow to stay in her good graces." He winked at me then. "So I'll need my apartment to myself if you know what I mean."

"Cameron, gross. We both know what you mean." A gagging sound escaped from Charlie and then she stuck out her tongue. "I guess Louis will just have to crash on my couch tomorrow then."

Even though I had already turned her offer down a little while ago, she successfully trapped me in a situation that I couldn't say no to. So I simply smiled. "If you're sure that's okay." I feigned a happy expression, but I was a little annoyed that she was going to get exactly what she wanted.

"Of course it's okay. It will be fun. We can eat popcorn and watch Netflix." Her lips tugged slightly up at the corners of her mouth, and I could tell she was trying to stifle the *I told you so* from coming out.

"Cam, you aren't really going to ditch me for some random girl and leave me to an adolescent slumber party, are you?" Maybe if I explained to him that I was having inappropriate feelings for his sister, he would disagree with the arrangement Charlie had come up with.

I only thought about that for half a second and realized how awkward that would be for each of us. I guess I would have to go along with this arrangement and do the best I could to keep my distance from Charlie. Although I knew that was going to be extremely difficult considering even when we weren't heavy in the throes passion, we couldn't seem to keep our hands off each other.

9

CHARLIE

My brother was so incredibly good at reading my signals. I loved him for that. He knew my secret, and I was so happy I had elected to tell him. Cam had accused me of crushing on Louis. Maybe that was right. Maybe the feelings I had were nothing more than what a girl feels over her teenage crush.

No, that wasn't it. I felt elation and happiness. I had all kinds of feelings when I was with him. I was totally in trouble.

Tonight I had to share Louis with my brother. I couldn't wait to have him all to myself tomorrow. I had become so familiar with his touch, as innocent as it may seem; sometimes I felt tense and unable to relax until he touched me. He held my hand and kissed me. And I don't just mean the times our mouths kiss.

I was able to take in those cleansing, healing, deep breaths when he kissed my temple or my head, or anywhere his lips touched. I couldn't inhale enough to take in the amount of oxygen my body required until he was near me. *How will I ever be able to survive without him? Now that I know I can breathe adequately only when he's with me, how will I live without him?* All humans require air to live. This is a fact. I know this to be true, because I am a nurse.

What didn't make sense was how I could survive when he was gone. My lungs couldn't have possibly taken in enough air. Now I realized that, before, I wasn't even living. Sure, I worked and spent time with my family, but my heart was dead. My life was empty. He left a void in me that was not capable of sustaining life. My life finally felt like *life* again. He'd been gone for five years and then brought me back to life in a matter of a few days. *I don't want him to leave.*

I didn't even mind sharing him at this point. If I could be near him, I could continue to live. I could continue to breathe. My heart could continue to beat. I hadn't *fallen* in love with him. I didn't fall off a cliff. I jumped. I crashed, collided, and plowed into love with him. A fall can be graceful. This was a head-on, impulsive, traumatic, bone-breaking impact. It happened without any warning. It was like a train wreck. I never saw the collision coming.

An unknowing smile pinched my cheeks. And not the demure smile of a respectable girl. This was a smile so wide it hurt my face. My lips stretched as far as they could without cracking. I was in love with Louis.

"Yeah, I know you got your way." I could hear Louis talking to me, but I watched his expression as he witnessed the smile that ran from one side of my face to the other.

"Charlie, don't be too girly at your slumber party." I heard my brother say next. "No painting each other's toenails and giving each other facials."

"How would you know what happens at a slumber party, Cam?" Louis questioned my brother, but I remained on the cloud floating near him.

"That's what Claudette and her friends would do,"

Cameron answered as if his response was completely obvious.

"And what did you do at slumber parties Charlene?" Louis calling me by my given name snapped me out of the euphoria I was basking in.

"You already know. You were there. I was always with you and Cam."

The guys and I rode to the lake and parked close to the shoreline. The sound of crickets and frogs sang loudly in the thick air. The humidity left a thin cloud on the lake, and I could smell the patchy fog. It had the same smell as fresh rain and left moisture on my bare skin. The guys carried the canoe from the bed of Cam's truck to the edge of the water while I was immersing my senses in my surroundings.

I held the flashlight. I had forgotten how dark it was during nighttime canoeing. The three of us climbed in and pushed off from the sand. Louis and my brother grabbed the oars and began to paddle us toward the center of the lake. I remained seated in the middle of the canoe while Cam took a spot at the bow and Louis sat behind me. I wasn't looking at him, but I could feel his eyes on me. Even though it was dark, I know he could see me. He could always *see* me.

There was a small amount of water in the bottom of the canoe where my feet were submerged, and I startled when something pinched my toe. "Oww!" A burning, stabbing, pain continued biting at my toes. My scream caught the guys' attention.

I turned the flashlight back on that I had clipped to the belt loop on my shorts and shone the beam toward my feet. And there, swimming in the small amount of water, was a crawfish near my foot. I quickly picked up the crustacean by its tail and tossed it in the lake.

"You have ruined all women for us, Lean Bean," Cameron said through his insufferable laugh.

"What do you mean?" I wasn't sure what precipitated that comment from my brother, so I exchanged looks with both men in the boat.

"You're never the damsel in distress. You don't need us to kill bugs. You don't scare…ever. You'll pick up a snake, or a frog, or a crawfish without it bothering you. You don't care if you mess up your hair or get dirt under your fingernails." I was unsure if he was paying me a compliment or stating things unfavorable about me. "You are every guy's dream. Right, Louis?"

Louis simply shrugged. He didn't respond with words. Not even one word. Not even a syllable. Not a sound. He didn't feel the same way about me that he used to. He didn't need me like I needed him. He clearly thought he could live his life just fine without me. I shouldn't feel sad, but I couldn't help it. My hope had vanished. Sure, he had said we were only going to be friends, but I guess part of me thought that we would take things slow and let our friendship evolve into something more.

I swallowed down the bile creeping up my throat and resumed my position facing forward. That suffocating feeling returned, and I couldn't breathe…until a warm palm pressed against my back.

Then I was able to fill my lungs with life again. Louis realized what his reaction did to me, and he was trying to comfort me. I could take in air again.

I intended to swivel in my seat so I could turn around and look at him, but hidden in the darkness of the night, something flew over my head. Correction. Something dove from the sky toward my head. "What the hell was that?" I said as I waved my hands around my head.

"I think it was a bat," my very matter-of-fact brother said.

"Nah, I think it was a hawk," Louis offered.

"Whatever it was, why did it drop from the sky and plunge toward my head?"

"You've seen the vampire movies." I don't know why, but my brother's response drew laughter out of me. Not a feminine giggle, but a roar of side-splitting hooting. My two favorite guys joined me in the fit of snorting and cackling merriment, and I realized there was nowhere else I would rather be. These two boys I once knew had grown into men, but they were still my best friends. They are my happiness. They were my life.

LOUIS

We dropped Charlie off at her apartment and drove toward Cam's place on the east side of town. My best friend remained quiet. This was not unlike him. He had always been one to take everything in before responding. He liked to weigh things carefully in his head before forming his thoughts into words, which was ironic considering how quickly he responded to a text message. I guess it was more difficult for him to say the words rather than tap them out on his phone. I knew he was alone in his head with his thoughts, so I just waited.

"So what's going on between you and Charlie?" He kept a tight grip on the steering wheel and focused straight ahead while he asked me.

"We've decided to be friends again," I said in the hopes that satisfied his curiosity.

"That's good." He responded curtly and promptly returned to the solitude of his own silence. Several moments passed by before he finally asked what was really on his mind. "Do you still love her...you know, like you did five years ago?"

Then I knew I was going to have to lie to my best friend. I wanted to say *no* and believe it. I really wanted to know what the answer was and say it out loud. Truthfully, I didn't know how I felt anymore. I loved her. Oh, how I loved her. But I didn't want to. I didn't want to let her hurt me again, so I should say *no* and believe it. "No. She's my friend. She doesn't want anything more and neither do I."

"Just don't be completely closed off to the idea. Both of you should just keep an open mind and let what happens happen." His comment took me off guard. I had no idea why he would say that to me.

"Has Charlie said something to you about me?" *Did she confide in her brother how she felt? What does she want from* us?

"I know it's none of my business. But when I stayed out of what happened between the two of you all those years ago, we all suffered. I lost my best friend and you two lost each other. I just don't want that to happen again."

I smirked and tried very hard to hold back my laughter. "You are forever the peacemaker...or the meddler. I'm not sure which supersedes the other."

I wasn't sure if he wanted Charlie and me to be more than friends or not. But I was sure he wanted all of us to be able to spend time together.

Run today? I read on my phone when I rolled over onto my side while lying on Cameron's couch.

Sorry. Too tired today. Maybe tomorrow? I hadn't slept well, and I really wasn't in the mood. I swear I don't know how she has the energy to run. All. The. Time.

Okay. See you later. I'll order pizza for dinner tonight. For some reason, that text sent a smile to my face. I would be eating dinner with her and sleeping at her house. The last time I'd fallen asleep on her couch, I was sitting up, but she was curled up with me. It'd felt amazing. The couch I was currently lying on was not as comfortable. Of course it wasn't. Charlie's warm body wasn't next to me.

That sounds great. Can't wait. After I hit the send button, I wondered if I sounded too eager. I certainly didn't want to lead her on, but I couldn't help but be excited about being with her again.

"Coffee?" Cam said to me, approaching from the hallway, entering the living room.

I sat up and nodded. "That would be great."

"I'm going to pickup basketball today at one. You wanna go with?"

I contemplated it, but since the blister was still open on my back, I decided maybe it wasn't a good idea. "Maybe another time. I want the burn on my back to heal a little more before I participate in contact sports."

"So running, fishing, and canoeing are okay, but no basketball?" he questioned with a lift of his eyebrow.

"I guess." I shrugged. It had made sense in my head.

"Uh okay. I really hope you aren't using that burn on your back as an excuse because you don't want me or anyone else to kick your butt." He flexed the muscles in his arms, and I couldn't help but let a chuckle slip out.

"Cam, some things never change. I can still beat you at any sport, anytime. I just didn't want to show you up."

"Whatever, we play again on Thursday at six o'clock. You and your burn should be better by then."

"I might be able to make that work." That was still a few days away. I was returning to the clinic on Friday and hopefully, I would be cleared to return to my job. But now I didn't feel so great about going back to work. I missed my job and my co-workers. I even missed my cousin and the landscape business. But I missed Cameron and Charlie more. The realization that I'd be leaving soon started to unnerve me. Plus, I still had to deal with whatever was going on with my mom. I still wasn't ready to think about that.

I watched Cam tap on his phone. He was probably sending another text message. I didn't inquire about who he was communicating with. It was probably the girl he was going out with tonight. I couldn't remember the name he had told me. But given that he didn't ever date anyone for very long, he probably hadn't committed her name to memory yet, either.

My phone pinged, and I turned it over to see the screen. It was another text from Charlie. **Going to be busy until around three. Wanna come over then?**

Sure. See you soon.

"Some of the kids from my school have a soccer scrimmage at ten this morning. I was going to go watch. You feel like going, too?" With Cameron being an athletic trainer at the local high school—the same high school we went to—he knew almost all the student athletes.

"Only if we go out to breakfast first," I suggested. "And we still haven't had coffee."

"I'll invite Charlie to go with us." I still found his brotherly inclusion of his twin sister funny.

"She was going for a run. I don't know that she'll be back in time." He tilted his chin and raised his eyebrow as if thinking, *how do you know what Charlie is doing right now?*

"She decided not to go. She said she was going to run with a friend, but her friend backed out." His questioning glare was still aimed at me. "Were you the friend she was going to go running with?"

"She literally just asked me, and I said I didn't feel like it today. We've been running a few times together, but I would hardly call us running buddies. Besides, I thought she always used to run by herself. She doesn't even like to talk while she runs, so she's not very good company." I wasn't sure why I was babbling like I was. It sounded like I was trying to cover the fact that I had been spending time with Charlie to her brother. I just figured if I didn't come up with something to say, that he would see right through me. He would see what his sister did to me. It would be apparent how I felt about her, despite my best effort of denying it to him and myself.

"If you're explaining, you're losing." He grabbed his truck keys from the kitchen counter and motioned for me to follow him.

I pulled my T-shirt back over my head, since I had removed it the night prior. Then I stood and walked in his direction. "What's that supposed to mean?"

"I wish you would cut the crap with me." His body pivoted with a force toward me, the jolt sent me backward a step. "Charlie is my sister, and you're my friend. I wish you two could just find a way to get along. It would be great if things could just go back to the way they used to be."

"Fine. Where are we going for breakfast?" I would deal with my friend's sullen disposition in an unexpected way.

"The Pancake Cabin, of course." He cocked his head and rolled his eyes in response as if I just asked him a rhetorical question because the answer was completely obvious.

Cam and I are heading to the Pancake Cabin. It would be great if you would join us. "Okay. I just invited Charlie to meet us there."

Okay. Be there soon. She responded just as quick as her brother does to text messages.

"She's on her way," I explained to Cam, and he grinned as big as the Cheshire Cat.

We arrived at the restaurant before Charlie, so we were already seated in a booth when she walked in. Cameron stood and greeted her with a hug when she approached us. I stood up next and hugged her as well. I may have held her for a moment longer than was probably acceptable from a friend, but I couldn't help it. I wanted to smell her hair and hold her close. I kissed her forehead and let her slide into the booth. I slid in next to her. It was just how I had envisioned it when the hostess led us to the table with the bench seating on each side.

I had her trapped in the space right next to me. She was wearing shorts again today, so I sat next to her and imagined what her long legs looked like under the table. I had only caught a quick glimpse of them. I rubbed her knee when the three of us were looking at our menus, and she placed her hand on top of mine. *What am I doing?* I quickly tugged my hand away. She did as well and continued to look at the menu.

No weird looks from her. No discussion of my intentions. She was being a little too easygoing. Maybe she was content with having whatever it was between us. Maybe she didn't need anything more. I could handle that. *Couldn't I?*

The waitress appeared and took our order. The three of us remained quiet for several moments. Cameron was the first to chime in. He always had to be the one to keep the peace.

"I saw Friday Furlough a few days ago." His voice finally broke the silence we had surrounded ourselves in. Friday was a girl we had gone to school with. She was a little crazy and socially awkward. We were always nice to her, but she was odd.

"What's she up to these days?" I asked, but I wasn't terribly curious.

"She's in medical school." He didn't seem very surprised

by her matriculation toward being a physician. Maybe because he had already had a few days to absorb that information.

"Wow!" Charlie piped in. "I knew she was smart, but I would never have figured she would be able to go into a career in medicine. She couldn't even look at the stitches I got on my knee from that fall I took on those rocks at the beach freshman year."

"I had forgotten about that." I found myself reminiscing about that trip.

"I fell because I was chasing you," she reminded me, and I pictured her running on those boulders alongside the ocean.

"I'm pretty sure you never chased me." I shifted my weight and turned toward her. "I was always the one chasing you." I waggled my brows at her.

Cameron's eyes widened, and Charlie blushed. Yet again, he needed to resolve those awkward moments that had seemed to be occurring with more frequency lately. "He's right. He was chasing after you and you slipped."

Charlie smiled and batted her eyelashes as if reliving the memory. "I remember now. You felt really bad about that."

"I did. It was all my fault that you had gotten hurt." I couldn't stop peering into her gray eyes. That magnetic pull she had over me reeled me in.

"And you said you would never be the reason I got hurt again." Her voice was merely a whisper, and I swear, if Cameron hadn't been at the table with us, I would have kissed her then.

A cough broke our connection when Cameron cleared his throat. "I'm starting to feel like a third wheel you two."

Charlie and I exchanged glances with each other and then eyeballed her brother. We both laughed and soon Cam joined in our amusement. "I like that the three of us are friends again. But the two of you can really make a guy feel out of place sometimes."

"Out of place? You left me alone with Louis in a bar the first day I saw him in five years." Reaching across the table with her long arms, she shoved his shoulder.

"And now look at the two of you." He waved his hand at the two of us. "Inseparable and totally in love with each other."

Charlie huffed out a laugh, but I saw the glare she cut in her brother's direction. "It's been fun getting to know each other again," I managed to say. "But I am sorry to disappoint you and crush the hope you have about having me as a brother. We're just friends." I squeezed Charlie's knee under the table again and she visibly flinched.

"Besides, Louis is going to be leaving in less than a week to go home. Who knows when we'll see him again." Her sorrowful eyes had that glassy appearance again. I could handle disappointment with Cam, but not from Charlie. I didn't like seeing her sad.

"Now that I have my friends in my life again, I think I'll be back a lot more often." I felt a squeeze on my knee then. I looked at Cameron. I didn't look at her. I knew that was her way of letting me know I had said something that made her happy. I did want her to be happy.

11

LOUIS

After breakfast, Charlie left the restaurant. I promised her I would see her around three. Cam and I went to the soccer scrimmage in an adjacent town. It was hot outside, and the heat from the weather sizzled against the burn on my back. Once the game was over, I was more than relieved to head to the air-conditioned cab of Cam's truck.

Cam drove back to his apartment and got ready for his basketball game. I figured I could really use a shower and some wound dressing supplies, but all my belongings were at my parents' house. Maybe I was just a coward because going shopping for clothes and dressing bandages seemed like a better idea than going to my parents' house. I figured I had some time to kill while Cam was playing basketball and before Charlie would be home, so off to shopping I went.

I drove my car to the clothing outlets that were about thirty minutes away. The drive was too quiet. I hadn't been alone since I returned to the eastern shore. I was used to being alone back home, but it felt strange to be alone here. I increased the radio volume in the hopes that the feelings I was having of loneliness would dissipate.

Once I arrived in the parking lot, I quickly busied myself with visiting stores and grabbing enough clothes to last me the next few days. There was a Target in the same area as the clothing outlets, so after dropping off the bags of clothes in my car, I visited Target for underwear, socks, toiletries, and bandage supplies. I even purchased a duffel bag to carry all my newly purchased items.

Feeling confident that I had everything I needed, I returned to Cameron's apartment to shower and change. He was already home when I arrived. I guess I had been gone longer than I thought.

"Honey, I'm home," I said, entering his apartment using the key he had given to me.

"You bought a lot of stuff. How long are you planning to avoid your parents?"

"I'm not sure yet, so I wanted to be prepared."

"After tonight, you're welcome to stay here as long as you like." He was sitting on the barstool at the breakfast bar that separated his kitchen from his living room.

"Thanks for letting me crash here last night, but I think I'm good. I'll find somewhere else in town. Or I can always go back home to my apartment."

"I'm sure Charlie would let you crash at her place."

I pretended not to hear him as I walked toward the bathroom so I could shower.

I arrived at Charlie's apartment at five minutes to three. I would have rather arrived at five minutes *after* three. Then I wouldn't have looked so obvious. Because by now, she must have figured out how much I want to be with her. She must know that being with her is the only thing that truly makes me happy. Honestly, being with her is the only thing that seems to make sense in my life right now.

The door swung open as I raised my fist to tap at her door. "Hey." I was pretty sure I hadn't knocked yet, but there she was, standing at the threshold of the entrance into her apartment.

"Hey," I eagerly returned. She opened the door farther and motioned me to walk inside. Her apartment wasn't as big as Cam's but it suited her. It was small and practical. "Didn't you and Cam live together when you were in college?"

"Yeah. But we need our own space now."

"Really? Why?"

She huffed and gave me a dramatic eye roll. "I wouldn't want to have to leave my home every time he had some girl over." Her annoyance turned to indifference quickly. "And it would be weird if I ever brought a guy back to the apartment."

Something about her last comment didn't sit well with me. I didn't want to picture her bringing some guy into her apartment, unless it was me. I had no right to be jealous, yet here I was, feeling possessive as hell. I tried to appear as if the statement she made didn't knife me in the gut as I casually set my duffel bag down on the floor in her living room. "What do you feel like doing before dinner?"

"We could go bowling or watch a movie." Her eyes lit up at her own suggestions.

"Or we could eat ice cream and walk along the board-walk." I would love to stroll alongside her holding hands.

"I'm in for ice cream, but have you forgotten how the boardwalk is littered with Junebugs this time of year?" Junebugs are what the locals referred to as the summer tourist population.

"Okay. Let's go get ice cream and go for a walk along the docks at the marina. I've been thinking of mint chocolate chip ice cream since the other day." And the strawberry cheesecake ice cream I tasted when she kissed me that same day.

"Sounds good. Let's go." The light in her eyes sparkled as she grabbed her keys and headed toward the door that led out of her apartment. She turned her head back toward me once and motioned for me to hurry. I didn't want to hurry. I wanted to enjoy every last second of our night alone together.

After our ice cream was finished, we went for a walk and held hands. It still felt completely natural, even though we weren't a couple. I was pretty sure she reached for my hand first, but I was happy to offer mine to her. We talked and walked with our fingers intertwined and after some time had passed, we agreed to head back to her apartment.

We ordered pizza and sat on the couch next to each other while eating several slices of pizza. It felt like old times when we ate pizza on the couch at her house. Yet it felt different, too. I felt different toward Charlie than I used to. She was the same person, but my feelings had changed.

I still loved her for her sense of adventure. She was unlike any other girl I had ever known. Cameron had hit the nail on the head when he said every guy would love to have a girl like his sister. She was never afraid to try something new. She was never worried about messing up her hair or nails, and she was confident. She didn't worry about how anyone thought of her looks.

I thought she was beautiful no matter what she wore. I loved seeing her with a ponytail in those shorts when we ran together, in her nurse scrubs with her hair in a long braid, or in a T-shirt and shorts and her hair pulled up into a messy bun piled on top of her head. And of course, I loved seeing her in those tight jeans and low-cut shirt with her hair left down in waves around her shoulders. I couldn't think of anything that she wore that would make me see her as anything other than beautiful.

However, sometimes things between us seemed so comfortable and easy, and other times, there was some crackling chemistry. I knew that I felt it, and I thought she felt it, too. It wasn't that I wasn't happy with her desire toward me, but I was not sure what would happen if we moved in to the *seeing each other naked* category.

I guess I could finally understand the dilemma Charlie had felt she was in when I'd confessed my feelings to her all those years ago. Right now, I felt like I was getting to know her again, and I certainly didn't want to screw that up. I would just keep our touching to holding hands and maybe a kiss or two. There would definitely be no sex.

I would probably have to tell myself that several times in the future.

"You want to watch a movie on Netflix?" With the gentle smile she was flaunting in my direction, I couldn't think of any place I would rather be or with anyone else for that matter.

"Sure. You pick." I adjusted my weight on the couch while she reached for the remote on her coffee table. When she leaned back on the couch, she lifted my arm and snuggled against me. Crap. I was in trouble.

The movie ended a few minutes ago, but she was sleeping so soundly, I didn't want to move. It was still early, but she had fallen into an easy slumber. With it only being eight thirty, I wasn't sure how that happened, considering she worked night shifts and didn't even start her job until seven at night. She must be tired. I certainly felt tired, too. Sleeping on Cam's couch last night left me exhausted. I never managed to get comfortable on that thing. But sitting on Charlie's with her head leaning on my chest was *so* incredibly comfortable. I had my eyelids almost closed when the chirp on my phone startled me. I reached for it on her living room end table and saw a text from my mother.

I know you're upset, but it's been two days. Can we talk? I had never been anything but respectful to my mother, for my entire life, but I couldn't talk to her right now without exploding. I still needed some time to let my anger settle down.

I'm not ready yet. You need to give me some time to digest things first. I didn't want to respond to her, but I needed some space. And she would give me space if I asked for it. She always respected me, too.

Okay. I love you. Call me soon. Charlie began to stir, so I kissed her head and stroked her hair.

"Sorry, I fell asleep on you again." Her sleepy voice instantly aroused me.

"I'm beginning to think you find me boring." I snickered while she peered up at me. Her sleepy, gray eyes locked me into that alluring gaze. I knew that moment I was going to kiss her. I wasn't going to be able to stop myself. So that's what happened.

My lips barely grazed hers when she gently parted hers, allowing me access to the inside of her mouth with my tongue. So much for no open-mouthed kissing. She tasted delicious and a cocoon of warmth enveloped me as I probed every part of her beautiful mouth. While I nibbled on her bottom lip, she tugged me closer toward her. Her graceful arms snaked around my neck, and I guided her down onto her back so I could position myself over her. We didn't break our kiss for what seemed like several minutes.

All the emotions I had been having for her over the last five years of my life was poured into that kiss. The passion, and lust, and love for her was expressed in our interlocking lips and intertwined tongues. When I heard a moan escape her throat, I knew I was going to be sorry for what I did next.

I pulled myself away from her and took in the sight beneath me. Her breathing was fast and frantic. Her lips were swollen from being freshly kissed, and those passion-filled gray eyes were pleading with me to continue.

"I really like kissing you." I realized my own breathing was labored as I spoke. "But I finally understand what you must have been feeling that night all those years ago."

"What's that?"

"I'm just getting to know you again. I like what we have, and I want to give us a chance as friends. Now that you're back in my life, I don't want to lose you again. And this…" I bounced my finger toward us lying on the couch. "is what caused us to lose our ability to be friends."

"I understand, really I do." Her chest heaved a prolonged breath before she spoke again. "But I really like kissing you, too."

I pulled myself into a seated position and grasped her shoulders, leading her to sit upright as well. Then I wrapped my arms around her torso and embraced her hard. There was so much I wanted to tell her. There was so much I wanted to show her. I pulled her into a tighter squeeze so I could feel her warmth radiate through me. Then I released her and placed my hands on the smooth skin of her upper arms and peered into the pair of eyes staring at me through long, curled eyelashes. Her gray eyes shimmered—glazed over with unshed tears. "So maybe we can kiss…every once in a while," I offered.

A fist struck me in the shoulder with a resounding smack. She hit harder these days than she did when we were kids. "Maybe we need some ground rules. You know, so we don't cross the line between friend and…you know."

Damn, she was cute. "Okay. First rule. Holding hands is okay. But massaging each other with our hands probably isn't a good idea." Having our hands roaming each other's bodies would lead to temptation for sure.

I could tell she heard what I said because she shifted uncomfortably in her seat, but she tried to act indifferent to what I had just stated. "Second rule. Closed mouth kisses are acceptable."

"That probably depends on where or what we're kissing." I arched a suggestive eyebrow up at her.

"A quick kiss on the lips is okay, but no lingering. A kiss on the head, or cheek, or hand is okay, too. But absolutely no open-mouthed kissing."

I wasn't sure I liked these ground rules very much. "Fine. Anything else?"

"Yes. Third rule. We are to keep clothes on whenever we're in each other's company."

Now she was just trying to kill me because by her stating that rule, I was doomed to think of her naked now for sure. "Fine. I just thought of another rule." She cocked her head to the side in curiosity. "Fourth rule. Sleeping together is okay, but *sleeping together* is not."

A pink glow instantly illuminated her cheeks. I swear she didn't used to get embarrassed so easily. "Fine."

"So now that's settled, what's next on the slumber party agenda?"

"We could play board games and drink beer."

I loved her suggestion. So we followed through with her idea. We played Trivial Pursuit and Yahtzee. Then we played cards. I wasn't sure how much beer either of us drank in those few hours. I was pretty sure there was a twelve-pack of bottles in her fridge at the beginning of our game playing. However, now there was only an empty box and two pretty intoxicated people in her apartment.

"I'm going to go and get ready for bed." Charlie attempted to stand but swayed slightly and appeared a little unsteady on her feet.

"Okay." Although I had more to drink than her, she was so much smaller than me. She easily weighed eighty or ninety pounds less than me. I thought maybe I should let her lean on my shoulder while I guided her into the bedroom, but I reconsidered that idea and took to just watching her hobble to her room on her own accord, safely, even with the drunken ambulation. Helping her to her bedroom was not a smart idea if we truly wanted to preserve the ground rules.

So I took to cleaning up the board games, cards, beer bottles, and putting away leftover pizza when I heard her call my name. I gingerly shuffled my feet down the hall toward her voice and opened the door to her bedroom. "You okay?"

She was beneath the covers on her bed, and she peeled back the comforter on the side opposite where she lay and patted the mattress with her hand. "Come lie down with me."

"You're drunk."

"You said we could sleep together." Her eyelids were drooping as she spoke. Whether I stayed or retreated back to the living room, I was convinced that she would be asleep very quickly.

"Okay. I'll lie down for a minute." That decision was probably not a good idea, but I couldn't think of why not at that moment. So I scooted beneath the covers and faced away from her. She slid down further between the sheets and draped her arm across my waist. Yep, definitely not a good idea.

But as I suspected, I heard soft snores escape from her

within a few moments. I debated getting up and going to lie down on the couch, but I couldn't figure out why I should. This had to be the most comfortable bed I had ever lain on. And soon, I was no longer able to keep my eyelids from falling shut. As the pull of a warm, calming slumber overtook me, I drifted into a dream about the girl that was once my friend and the woman she had become.

I opened one eye to examine where I was. I knew by the floral smell of the sheets, I wasn't at my apartment. I wasn't at my parents' house, either. I opened my other eye and rolled over onto my other side. There was a wrinkled spot where Charlie had slept, but it was currently empty. Then as if I wished for her to appear, she entered the bedroom.

"Hey, sleepyhead."

Was she always this cheerful in the morning? "What are you doing up so early?"

"Early? It's eight o'clock." *Has she always been a morning person?* "You promised to go for a run with me, remember?"

I had to think back to when that would have happened. "When did I do that exactly?"

"Remember? You said you didn't feel like running yesterday, but you would today."

Maybe I did remember something like that. "Fine." But I still moaned and whipped the covers over my head.

She playfully pulled them back down. "Come on. We can go out to breakfast after our run. I know my bed is super comfortable, but it's time to get up."

Now she was just being annoying.

After a glass of water and some ibuprofen, I managed to change into some mesh shorts and tie my sneakers. I had my shirt off when Charlie entered the living room. "Put a shirt on, Coleman."

"Does this really violate the third rule?" I watched her nod in agreement. "What about when we go swimming? Will I have to wear a shirt then, too?"

She huffed and turned on her heel away from me.

Again, it was adorable when I got her riled.

It was a long and silent five-mile run. She still doesn't talk to me when she runs. So she remained focused, and I just followed alongside her. We ran through the park today instead of through our old neighborhood, which I was especially grateful for. I didn't want to have an inadvertent run-in with either of my parents.

"Hurry up and shower. I'm starving," she said to me once we returned to her apartment.

"Fine, but no more breaking the third rule. No sneaking in while I'm in the shower this time." I raised my eyebrows up and tossed her a suggestive grin before walking down the hall of her apartment toward the bathroom.

Once we had showered, we went out to breakfast at the Pancake Cabin again. I was pleased with her suggestion. I had forgotten how good their food was until we had eaten it yesterday.

"When are you planning to talk with your mom?" she asked in between bites of her French toast.

"Maybe tomorrow." I still didn't exactly *want* to hear what my mom was going to say. But at least now I thought maybe I could hear it and not explode. Charlie had a way of calming me.

"I have to work tonight, but you're welcome to stay at my

place." She took a sip of orange juice and then those gray eyes darted directly at me. "I'm pretty sure you like my bed."

"It is more comfortable than Cam's couch." Although I was pretty sure her bed was so comfortable because she was in it with me. Pretty much anywhere I slept, next to her was the most comfortable place I had ever slept.

She fumbled with something in her purse and then slid a key across the table to me. "You can have my spare key."

I stared at the key in front of me, but I didn't move or speak.

"It won't bite you, Louis. Take it." She picked up the metal object and reached for my hand. Then she faced my palm up and placed the key in it and closed my fingers around it. "Are you going to say anything?"

I wasn't sure if I could speak at that moment. She basically gave me access to not just her place, but to her whenever I wanted. That could be extremely dangerous.

"Geez Louis, you act like I just asked you to move in with me. I'm just letting you have a key in case you ever need a place to crash." My hand was still curled around the key, and she was still holding my hand in hers. "I can take it back if it makes you uncomfortable."

I quickly retracted my hand with the key from her hold. "Thanks." I cleared my throat for no reason, other than in an attempt to clear the air that was thick with awkwardness. "It would be great if I could sleep there tonight."

A satisfied smile crossed her lips. Crap. I was in trouble for sure.

12

LOUIS

I spent the rest of the morning with Charlie, but when she went home to take a nap before work, I texted Cam. He invited me to the local college football game with some of his friends, so we went. Afterward, we grabbed a burger and returned to his apartment to watch another football game on his television.

"So what's the plan with your mom?"

"Thinking maybe I'll go talk with her tomorrow." I opened Cam's refrigerator and saw the only beverages behind the door consisted of beer and water. "Would it kill you to have some soda in here?" I grabbed a water bottle and unscrewed the cap before taking a long swallow of the cold liquid.

"Next time you decide to crash, I'll make sure I stock my fridge with cola." A low rumble of a laugh erupted from him. "Hey, I'm planning to do a coffee run for the ER nurses tonight. You wanna come with me?"

I contemplated what to say. I wouldn't mind seeing Charlie again, but I certainly didn't want to smother her, so I reconsidered. "Nah. Thinking I'll get to bed early. Tomorrow probably won't be much fun."

"Need a place to crash? You're welcome here as long as you like."

"Thanks, man, but I'm just going to stay at Charlie's. She's working tonight, so I'll have her place to myself."

"Um. Okay." He changed his position to face away from me, but I knew he was hiding a smirk. He knew something, or he thought he knew something. I felt the need to explain my relationship with Charlie to him for some reason. But then again, what was going on with his sister and me was between her and me. I didn't owe him any explanation, especially when I wasn't entirely sure myself.

The faint smell of coconut tickled my nose. And I felt a comforting warmth wrap around me. I managed to open my sleep-filled eyes and saw Charlie sliding under the covers next to me. "What are you doing?" My voice cracked and whispered from being dragged out of a peaceful slumber.

"What does it look like?" I peeked under the covers and saw she was wearing shorts and a T-shirt.

"It looks like you are climbing into bed with me."

"Duh." Her head shook playfully. "I've been up all night, so it's time for me to go to sleep." Our bodies were lined up facing one another as we took refuge lying beneath the covers. "You can stay, but you're breaking the third rule."

In my half-asleep daze, I tried really hard to remember what the third rule was, but when I glanced at my chest and noticed it was bare, I recalled which rule I broke. "Are you really going to make me put a shirt on?"

"Breaking one rule may lead to breaking others..." Her face remained uncovered but she fumbled beneath the blankets for a moment before she pulled out her shorts. When she tossed them onto the floor, a scratchiness from within my throat developed. I found myself speechless as I thought about her nakedness beside me, only hidden by a mere sheet and comforter. "Don't look so surprised, Louis. I have underwear on. If you're going to sleep in what you are comfortable in, then so am I." With a quick flip onto her opposite side, she faced away from me causing her hair to fan out over her pillow. She snuggled up against me with her backside, though. She knew exactly what she was doing.

I lay there completely awake and aware that her bottom was nestled on top of my crotch. I kept imagining what her panties looked like, and on impulse, I rubbed my fingers along the silkiness of her bare leg.

"Now you're breaking the first rule." Her voice was sleepy, yet sexy, even mixed in with the yawn I heard.

Damn those rules. I slid my hand around her waist and followed the smooth skin of her bare arm to find her fingers. "Nah. I was just trying to find your hand, so I could hold it."

She sighed and within moments, I could hear her breathing even out. I inhaled her coconut scent and fell back to sleep for an additional hour, spooning her with my arm still draped around her midsection.

I awakened in the same position. I stayed in in that spot, curled up with her for several minutes, but figured it was time to get up. It was difficult to leave the warmth of her body and the coziness of her bed, but somehow I managed to crawl out from the cocoon of covers I was enveloped in.

It was almost nine, so I texted my mom that I wanted to meet with her. She asked for me to come by the house, so I showered and changed. I kissed Charlie gently on the cheek before I left and she didn't stir. I still watched her for several moments before I left. Having the key to her apartment made it easier to leave somehow. I guess because I knew I could come back anytime I wanted.

Both of my parents were sitting at the dining room table in their home when I entered the house. It was ten o'clock on a Monday morning. *Why aren't they at work?*

"Thanks for coming by to speak with us, Louis." My mother's voice wavered slightly when she glanced in my direction and then directed her gaze to my father.

My father sat at the table in his dark gray suit, but a bright red tie caught my attention. I wondered who had picked out that tie. It was way brighter than his usual, neutral, low-key ones.

"Sit down, son." My father motioned for me to join them at the table.

A wave of nausea hit me in the gut. A similar scene played out when they told me my grandmother…my father's mother had died. *Did someone die? Why were they waiting until now to tell me?* That would definitely be a reason for them to miss work. My father *never* missed work.

I finally took a seat next to my mother, across from my father. I always thought he was such a massive presence, but as I sat across from him, he seemed smaller. His sullen demeanor made him appear like he lost some of the gumption he used to have.

"Louis, I don't know how to tell you this." The solemn look my mom displayed had me concerned. Her eyes followed my dad at the other side of the table, and he nodded for her to continue. "Your father and I are getting divorced."

Those words hit me harder than a punch in the abdomen. A choking sensation wrapped around my throat, and I couldn't breathe. The air that occupied my lungs had escaped and couldn't be retrieved. I tried to suck in a deep breath, but I couldn't inhale forcefully enough. Dizziness swept in, and images became fuzzy.

"Grant, go get Louis a glass of water. He looks ill." *Gee, thanks Mom. I must look as bad as I feel.*

My dad quickly returned with the water and sat it on the woven placemat on the table in front of me. I lifted the glass to my lips but it felt heavy in my hand. My body shook as I attempted to swallow the water, while also concentrating on not choking.

When I finally found that deep breath I craved, I drew in some air and exhaled slowly a few times as I attempted to digest the information I was provided. "What happened?" My parents exchanged glances, but my dad was the first to speak.

"We grew apart years ago." He combed his hand through his thick dark hair that was just beginning to gray at his temples. I hoped I got his hair.

"Honey, we separated a few years ago." I could hear my mother's voice, but I couldn't seem to look in her direction. So I stared at the water glass in front of me while she spoke. "We wanted to tell you in person rather than over the phone, but you came home so infrequently and for such short periods of time, it just never seemed like the right time."

A flash of anger seeped out of me. "So this is my fault!" I shot up from the table and paced the carpeted floor.

"Son, that's not what your mother is trying to say." *Why was he even talking? He was hardly ever home anyway.*

"You two just blindsided me. I had *no* idea your marriage was even in trouble, and today I find out you're getting divorced. How long has this been going on? When did you get separated?" I halted the pacing, but the volume of my voice had increased from a surprised to an angry octave.

"Almost three years ago." My mother hung her head after her statement.

I couldn't help but scoff at her admission. "Three years? Three years? Three years! This has been going on for three years, and you two didn't think this was something that you should let your only child know something about?" Both of my parents stared at me with blank expressions. Their nonverbal communication was not sufficient for me. "Well?"

"We wanted to tell you, son, but we didn't want to upset you." My dad's words seemed so matter-of-fact. His calm and casual attitude had me wondering if he was dating someone, too. I also began to question if he knew my mom was with someone else.

"You didn't want to upset me? Well too bad! I am upset. You were right. You *did* upset me." My blood was boiling and anger seeped out of my pores. "So, separated. Dad doesn't live here anymore?" They both shook their heads. "So where are you living, Dad?"

"In a condo on the south side of town."

"Are you living by yourself?" I had to know.

"I live by myself, but I am seeing someone." I wished I was still at the table so I could throw the glass of water somewhere. "I know you saw your mother with Marshall the other day."

What the hell was wrong with the two of them? They had gotten separated and started dating new people without ever telling me. "I have to get the hell out of here." I dug my keys out of my pocket and headed for the door. I was glad my parents didn't try to stop me. I needed some air.

I didn't know where to go. I was so angry that I probably shouldn't be driving. Some idiot blew through a stop sign, and I began following him. I wanted to snatch him out of his car and beat the crap out of him for his reckless behavior. Somehow, I managed to get that thought out of my mind and abandoned the ambush I planned in my head.

I drove to the marina and parked my car. When I began a

stroll to calm my frayed nerves, I stumbled into the wake of a couple's cigarette smoke, and I blurted out, "You assholes don't need to poison everyone's air." I was prepared for the man to turn around and threaten me, but they just laughed and continued to puff on their nicotine-filled tobacco sticks. I could have totally kicked his ass and enjoyed doing it. I was itching for a fight. I needed to get a grip. I was going to get myself in trouble if I didn't find something to calm me quickly. So I headed to the only place I knew might help me compose myself.

I knew she hadn't been asleep for very long, but I needed her. She wouldn't mind, that's what I told myself as I drove to Charlie's apartment. She gave me a key to her place, so I figured she expected me to use it. I drove faster than I probably should have, and I stormed into her apartment as soon as I unlocked the door.

13

CHARLIE

The door being shoved open forced me awake. I was grateful the masculine body storming into my room was Louis and not a criminal. But he didn't look like himself. His breathing was noisy and his nostrils flared. I had never seen him like that before. His clenched fists swung at his sides while he stomped forward. A suppressed rage skimmed just beneath the surface, and I was fearful that he might explode at any moment. His tightened expression made my muscles quiver.

"What's wrong, Louis?"

"My parents are getting divorced. They have been separated for three years and decided now was the time to finally tell me." The tone of his voice was deeper than usual and his face was flushed.

With passion and intensity marring his facial features, he bounced onto the bed with me causing the mattress to shift beneath me. Those blue eyes were dancing before me for only a moment when his lips assaulted mine. He kissed me hard and frantically as he devoured my mouth with deep sweeps of his tongue. The betrayal he was feeling soaked into

114

my soul. He was lonely and hurt, and I knew he needed me. Screw the second rule.

My body responded quickly to his needs. Even though I was sound asleep just moments ago, my senses were fully awakened. Every part of me had a heightened awareness of Louis. A tingling sensation swept over my body and a delicious aching formed in the pit of my belly.

My trembling hands reached around to his back, and I began to trace my fingers up and down the cotton of his shirt across the ripples of his back. I didn't palpate any bandages during my survey, so I continued pressing against him.

Louis soon followed in my quest for discovery as he explored my exposed skin with his hands. So much for the first rule. *Did I actually agree to these rules?* Clearly I hadn't realized what I would be missing. Still with our mouths fused together, he reached beneath the covers and brushed the back of his hand over my bare thigh. I couldn't help but moan with gratitude. His touch sent a fire of desire through my bones, blended with a lightness, like being lifted into the air on a cloud of delight.

A throaty moan escaped him and dampness developed in my underwear. He broke our kiss long enough to pull his shirt over his head and toss it onto my bedroom floor. His respirations were still erratic and his blue eyes were holding me captive with an intense stare. Emotion was etched on his face, but I wasn't sure which emotion was there. *Was it passion or lust? Was it sadness or regret? Please just kiss me some more.*

I reached up to his muscled chest and pulled him over me while bending my neck back, exposing the sensitive skin for his touch. He pecked my neck with a trail of ardent kisses while his warm hands slid underneath my shirt. I wasn't wearing a bra, and he seemed to be happy about that revelation because without any wasted time, he was soon caressing my breasts with the pads of his fingers. I needed to feel his skin flush against mine and a layer of cotton created an unwanted barrier. As if he could read my mind, he tugged at the bottom of my shirt. I assisted him by pulling it over my head, and he tossed it to the floor with his own discarded shirt. The third rule was definitely broken now.

He dragged his lips away from my neck, but while still handling my swollen breasts, his cobalt gaze pulled at me, urging me to look at him. I observed his slack jaw as he released the hold of my aching mounds and grabbed the sides of my face before sliding his fingers down my cheeks. "You are so gorgeous, Charlie." His breathing remained uneven and heavy.

I didn't know what to say. I just grinned widely and proceeded to pepper light kisses over his broad chest. When I licked his nipple, he winced and quickly drew the covers back to reveal me in nothing more than my pink lace panties.

I grabbed the erection that was building in his shorts and he enveloped one of my taut nipples into his mouth. I screamed his name, but he never released the firm hold his mouth had on my rosy bud. While he performed magnificent twirls with his tongue around one of my nipples, he was gently squeezing the other between his finger and thumb.

I had to have him then. "Please, Louis." I wanted him desperately—no, I *needed* him. *God, I had to have him.*

He tugged at the hem of my panties and swiftly pulled them down to my ankles. I kicked them off and located the waistband on his shorts. He rid himself of his shorts and underwear while simultaneously trailing kisses down my abdomen.

"Stay right where you are," I huffed while rolling over to my side and reaching into the top drawer of my nightstand.

I grabbed the foil wrapper and tore it open with my teeth. Louis grabbed it from my hand and applied the latex material to his full erection, while I admired his nude form. I had no interest in any more foreplay. I needed to feel all of him. I knew from that moment that he was the only man that could fill the void that was left in the empty pit of my heart.

I reached for his shaft in the hopes of guiding him to the place where I needed him to be, but he had another plan. He hastily impaled me with his arousal, stealing my breath away. He wasn't gentle, but he didn't hurt me. I stretched and adjusted quickly to accommodate his size and girth. As his thrusting began moving in a rhythmic pattern, I felt like I would leave the earth and float away on that cloud that I was on. When my climax rumbled within me, rippling waves of ecstasy shook throughout my body.

Bursts of light exploded behind my closed eyelids as I felt myself tighten around him while the walls of my inner core quivered from the best orgasm of my life. His body stiffened with his own release and he collapsed on top of me. He tried to prop himself up on his forearms to keep from crushing me, but his exhausted body didn't cooperate. So much for the fourth rule.

The thumping of his heartbeat against my own chest was comforting and spoke to my own heart. I knew I was meant to be with him. Without hesitation, I whispered "I love you" as I trailed my fingernails up and down his arms.

I didn't expect what happened next. Louis rolled off me and headed to the bathroom without a word. The cool breeze left from the wake of his rapid departure left me feeling extremely naked without the warmth of his body hovering over me. I pulled the sheet back over my body to cover myself and extinguish the chill left in the air. When he left the bathroom, I figured he would return to my bedroom —to my bed—with me.

But instead, I heard footsteps moving away from my room down the hallway. *Maybe he was thirsty?* I heard some fumbling around in my living room, so I decided to get out of bed and see what he was doing. But before I climbed out of my bed, I heard the heavy door to my apartment swing open and click shut.

What the hell just happened? I mean besides the rule-breaking, mind-blowing sex we just had. With an exaggerated sigh of frustration, I rolled back over in an attempt to return to sleep, but I couldn't resume my previous slumber because the tears forcefully flowed like an angry river down my face and loud sobbing ensued. *Those damn rules were supposed to prevent this from happening.*

I managed to fall back to sleep somehow, but I wasn't sure for how long. I stayed in bed when I awakened again, thinking back to last night and how disappointed I had been when my brother showed up with coffee and Louis wasn't with him. Seeing him last night would have made my night. Seeing him in my bed this morning, certainly made my morning. When he stormed into my bedroom and sexually devoured me, I had my hunger for him satisfied, but that was swept away now. *How could we be so fiercely connected one minute and completely distant and apart the next?*

I needed an explanation. Maybe he was just feeling too emotional and needed some time to adjust to his feelings for me. I wanted to talk to him and find out what was going on in his gorgeous head. But I had never been the type of girl to chase after a man. If he wanted to talk to me, he knew how to reach me. *I gave him a freaking key to my apartment! What was I thinking?*

I was thinking that I loved him, and I wanted him to stay with me. I yearned to give him a place to go where he felt safe, and I intended to be the person that provided that for him. As I peeled myself out of bed and picked up my discarded panties and shirt on the floor, I decided to shower before putting clothes back on.

As the hot spray of the shower beat against my skin, I could still feel his touch on me. I could still smell him. And Lord help me, I could still taste him. The taste of him still lingered on my tongue. My breasts felt swollen and my nipples felt slightly abraded from his day-old stubble. Between my legs had a pleasurable soreness, and I wondered why I was washing him off.

I dressed in a tank top and comfortable yoga pants. When I picked up his clothes next to my bed, I couldn't help but pull them to my face so I could smell his intoxicating scent. *I was acting crazy.* But when I walked out into my living room, the bare spot where his duffel bag once sat stared at me like the empty hole he left in my heart. *He was really gone. He wasn't going to come back.* And I wasn't sure that my shattered heart would ever be able to feel whole again.

When shit happened in my life, I always ran to Cameron for comfort. He always knew exactly what to say and do to make me feel better. He knows me better than anyone, but for some reason, it didn't feel right running to him this time. I would have to deal with this on my own. I'm a twenty-three-year-old woman. I shouldn't need anyone. I don't need a pity party, and I don't need to rely on someone else to make me feel better. I could move forward without needing to *feel* anything.

So I went about my life as best as I could. I was off Monday night, but I went to work Tuesday and Wednesday night. I did my best to avoid Cameron. I knew if I saw him, he would see right through me. He would know exactly what was going on. He would take one look at me and know his best friend had broken my heart. More accurately, he would know Louis destroyed me. He would see an empty shell of the person I used to be without the love of my childhood friend.

I successfully managed to dodge Cam's texts about bike riding, fishing, and canoeing explaining that I needed to nap because I had to work. I still jumped to see if Louis had texted me every time my phone pinged even though I knew I was being overly hopeful.

After three days of avoiding my brother, he threatened to drag me out of my apartment if I didn't meet him at the gym. So I went. I don't know why, but I agreed to go.

However, when I walked into the gym for pickup basketball, not only did I see my brother, but I also saw the man that had ripped out my heart and consumed my soul. The color drained from his face when he caught sight of me. And in a millisecond, he left my brother's side and bolted across the gym to the door leading to the outside.

I wanted to run after Louis and force him to tell me what was going on. I deserved to know what had happened to make him leave me. As all those thoughts scurried through my mind, I felt water welling up in my eyes and a wave of nausea overcame me. I had to get the hell out of there. I didn't want to run into Louis in the parking lot, so I walked out of the gym on the opposite side of where he exited.

"Lean Bean!" I could hear Cameron calling behind me, but I wasn't interested in speaking to him. I continued my speed walking and took off into a jog that quickly developed into a sprint. I ran to my car and left my brother behind.

I hurried home to wall myself off from the world of Louis. I struggled with my stupid key in the lock because my hands were shaking so badly upon arrival at my apartment. My legs felt like liquid as I tried to lift them into some kind of gait until I could finally collapse on my couch. Once I reached my destination, I had lain on the cushions on my belly with my eyes closed for several minutes.

Unfortunately, I was alone with my thoughts again. And I continued to think of the emptiness inside me as a hole. But a hole would be void of any feelings. I didn't have a void. I was full. I was full of doubt, loneliness, and shame. I was so hurt, yet so full of love for Louis, I couldn't make sense of it all.

The sound of a metal key being inserted into the deadbolt of my apartment door caused my heart rate to accelerate and chilly perspiration caused my skin to erupt with gooseflesh. I jolted upright on my couch and forced myself to take in a deep, cleansing breath. I wasn't expecting to see a man appear before me once the door was shoved open, and I certainly wasn't expecting the man to be my twin brother braced in the doorjamb of my apartment. Yet, there he was wearing his best pity face. *Had I given a spare key to every man in my life?*

14

CHARLIE

"Lean Bean." His voice was soft and sweet while his face was drawn into an empathic frown. His gentle foot-steps approached me, and normally this would comfort me, but this time I really just wanted him to go away. That wall I was so desperately trying to put up was closing in on me.

"Cameron, I'm fine. Can you please go?" I slouched back down and plopped onto my comfortable couch.

"What happened?" I wasn't facing him, but I felt the weight of his body sink into the cushions, so I knew he had sat down next to me.

"I don't want to talk about it." This was the only time I could think of in my whole life that I didn't want to talk to my brother. Even when we were kids, I couldn't stay mad at him for very long, because there was always something I wanted to talk to him about. He wasn't even the older twin, but for some reason, I always went to him for advice on everything. He was always wise beyond his years, and he could somehow constantly make sense of even the most confusing situations.

His firm hands rubbed against my shoulders while I

remained prone on my couch. "I don't ever recall seeing you with a broken heart before." It was eerie and extremely disturbing that he *always* knew what was going on before I said anything.

"You don't know what you're talking about." I was going to deny it to him even though I was pathetically talking into the couch cushions, too depressed to even lift my head up when I spoke.

"He told me about his parents." When I didn't respond, he continued. "But he didn't tell me about the two of you."

Cam's last statement spoke volumes. I wasn't significant enough in his life to mention anything about me to my brother. Louis obviously didn't feel the same about me that I felt about him. I didn't think he would tell my brother about our one afternoon of passion exactly, but maybe he could have said something like, *I'm in love with your sister, and I don't know what to do with those feelings.*

"I would pick you if I had to make a choice." His heavy sigh told me that he had something else on his mind.

"I would never ask you to make a choice between him and me, Cam." I continued to talk into the couch cushion and face away from him.

"I know you wouldn't. It's not in you to give an ultimatum. You are both my best friends, but *you* have always stood by me. I can't say the same for Louis." I sat up, breaking free of the shoulder massage. Cam's sagging body posture and the saddened features stretched across his face weighed me down with guilt.

"The only reason he left was because of me! It had nothing to do with you." Great. The tears appeared again. *Hadn't I shed enough water over this whole thing already?*

"Maybe I need to remind him that this thing that is broken with the three of us needs to be fixed. I'm not going to stand by passively this time. I shouldn't have five years ago." His head tilted slightly to the side and he stretched his arms out and wrapped them around me.

I sank right into his embrace. Somehow his tight hug made me feel safe enough to let all my emotions free. I could hear my own gut-wrenching sobs as I shed too many tears to see straight. And my brother held me, sitting on my couch, while I extinguished my soul from the plight Louis had bestowed on me.

"Are you going to tell me what happened?" Our embrace broke as he pushed me far enough away that he could look me in my water-filled eyes.

I shook my head no. "This isn't the kind of thing a girl talks with her brother about."

"What do you mean, Lean Bean?"

I giggled at the rhyme he had just made through my hiccupping sniffles.

"You used to tell me everything." He stood and concern washed over his face. I could feel his disappointment. He always had been my confidant. "I guess I'll just have to go pay Louis a visit then."

As he turned to leave, I begged him not to speak to Louis. "Please, just let me deal with things for a few days before you talk with him about this. I promise I'll tell you everything…eventually."

"I've never felt like I needed to save you from being wounded by a man. You never acted like you cared enough about any man to give him an opportunity to hurt you. But seeing you like this, Charlie, makes me want to beat the crap out of my best friend." That was probably the sweetest thing my brother had ever said to me. "If you decide that whatever is going on between the two of you is beyond repair, please just don't shut me out. I can live without my best friend, but I can't live without my twin. Because if I'm being completely honest, he isn't my best friend…you are."

I hauled my wilted body up and stood to give Cam a quick hug. "You are the best brother a girl could ever ask for. We're twins. No one could ever separate us." I tried my best to reassure him before I broke the news. "I'm going to be gone for a few days. I need some time to think everything over."

"Where are you going?" His puzzled look almost made me feel like I should offer additional information.

"I promise, I'll tell you everything once I get back."

"We never had secrets between us before. I'm not sure I like this." His hand rubbed over his face. "You better have your phone with you at all times. If you aren't going to tell me where you are going or what's going on, you better at least respond to my text messages."

I laughed at his silly request. "Of course I'll respond to you. You're my favorite person in the whole world." I have always been glad he stayed single because I liked having him all to myself. I'm not sure how I'd be able to adjust to sharing him with *anyone* else. Luckily for me, Cam has never looked for anything serious. However, because of that fact, my brother was *not* the person I needed right now.

Sometimes a girl needs her sister. I had never gone to Claudette for advice on *anything*. But this time, I really needed her advice. I really needed to hear from a female. And truly the only female I trusted enough to tell me the truth was my sister.

I drove the hour it took to reach the Delaware beach town my sister lives in. I probably should have called before just showing up, but I knew where she would be. She lived in a beach town, and it was summer. This translates to lots of business for the residents, but it also means all work and no play. The residents of the Delaware beach towns work almost every day during the summer months, so you'll very rarely find them lounging on the beach or frolicking in the ocean.

Much like the Junebugs of Maryland's eastern shore, the tourists invade during the warm months and nearly triple the population of the otherwise quaint towns. They flood the coastline and litter the beaches with their presence. Finding a small spot in the sand to sunbathe or relax with a good book is no small feat for anyone during this time of year.

So I entered the bakery-coffee shop where my sister was the general manager and observed her frantically taking orders and packaging pastries. It was nearly eight o'clock at night on a Thursday. *Why were there so many people in need of coffee and muffins at this hour?*

I stood in the common area and glanced at the mugs on display for purchase until a high-pitch squeal rang out behind me, and I was embraced in a bear hug that nearly toppled me over. "Char!" Only Claudette could get away with that lame nickname. It reminds me of charcoal. I would have turned around to face her, but she plastered her cheek to my back and was literally squeezing the breath out of me.

She finally released me, and I looked at her sparkling blue eyes. My gray eyes always seemed so dull in comparison to her dazzling cobalt ones. She also stood at least two inches shorter than me. Even though she was the oldest of the Callahan offspring, she was the most petite. She had our mother's stature as well as her wavy blond hair. Cameron had the height of our father and his dark brown hair with hazel eyes. I fell somewhere in between. I didn't seem to favor either one of our parents. My hair was a lighter brown than Cam and my dad. And I lacked the petite frame of Claudette and my mom. Thankfully I wasn't as tall as the men in my family. I would have been teased and called an amazon woman for sure if I was.

"What are you doing here?" Excitement was bursting through my sister. Her eyes were shining and a smile stretched across her entire face.

"I came to see you." Burning crept up my throat and a squeezing sensation spread throughout my chest, but I quickly sniffled the emotions back.

"I'm planning to leave in about an hour," she said as she walked back toward the counter. "Why don't you go back to my place and relax? I'll pick up takeout burgers and meet you there." She pulled her purse out from a cubby behind the counter and dug into its contents until she retrieved her keys. Unwinding around the overlapping circles, she removed the key from its ring and handed it to me.

I happily took it from her and drove to her cottage in town. I parked and walked into the small bungalow with my suitcase in tow. Craving a beverage to moisten my dry throat, I searched her fridge. The interior door shelved five bottles of wine. *Geez, Claudette. How many bottles does one person need?* I guess she's someone that could benefit from a wine fridge.

I decided to fill a glass with tap water and sat on the couch, flipping through the channels on her television with the remote in my hand until she returned home less than an hour later. I hadn't found anything worthy of watching on television when she finally entered the living room through the front door.

She set down a brown paper bag on the coffee table my feet were propped on. I removed my feet from the area when she pulled out two Styrofoam containers. "I got a bacon cheeseburger for you." She pushed the square container toward me. The scent of a delicious juicy patty wafted through the air.

"And you got a plain burger piled high with shrubbery for yourself." I laughed and she quirked her eyebrow up.

"Some things never change." I guess my sister paid closer attention to my likes and dislikes than I had originally thought. "So what's up, Char? How have you been?"

"I need some advice." My comment elicited an excited gasp to whoosh from my sister and she pointed a finger to her chest.

"You want advice from me? I need to mark this on the calendar. I thought Cameron was your BFF." She opened her food container and sat on the couch next to me.

"Can we uncork one of those bottles of wine you have in your fridge? I may need some alcohol." Although Claudette seemed genuinely thrilled, sadness overloaded my core. I came to my sister for her advice in healing a wounded heart.

In only a moment, my sister abandoned her burger and retrieved a corkscrew and bottle of wine from her fridge. She approached me with a poured glass grasped in each of her hands.

"You are entirely too efficient at that." I easily extracted one of the glasses from her hold. "I worry you might like wine too much."

"Maybe I just never seem to have a reason to drink it, so the bottles sit in there unopened." She stuck her tongue out at me just like she used to when we were kids. Cameron was absolutely the more mature of my two siblings.

I took in a long breath and exhaled forcefully. But once my gaze found hers, burning developed within my eyes and I knew tears were forming. *What's with all the tears?* Women cry when they're happy. They cry when they're sad. And a woman like myself, cries when I'm angry. With so many reasons to cry, how could one keep track of why she was actually crying? However, there was no doubt in this situation. I cried because of overwhelming sadness.

"What happened, Char?" My sister's excited expression transformed into a sympathetic one, but she managed to maintain a half-clenched smile as she brushed a stray tendril of my hair behind my ear.

"You remember La-La-Louis?" My quivering lips vibrated as I stuttered. I hadn't realized how difficult it would be to even acknowledge his name.

"Of course. He was Cameron's best friend." A blank stare reflected back to me. "The three of you used to be inseparable."

Visions of Louis and me with intertwined legs and connected bodies took up residence in my mind at her comment. "Yeah, well…"

"Have you seen him?" She must be hungry because she quickly tossed the sympathy aside and resumed eating her burger.

"Oh, I've seen him all right." And I definitely liked what I had seen.

"I heard he moved after high school and hadn't been back home since." She talked while she chewed. She had always been so ladylike, I was surprised her manners weren't on point all the time.

"Well, he came home two weeks ago." Her burger dropped back into the food container with a soft swish while confusion mixed with inquiry occupied her expression as she turned toward me. With her legs crossed, she pulled them up into her chest presumably getting comfortable for the story she knew was going to follow.

She sat silently while I told her about the CPR on the old man at the grocery store, the beers at the bar, the forgiveness, our running together, the innocent flirting, and the not so innocent touching. I explained the rules that we made and seeing his mother kissing another man. I told her about our ice cream date and that he stayed at Cam's house one night and mine another. Her eyebrows lifted when I told her about sleeping in bed together, but she remained quietly listening.

Then I told her that he found out his parents were getting divorced, and how he came over to my apartment and entered with the key I had given him. When I finally told her about the lust we could no longer deny, she bit her bottom lip in anticipation of the rest of my story.

"So we slept together and then he left." Tears rolled down my cheeks and my sister grabbed a tissue from the box on her end table to hand me.

"Sweetie. I'm so sorry. Did he say anything before he left?" She brushed the hair off my face again.

I thought back to that afternoon. I hadn't remembered that *he* said anything. "I told him I loved him, and he took off."

Laughter rang through the air as my sister chuckled at me. I sat in my car driving for an hour and waited another hour for her to get home so that I could sit on her couch with a broken heart and have her laugh to my face. "Char, you can't say that to a guy the first time you have sex with him. That is, unless you're looking to get rid of him. No wonder he ran away." She threw me a wayward glance. "I'm surprised Cameron didn't tell you the same thing."

"I haven't talked to Cam about this." I blew out a breath and faced her. "Claudette, I came here looking for advice. I'm in love with Louis. I want to be with him, and I was hoping you could help me figure out how to do that."

She took a swallow of her wine and resumed consuming her burger. I wasn't sure how she could keep eating while my life was in crisis, yet she did.

15

CHARLIE

I let Cameron know I had been staying at Claudette's for the last couple of days. I found it better to text him rather than speak to him. He already knew something was bothering me. He probably knew *what* was bothering me or had a pretty good idea, and he was likely upset that I went to Claudette. He was *always* my go-to sibling for the good and the bad.

It was relaxing at Claudette's place. I liked being away from everything for a little while. It was good to be away from Louis and work, and it was enjoyable having some time to myself. My sister worked every day, so I had plenty of time to sort things out in my mind. I ran on the beach every morning for three days. Those runs were quiet and tranquil. I didn't have to watch for car or bike traffic. The only noise other than the squishing sound of my feet into the sand came from the waves crashing on the shore early in the morning. The Junebugs weren't out on the beach at sunrise, so it was quiet, and I didn't trip over anyone while I jogged along the water's edge.

The saltwater smell hung in the air and the beach surface

was soft in contrast to the pavement I usually ran on. A gentle breeze was always blowing at the early hour on the shoreline as the sun rose from the horizon and painted a picture of purple, orange, red, and yellow in the sky while reflecting on the water shining bright light and emitting radiating warmth. *Why hadn't I ever thought to run on the beach before?*

One morning I did have an encounter with some seagulls that were fighting over trash that some tourists had left behind during their daily beach excursion. Their squawking was loud, but I put in my earbuds with music playing to drown out the noise. Once I passed the birds, I removed my earbuds so I could listen to the ocean again.

It was good to visit with my sister, too. Every night she came home from work and we drank wine and ate together. I was pretty sure she only had one bottle of wine left when it was time for me to return home. I decided I'd have to buy more the next time I came to visit. After my few days of peaceful comfort, it was time to leave the refuge my sister had provided me when I needed it. So I packed up my suitcase and began my long drive.

It was Tuesday when I left Claudette's house, and I was due to return to work on Wednesday night. I hoped it would be coffee night. *Maybe I would nudge Cam toward that.* I got up early to avoid traffic on the road. I was exhausted and didn't feel up to dealing with all the people on the highway, so I decided to forego my morning beach run in order to get on the road early.

When I arrived at the apartment building, I walked up and dejectedly sat outside of the door because I realized I didn't have a key. I could call someone about the situation. Surely, Cam would be happy to help me with my predicament. But I didn't know if I was ready to talk to him about everything yet, and that's exactly what would end up happening if I called him. So I sat there for several more moments.

The minutes ticked by and soon it was almost an hour. I stood to leave and return to my car, but as if I had willed him there because I was thinking about him, the most gorgeous man I had ever seen approached me wearing a navy blue firefighter uniform. He told me he would be going back to work on Monday as long as he had been cleared last Friday by the doctor. So there I was after his first twenty-four-hour shift back after two weeks of medical leave wanting to make things right with him.

"What are you doing here, Charlie?" The moisture from my mouth evaporated and my fearless front dissolved. I couldn't get words out. So, taking my nonverbal stance as a response, he pushed past me and inserted his key into his apartment doorknob.

Once the door opened, I followed him inside, closing the distance between us. Digging deep into my core, I managed to find a shroud of courage, so I took in a deep breath and stood straight and tall toward him. "I needed to see you."

He turned his body to face me with a scornful look held firmly across the chiseled features of his face. *How had I thought my feelings were reciprocated by him?*

"I wanted to make sure you were okay." I decided to draw from whatever inner strength I had and conjure up some bravery to speak to him about the situation between us.

"I'm fine. Are you okay?" I don't know why he asked. He already knew the answer. He knew I wasn't okay, or else I wouldn't be there.

"No. I'm not okay." He stood only an arm's length away from me, so I reached toward him and placed my hand on his shoulder. He promptly pulled away from my touch. That rejection stung. "What is with you?" His dismissal toward my affection brought on a pool of tears within my lower eyelids.

I could feel the wetness hovering and knew their descent out of my eyes and down my face in slow streams was eminent. "You told me you loved me five years ago, and then you ran away. I told you I loved you five *days* ago, and then you ran away. What is it with the running away from me?"

The emotionless gaze from his cobalt eyes pierced my breaking heart. "I don't know what love is. I thought my parents had it, but here they are twenty-five years later, and they're getting divorced. I'm not interested in anything that has to do with love." His facial features were stern and unfeeling. His happiness was gone. The smile that I used to see and melt over was gone. His appearance was no longer a reflection of the same person I had spent time with over the previous two weeks. He was a stranger…an angry stranger. "You need to go."

"Why?" I swiped my fingers across my eyes to keep the looming tears from falling out.

"Because I can't give you what you want." His matter-of-fact tone was in such a nonchalant manner, yet I had no idea what he thought I wanted.

"So you can't be my boyfriend?" I figured that's what he thought I wanted.

"That's exactly what I'm trying to tell you."

"Okay. So how about my friend? Is that off the table?" I wanted him in my life. It didn't matter to me in what capacity. I just didn't want him to walk away from me for another five years. Truly, I didn't want him to walk away from me for another five days.

"I think we've proven that we can't just be friends." He brushed his fingers through his blond hair. "Remember the rules?"

"Yeah, I remember." I knew I was going to regret what I was about to say. "I wasn't the one that initiated breaking the rules. You were!" I was hurt and angry—a deadly combination. I knew I shouldn't have said that because I was about to get exactly what I didn't want—for Louis to be out of my life again.

I was completely bewildered when he slumped his shoulders forward and hung his head low. He didn't yell at me as I expected. Feeling as though his demeanor could detonate at any moment, I approached him cautiously. Then I slowly brushed my hand against the bristly hair of his forearm.

He gradually pulled his head up and dragged his eyes into a gaze in my direction. "I'm sorry about what happened. I got carried away." I could feel the shame in his words, tone, and body language. He shouldn't feel ashamed.

"I'm not sorry about what happened between us. I told you how I feel about you. The only thing that I regret is how I chased you away…again." He wrapped his strong arms around me, and I nestled into his chest within the comforting embrace. I pressed my face against his uniform shirt and inhaled his scent as a kiss touched the top of my head.

"We aren't any good together, Charlie." *How could he say that? Did he not remember the last two weeks like I had?*

"You're wrong. We're perfect together." I encircled my own arms around his waist, but he quickly began to struggle free from my grasp.

"No. We're not. You need to go. I had a rough shift back at work, and I don't need this right now." He was stronger than me, so he easily pulled out of my hold and stomped out of the living room area and toward the back of his apartment. I assumed he was headed to his bedroom. I followed behind him after a moment once I realized he wasn't coming back.

I saw a closed door in his hallway and swiftly turned the knob. The knob didn't budge, though. It was locked. "Louis. Let me in, please. I want to talk with you." There was no response, just deafening silence. "Will you at least let me know you're okay? I won't leave until you tell me."

"I'm fine, Charlie. Go home." His icy, muffled voice rang in my ears. I had been dealing with his mixed signals for two weeks at that point. Maybe I was better off without this confusion in my life.

"Well, unlike you, I don't leave without saying goodbye." I knew he was hurting, but I was hurting, too. I couldn't seem to stop myself from lashing out at him, however. When he didn't reply, I shrieked out a final "Bye!" and strutted out of his apartment.

After I was safely in my car, I let the tears flow. Sadness swept over me and replaced the anger I had felt standing in his apartment. My chest heaved deep sobs and my vision was blurred from the waves of water clouding them like a rainstorm so severe the precipitation came down in sheets and sometimes blew horizontal.

I wasn't sure how long I sat there. Maybe minutes, probably longer. Once my shaking and sobbing subsided, I put my key in the ignition and started the drive that would surely be the longest two hours of my life. I was leaving Louis. I didn't know if I would ever see him again. I was sad because he was in need of support, and he didn't want it from me.

I fetched my cell phone out and sent a text to my favorite person. **I'm ready to talk. I'll be home in a couple of hours. Can you come over?** I needed my best friend. I no longer cared if Louis and I disrupted the friendship between Cam and the person he grew up with. I was going to tell my brother everything in person, not on the phone. I needed to get the weight of the Louis burden off my shoulders.

16

LOUIS

I was an asshole. But I didn't see how I could get out of the situation without being an asshole. I wasn't interested in the L-word bullshit. It had ruined me five years ago, and I wasn't about to let that happen again. So I had to be an asshole to get her to go away and leave me alone. If I wasn't a jerk, she would have tried to stay, and I didn't want her to. I wanted her far away from me.

Everything was fine when I was away from her. I had a life, a career, and I had gotten an education. I just needed her out of my life again and everything would be fine. I had everything anyone my age could ever want. I didn't need a girlfriend. There were plenty of girls that would go out with me. There were plenty of girls that would land in my bed if I wanted them to.

So why in the hell couldn't I stop thinking about Charlie? I hadn't known how much I missed her until I saw her again. When I saw the woman she had become as I was standing in that grocery store cereal aisle, I couldn't believe the sight before my eyes. She had developed into a woman even more beautiful than I would have ever imagined. She always had a slender frame, but now she had a slight curve to her hips and a soft swelling of her breasts. She walked like a woman now too, not with the lankiness of the tomboy I had grown up with. She no longer had any awkwardness about her. Even though I had adored that years ago, I was very much attracted to the confidence she radiated now. Her skin was delicately soft, and she smelled like coconut. I loved the warmth of her body, whether it was merely holding hands or with her pressed against me, I loved how it felt to touch her.

I really needed to get a grip. I had told her to go because that's what was best. *But was it really going to be for the best if I never kissed her again?* I loved her lips. I loved her mouth. She tasted like heaven and every time my lips touched her, I felt a fire ignite deep within my core. I couldn't keep thinking about her like this. I would end up bitter like I was five years ago when she told me she wasn't in love with me.

She was right. Now that she told me she loved me, I felt the panic to get away again. I don't understand it. I just know I can't be around her. I know that one of us will be hurt if we don't stay away from each other. I certainly didn't want to get crushed again like I did all those years ago. So unfortunately, she needed to be hurt a little now to avoid a much larger hurt years from now...just like what happened with my parents.

If my parents hadn't been happy for so long, why hadn't they ended things before now? Why did they continue to torture themselves for years, rather than pull the bandage off quickly? Well, that wasn't going to happen to me. I would rather stop this ultimate wrecking ball from crushing me or Charlie. Truth be told, I didn't want her to be hurt down the road. As bad as I felt being the cause of her pain now, I don't think I could bear being the source of her pain years later. I cared about her too much for that. Hell, I was still in love with her. *Shit.*

I went to work at the firehouse, and I worked for my cousin's landscaping business nearly every day for three weeks. My mother had texted me a few times asking how I was. I merely responded that I was fine, but I didn't exchange any more dialogue than that. I wanted her to know I was alive, but I didn't feel up to talking to her anymore about the inevitable divorce. I wasn't exactly sure when that would happen, either.

I guess since I *saw* my mother with someone other than her spouse, I still held some resentment toward her. I knew my dad had said he was seeing someone as well, but it hadn't been shoved in my face. I was going to have a hard time getting the image of my mother kissing that man out of my mind. Since I had that picture permanently tattooed on my brain, it felt more real with her than it did with my dad. It wasn't fair because the decision was mutual, but I probably just expected more from my mother.

When I was growing up, my mother was always the one who was there for me. My dad worked all the time. I realize now, it was probably because he wasn't in love with my mom, so he'd spent his time elsewhere. But because she was always there for me, I confided in her. I thought I had a special relationship with her. So I felt like she betrayed me by not telling me about their separation and ultimate divorce. Since I didn't have any siblings, it was always just my mother and me. Maybe being away for so many years had changed our relationship. Perhaps she didn't feel close to me anymore. I was pretty sure I would forgive her one day, but I couldn't imagine it would be in the near future.

My father and I never really had much of a relationship while I was growing up. We had dinner together as a family a couple of times per week when he wasn't working late, and we went on one family vacation together per year. He never went to my soccer or lacrosse games. He did attend my graduation, but he never went to any other school-related activity. He didn't even have "the talk" with me. My mom did. It was painful, but I endured my mother talking to me about sex, and condoms, and sexually transmitted diseases. She also talked with me about smoking, and drugs, and alcohol. I guess I'm fortunate that I had one parent talk to me about all those high-risk behaviors and how to stay safe.

As I lay on my empty couch in my lonely apartment, I contemplated going to see my dad. I don't remember a time that I really talked to him about much of anything. I had no memory of discussing anything of importance with him. I was pulled out of my drifting thoughts with a buzz from my cell phone. There was a text from Cam.

Are you EVER coming home again?

I hadn't called or texted him since I left. And this was the first time he had reached out to me. I didn't know what to say back to him. But I figured if I didn't respond, that was the same as saying his friendship didn't matter to me.

Eventually. Just need some time to myself for a little bit. Not ready to see my parents again yet. Hopefully he would understand I wasn't avoiding him. I was avoiding my parents…and Charlie, but I wasn't about to admit that to him. I was curious if she said anything to him about what happened between us.

Okay, man. I get it. Just let me know when you're in town again. It was good to have my friend back here. Relief washed over me knowing he still wanted to be friends with me.

Will do. Whenever I was ready to go back to my hometown, I would at least have someone to go have a beer with. And I had a feeling whenever that was, I would probably need more than one.

Two more weeks passed before I felt like I accepted the situation between my parents enough that I could go back and talk with them. I felt like it was better if I saw each of them individually, rather than together. So I called my dad first. Surprisingly, he answered on the second ring. My call didn't go to voicemail. I didn't have to leave a message.

"Hi son. How are you?" *Did he expect me to say "I'm doing good" or "Fine?"*

I decided to ignore his question and get straight to the point. "Dad, I was wondering if I could see you sometime. You know, to talk about things."

"Of course, son. When would you like to meet? We could go to dinner. Or lunch?"

"I know you're probably busy with work. So let me know when there is a convenient time for *you.*" I paused, half expecting him to check his calendar and appointment book.

To my surprise, he replied to me immediately. "I know I probably worked too much when you were growing up, and I wasn't there for you all that much. But you are my priority, and I will always make time for you. Are you in town now? I can meet you now. Or I can meet you tomorrow, or the next day, or the day after that." He waited a beat before continuing. I was too stunned to respond, so he resumed speaking. "Louis, things in my life have needed to change for a while. I know I probably don't deserve a chance to be your father now, but if you could find it in your heart to let me try, I would like to show you how important you are to me."

Of course I would give him a chance. He's my dad, and I had initiated the meeting. So I met him for dinner two days later after another twenty-four-hour shift. I was prepared to spend the three days I had off individually with my mom, my dad, and maybe Cameron.

Heading to meet my old man for dinner. Might need a beer afterward. You up for it? Since I hadn't spoken to my mother yet, I might need a place to stay for the night. Maybe Cam would help me out again. Lord knew I wouldn't be asking Charlie for a place to stay.

Of course! Just say when and where. He ended his text with a smiley face. That absurdity drew a chuckle out of me. I never would have thought my childhood best friend would be texting me smiley faces twenty years later.

I'll text after dinner. And after another response of merely a smiley face from Cam, I decided there was no need for an additional response from me. I merely shook my head and shoved my phone back into my pocket before driving to the restaurant where I had agreed to meet my father.

When I pulled into the parking lot, I scanned the area for his car. I wondered if I had arrived before him. I didn't see his car, but I decided to go into the restaurant anyway. No need to wait in my vehicle outside. So I dragged my reluctant body inside and met a pretty blonde at the hostess stand.

"Looking for someone?" I know her cheerful disposition was well-meaning. And had I not been in such a sullen mood, I might have considered answering her with a smart-ass comment such as "Not anymore," and then flash her a devilish grin and a raise of my eyebrow. But I was simply not interested in any playful banter.

So I skipped the flirting and went straight to the point. "Actually, I'm looking for my dad. I'm just not sure if he's here yet." I performed a quick inspection of the tables behind her in the bar area and didn't see my father.

"There was an older gentleman in a suit that I sat just a few minutes ago. Said he was waiting for his son." The bright smile she flashed me never faded.

"Old guy in a suit. Yep. That sounds like him." I returned a half smile in her direction.

She motioned for me to follow her and led me to a booth on the opposite end of the restaurant. I saw my dad seated facing me, wearing his own goofy grin. I slid into the booth across from him and thanked the hostess for leading me to the right table.

"Hi, son. I'm glad we were able to meet." His business meeting tone conveyed a deal negotiation, not a dinner with his offspring.

"I'm glad it worked out." Even though he said he wanted to be here, I imagined it was difficult for him to get away from work. He used to take work with him everywhere. He didn't have to be at his office to work. I half wondered if he would end up pulling his laptop out during our meal, or at the very least answer emails on his phone while we had a conversation.

"I know I am not very good at this." He pointed his finger at himself and then to me. "But maybe I just need more prac-tice. I hope this isn't the only time you hang out with your old man."

"Dad, I didn't call you to 'hang out.' I called you so that I could talk to you about what happened." The puzzled look on my dad's face glared at me as I spoke. "What the hell happened between Mom and you?"

"I'm happy to discuss anything with you, son." His gaze quickly shot down at his menu. "Let's order and we can talk about whatever you want."

I was annoyed by his dismissive response. Although, I should have grown accustomed to his brush-offs at this point. He had been dismissing me my whole life. It always seemed like work was more important than me or anything in my life. So I glanced down at my menu as well and decided which burger I wanted to order. Once the waitress arrived to retrieve a drink order from us, I informed her we were ready to place our food order as well. The sooner we ordered dinner, the sooner I would get the answers I wanted.

Once she had penciled our orders onto the pad she was holding in her hand, she shoved the pencil in her ponytail and strutted away from the table. She was cute with curly blond hair and a sultry saunter to her walk, but I wanted to remain focused. So I dragged my gaze away from her for fear of being distracted.

"I know you're confused and upset, son." The set of eyes staring at me were so similar to mine that it was like looking at my own reflection in a mirror. "The relationship between your mother and me has always been simple, yet complicated."

"That doesn't make any sense, Dad." My aggravation was churning, and I didn't think it would take too much more for it to slip over the edge. "Tell me what happened to the two of you."

"Where would you like me to start?" I hadn't anticipated it being a long story. I kind of imagined it would go something like, "We decided we didn't love each other anymore, so we separated." It couldn't really be more than that.

"I guess I'll start from the beginning." The waitress arrived with a beer for my dad and an iced tea for me. I needed to be as sober as possible to hear what he had to say. "You know your mother and I met in college." I nodded. Of course I knew that. My mother had told me a thousand times. "We were friends, mostly. We spent a lot of time together. You know we ate together at the dining hall. We had classes together. We went to an occasional football game together. However, we never really had chemistry."

Was he seriously going to talk with me about this? I hoped he wasn't going to discuss his sex life with my mother. I tried to remain expressionless, but I am sure my discomfort with where the conversation was going was apparent on my face.

"But because we spent a lot of time together, we decided to make a go of things. I took her out on an official first date, and then I guess we were officially a couple. We were no longer eating meals together because we were friends. We were eating meals together because we were boyfriend and girlfriend. It was several months later when we finally became intimate."

That was too much information. I coughed loudly and shifted on my seat in the booth. He really *was* going to talk about his sex life with my mother to me.

"We were comfortable with each other, so it kind of happened, and we were okay with it." My dad took a swallow of his beer and then looked me square in the eyes. "After we graduated, I proposed to her."

"Because you were in love with her?" *At some point, they had to have fallen in love with each other, right?*

"I have always loved your mother. She and I are very good friends. We still are."

"Dad, I'm getting confused. Were you in love with Mom when you proposed?" I held my iced tea glass in my hand because I wasn't sure what I should do with my agitation. I knew I would begin to fidget soon if I didn't get a hold of my emotions.

"I didn't know what it was like to *fall* in love with someone. I loved your mom, so it felt like the right thing to do was to marry her. We managed to keep our friendship, but that was really all we've ever had. There was never that amazing connection, that heart-stopping adrenaline rush you get when you see each other after being apart, the magical butterflies in your stomach you get before you're about to kiss each other."

"Gross, Dad." I wasn't sure if I'd be able to eat my burger if the conversation continued down that path.

"Son, we settled for friendship because passion can fizzle, but we knew we would be friends forever."

"But you aren't going to be husband and wife forever." I know I sent a scowl in his direction. I wasn't sure where all my displaced anger stemmed from.

"Believe me, we didn't make that decision lightly. We talked about it for hours, days, months even. We decided to try a separation. Once I moved out, we would text each other because we missed each other. But it was good for both of us to see what else was out there."

"So if absence made the heart grow fonder, then how did you end up at the place where you are now…making a decision about divorce?"

My father's response was postponed by the arrival of our food. The waitress asked if we needed anything. I think she made some suggestions about ketchup and steak sauce, but I shook my head no. I wanted her to leave as quickly as possible, so I could return to the conversation at hand.

"We each met someone, son." Then he lowered his head as if he was embarrassed to speak anymore.

"And?" I may have raised my voice slightly because my dad popped his head up in attention at my questioning word.

"We both found a person that makes our heart race wildly. I can't wait to see Holly again when I'm away from her, and your mother feels the same way about Marshall."

"Ohmigod, Dad. Have you all talked with each other about this?" I couldn't believe what I was hearing.

"Of course we have. Your mom is my best friend." He said it so plainly, as if all this was a very easy explanation.

"But isn't marrying your best friend what is supposed to happen?" I was terribly confused. Again, I was sure my look of disbelief was apparent.

"Son, you should marry someone that is your friend *and* gives you the butterflies. If a woman can't be both, then your marriage will likely not last." He smiled at me for the second time since I had arrived at the restaurant. I don't know if I had seen my father smile twice in the same day ever…in the last twenty-three years. "Look son, I certainly am the last person to get love life advice from, but please learn from my mistake. Make sure you find the one that causes your heart to do somersaults. Find a woman that you can live with, but make sure she's the one you can't live without." He cut into his steak and took a bite.

I followed suit and bit into my burger. We sat in silence. The only sounds were from eating our dinner. I tried to take in what my dad had said. He married his friend, but that's all they were. *How was that even possible?* Although if the new woman in his life was the reason for this difference in him, then maybe there was something to what he was saying.

While I was eating, I reflected back to life with my parents. They were always cordial with each other. I had remembered hearing from kids at school about arguments their parents had. But other than an occasional disagreement, my parents never had any really big fights. They always got along well.

However, I didn't ever remember them being overly affectionate with each other. They may have given each other a hug, but I couldn't say that I ever saw anything more than a chaste kiss on the cheek from them. I certainly never heard them having sex. I know both Cam and Charlie had told me they could sometimes hear their parents. I shook my head quickly to try to get the image of my parents having sex out of my head. It had taken up residence there since my dad had first mentioned it.

"So tell me about what's going on with you." My father finally broke me out of my silent reflection. "You dating anyone?"

I scoffed at his comment. "Uh. No."

"You're young. You'll find a woman that makes you happy."

I shrugged off his comment. I had met plenty of women that I had chemistry with, but not one that I wanted to spend time with when we had our clothes on. Well, that is except for… no. I wasn't going to think about her. I needed to stay away from her. It could never work between the two of us.

"Something else on your mind, son?" I must have appeared pensive because my father picked up on it. "There is a woman, isn't there?"

My withdrawn body language again didn't go unnoticed. "Dad…"

"It's okay, son. We don't have to talk about it. I know it's your own business. But just consider what I told you. The one for you makes your heart race *and* is your friend." He reached across the booth and touched my shoulder. I hadn't realized how long his arms were until that moment. "And in the end, everything works out just how it's supposed to."

I texted Cam before I even left the parking lot of the restaurant. I needed a beer, or two, or three. I'm not sure how, but Cam arrived at the bar before I did. He lived closer to the bar than the side of town I had dinner with my dad, but he must have been literally waiting by the phone for me to text.

As I walked in, I saw he already had two beers on the high-top table where he was sitting in the bar area. It reminded me of the last time I sat with him at this same table. That was when Charlie and I had discussed that night five years ago. We had agreed to move on from there, yet here I was away from her again.

"Hey, man!" Cam greeted me enthusiastically as I approached. It was good that he seemed genuinely happy to see me. I wasn't sure what Charlie may have told him, and if she had said anything about me, I knew I was going to come out looking like the asshole I was.

I did the obligatory fist bump and sat on the stool at the table with him. "Thanks for the beer." I nodded at the beverage sitting in front of me.

"I figured you may need it after dinner with your dad." He shrugged before taking a pull from his beer. "Are you in town for a little while?"

"Maybe a couple of days. Just for the weekend."

"You're welcome to crash at my place whenever you want." His comment reminded me why I had never had a best friend like Cam. I didn't even have to ask for a favor. He just knew and offered.

"That would be great. I'm definitely not ready to stay over at my mom's again yet." I lifted the glass bottle to my lips and poured the cold liquid down my throat. "And I don't even know where my dad is staying, or what kind of accommodations he has. It never came up during dinner."

"Well, I always have a couch for you whenever you need it." He slapped me on the back and then took in a deep sigh. I knew something was on his mind, but he was hesitant to speak about it. I could tell he wanted to say something to me, but his reluctance had me a bit concerned. "Despite whatever goes on between you and my sister, I want us to stay friends."

Damn. She *had* said something to him. "I'm really sorry, man." This conversation had grown awkward and weird fast.

"She told me everything. I left you guys to figure things out without my interference five years ago and you ended up apart." He blew out another exaggerated breath. "Then I forced you guys to mend your relationship, and you still ended up apart." His sorrowful eyes stared back at me. "I'm sorry that I may have pushed you two together. I guess I wanted my two best friends to be best friends, too. But if you aren't going to be friends, then at least don't ever make me choose between you and Charlie."

"I would never do that! She's your sister...your *twin* sister." I ran a frustrated hand through my hair. My agitation was taking hold again. "And I'm not going to be one of those guys that bad-mouths her. I don't even have anything bad to say about her anyway. She is amazing, and I screwed things up." *What the hell was I saying?*

"It's never too late to right a wrong." He held his glass up in a salute before finishing the amber liquid. He placed the glass back down on the wooden table with a small thump. "She doesn't have a bad word to say about you, either. It's so obvious that you two are into each other."

"It sounds an awful lot like you're trying to play matchmaker, Cameron. I thought you weren't going to push us together anymore." I relaxed a little and smiled at him because I couldn't help myself.

"Is it wrong to want you two to be together?" he said before signaling the waitress for another draft.

"I just don't think it's meant to be." Even though she was the only woman that I had ever considered a friend *and* she made my heart race wildly.

"Well then, I won't have to see you fight off the other guy for her affection." His eyes squinted slightly when he made his comment.

"What are you talking about, Cam?" He was being way too vague.

"Charlie is seeing someone."

My heart rose up into my throat, and my breath was squeezed right out of my lungs. Blurred vision and dizziness developed, but not from the beer. I hadn't even had a full glass yet. I was unsure what to do with the information he had just shared with me.

A wave of nausea seeped through from the emotional punch in the belly thrown at me. *One little comment couldn't possibly have this much of an effect on me, could it? And I had no one to blame but myself.*

17

CHARLIE

The drive home was long. It felt so much longer than two hours with everything crawling along in slow motion. My crying stopped halfway home, but as soon as I saw my brother's truck in the parking lot of my apartment complex the crying resumed. By the time I entered my apartment, I was a blubbering mess. Cam jumped off the couch and swiftly moved toward me. He wrapped his arms around my shoulders and hugged me while I let out more loud sobs. *I don't know where all the water came from, surely I should have dried out by now.* He just stood in my living room, holding me in a comforting brotherly embrace as time ticked by.

He didn't let go until my sobs were mere sniffles, and I had thoroughly saturated his shoulder with the avalanche of tears that escaped my eyes. "Thanks for coming over."

The worried look on his face made me feel guilty for bringing him into this situation. "Why don't you come sit on the couch and tell me what happened." He grabbed my hand and pulled me in the direction of my sofa.

I sat down with a plop against the cushions. "I don't even

152

know where to begin." I took a deep breath in and released it slowly.

"I'm here to listen to whatever you want to tell me." He sat next to me on the couch, still wearing that look of brotherly concern. "Do you want me to make you some tea? Mom used to do that for us when we were upset."

I huffed out a laugh at his suggestion. As if anything was going to heal my broken heart. "No thanks. But I appreciate the offer."

He sat quietly, waiting for me to fill the silence. He had always been uncomfortable around crying women, but he tried not to show it during my waterworks display.

"I fell in love with him, Cam. I know it's stupid and too fast for that to happen, but it happened, and I did." The burning in my throat occurred again as if I was going to expel more tears. I don't think I had ever cried that much in my life.

"Do you want me to hurt him? I can you know." His grim look was stern as his clenched jaw twitched.

I scoffed at his comment. "No. He's already hurting. He doesn't need you to add to it."

"So he's hurting and you're hurting? How did you both get to here? I thought you two were getting along fine."

I rolled my tear-filled eyes. "We *were* getting along. It was amazing. Once we got past what happened five years ago, we decided to work on being friends again. However, we developed an attraction to each other during the time we spent together." Cam's shifty look indicated he was uncomfortable with the conversation—even more uncomfortable than my crying had already caused. "If this is too weird, then we don't have to talk about this. We can just watch a movie or something."

"Lean Bean, I'm here for you. And like always, you can tell me anything. Please remember that." I'm glad he reassured me, because I really wanted to talk with him about this. He had always been my best friend, and he always knew how to make me feel better.

"We began to run together. You know I don't like to talk when I run, but he didn't seem to mind. He simply seemed to enjoy being with me, and I was happy to have the company." I grabbed a tissue from the box on my side table and wiped the dripping snot leaking from my nostril. *I would die if any other man saw me ugly cry like this.* "We went out for a couple of meals. We ate ice cream. We held hands. We cuddled on the couch and fell asleep." I needed to take in a deep breath for the next part of the story. "We kissed each other. Like the ohmigod this is the best kiss I've ever had kind of kiss. But because we were trying to get used to being friends again, we decided to come up with some rules so we didn't get carried away."

Cam's curiosity was obviously piqued because he straightened his posture. "Rules?"

"Yes. Rules." I filled him in on rules one through four. Hand holding was okay, but no caressing each other with our hands. Closed mouth kissing was okay, but no open-mouth kissing. Our clothes always stayed on when we were together. And of course sleeping together was okay, but no sex.

"And how did that work out?" He smirked because he knew I was going to admit to breaking every one of those rules. It was better to see him smirk than continue to carry the worried look he had been wearing since I got home.

I slapped him on his shoulder. "He slept in my bed the night he stayed at my house, but we didn't have sex." Cam wiped his hand across his brow in relief. "We didn't have sex until the day he found out about his parents' divorce."

A visible shudder went through my brother. "And then

what happened?" He cringed slightly as if I was about to deliver news he didn't want to hear.

"I told him I loved him and he left, walked out on me, left me alone and naked in my bed without even saying good-bye." Cam rubbed the back of his neck. I held up my hand in his direction to stop him from saying anything. "I know. Claudette already told me that I shouldn't have said I loved him right after sex. It sounds desperate and clingy."

"Maybe with someone else, but Louis loves you, too." More tears escaped my eyes.

"Did he say that to you?" I already knew the answer. My brother was just trying to make me feel better. That was his job… to make his twin feel better. He slumped his shoulders forward and hung his head low. "I know he didn't tell you that because that's not how he feels. I left Claudette's house early this morning so I could go see him."

"And I guess that didn't go well."

I snorted a fake laugh as a response to his statement.

We continued to talk for the next several hours. I was already feeling better by the time he left. I decided to grab some junk food to drown my sorrows after I said goodbye to Cameron. When I opened my freezer, I saw several quarts of ice cream. It was ice cream I hadn't purchased. Of course, that is why my brother is truly my best friend.

Found the ice cream stash. You're the best. As I have come to expect, he responded with a smiley face text.

I ate ice cream and fell asleep for twelve hours. I woke up early the next day, so I decided to go for a run. I only made it three miles before I turned back and headed home. Running wasn't the same anymore. Louis had ruined that for me. I considered going to the gym to run on a treadmill like

Cameron. It just wasn't the same outside without Louis's feet padding along next to me. I could still hear his increased breathing even though he wasn't with me that morning.

Wanting some warmth and comfort, when I got back to my apartment instead of hopping into my shower, I grabbed my purse and hopped into my car instead. I decided to treat myself to coffee and a muffin from the local coffee shop.

There were way more people at the coffee shop than I had expected on a weekday morning. If I had thought I would have to stand in line with a lot of other people in their search of caffeine and sugar, I would have opted to take that shower before I left my apartment.

"I guess I should have gone to Dunkin' Donuts." I heard a voice over my shoulder say.

I turned around to a very attractive man around my age standing behind me. He was dressed in khaki shorts and a golf shirt, and his wet hair was combed in place as if he was fresh from a shower. I must have looked like a disaster compared to the well-put-together guy that just made the Dunkin' Donuts comment. "You still can," I responded finally after adequately checking him out.

A small laugh emitted from him. "Yeah, I suppose I could." After I threw an eye roll, I turned around from him and faced forward again. "I'm Travis, by the way." I swiveled on my feet again to face him.

"I'm sorry if this sounds rude, but you're obviously a morning person. I am not. I really don't like to speak to anyone before nine." He was a good-looking man with dark hair and eyes the color of coal, but I really just wanted to be left alone.

"It's Charlie, isn't it?" *Why was he still talking to me? And why did he know my name?* I turned around to face him once more as the line inched toward the cashier. "I'm a teacher at the high school. I'm friends with your brother."

Of course he was. Everyone was friends with Cameron. I smiled at him awkwardly, obviously aware of how rude I had actually sounded. And now he would probably go tell my brother how I was rude to his friend. I had promised him I wouldn't brood over Louis, yet here I was, being rude to the first man to speak to me since I came back home. "I'm really sorry for not engaging in friendly, casual conversation to pass the time."

"I'm not offended, really. And I wasn't trying to hit on you if that's what you think." *Where had that come from?*

"Are you saying that because you were, but you don't want me to know you were?"

A megawatt smile shone in my direction then. "I don't know how to say this without sounding rude, but you're not exactly my type."

"You probably go for freshly showered blondes, rather than brunettes that just ran several miles and are saturated with sweat." I knew I looked a mess with my unruly ponytail, a glistening sheen over my skin from perspiration, and my non-matching tank top and running shorts.

He laughed again. "You make me laugh, Charlie. I like that about you. Do you feel like getting coffee again sometime?"

What harm could there be in that? Louis and I weren't together, so coffee with a cute guy couldn't hurt. "Sure. I'll shower and be more presentable next time." I returned a smile to him as I approached the counter to order. I spouted off my request for coffee and a blueberry muffin. As I glanced over my shoulder at Travis, I watched him cover his mouth in an attempt to stifle his laughter. "Did I say something else funny?"

"No. You just ordered the same as my usual." He winked at me and handed me his phone. "Enter your number, and I'll text you."

He seemed nice enough, but he didn't make my heart

pound in my chest. He didn't take my breath away. Dammit, Louis. He quite possibly ruined me for other men. I programmed in my number and handed his phone back to him. Travis punched some things into his cell, and I felt my own phone vibrate.

Coffee tomorrow? I glanced down at my phone and looked back up at Travis.

It made me smile that he texted me while I was standing right next to him. **Sorry, can't. I work tonight. How about the day after tomorrow?**

Sure. How about 9am when you feel like talking to people?

I smiled and even let a giggle escape. **Sounds good. Same place?** I felt my phone vibrate almost immediately, but one of the baristas called my name because my order was ready, so I didn't look down at my phone right away. Travis took two side steps in my direction as his name was called only a moment later.

"See you day after tomorrow," he said to me as he picked up his coffee and the bag that contained his muffin. "I'm off to play a round of golf." He gave me a friendly wave and swung the door open to leave.

I moved away from the counter and looked down at my phone.

It seems only right, since this is our place now.

I wasn't sure how to take that text. I hoped he knew it was just coffee. I certainly wasn't looking for anything more. I knew I looked a mess, but he still wanted to hang out with me. I guess I should feel good that looks weren't important to him. At least I'd be able to be myself around him. And he played golf—that was the only sport I think Cameron hadn't played. *Maybe I should ask Cam about Travis.*

So I texted him after I got back to my apartment. I still hadn't showered. I decided to drink my coffee while it was still hot and eat my muffin before I did my best to wash away my lingering Louis sadness.

You know a teacher named Travis? He's a teacher at the high school where you work.

Yeah. He texted me about you a little bit ago.

Interesting. **He did? What did he say?** I should just call my brother. It is stupid how we engage in the texting back and forth. But before I could even pull up his number, I saw his name and number dance across my screen. Of course he knew I was thinking about speaking with him on the phone. He *always* knew what I was thinking. "Hey, Cam."

"Hey, Lean Bean. I didn't realize you were ready to get back on the horse."

I chuckled at his comment. I knew he was thinking about how I was just crying to him over a guy yesterday, and today I already made a date with another. "I learned from you."

"Ouch. Are you saying I'm insensitive?" I knew he was messing with me.

"No. You have always made your intentions perfectly clear. The poor girls just always think they can change you." I could almost see his grin after my comment.

"So, Travis, huh? He texted me to ask me if I would mind if he asked you out."

"And what did you say?" *Was this before or after he asked me?*

"I said I didn't mind, but that you would probably turn him down." I guess going back to yesterday and my crying that was probably what he honestly thought.

"I said I'd have coffee with him."

"Yeah, that's what he said. It shocked the hell outta me. There haven't been many times you surprised me, but you surely did." I could hear his laughter coming through the line.

I guess that was true, though. He had always been one

step ahead of me. He practically always knew what I was going to do before I even did sometimes. "Is he a good guy?"

"He is. He's had a rough year, but he's a good guy. Not sure that he is looking for anything serious, but even if you're back in the saddle, you probably shouldn't jump into anything serious right now anyway."

"Cameron Callahan, are you trying to tell me what I should and shouldn't do?" I snickered.

"You and I both know even if I did, you'd do what you want anyway." I loved our friendship. We could be brutally honest with one another and never fear judgment or righteousness.

"I'm going to see him the day after tomorrow. I'll let you know how it goes." A wide smile tugged at my face. I guess I could learn from my brother's dating attitude. *The best way to get over someone, is to move on to someone else.* Even though I didn't consider myself shallow like him, I recognized there was nothing wrong with enjoying someone else's company.

So after an uneventful shift at work and a day of rest, I was back at the same coffee shop waiting for Travis. I sat at a table trying to decide if I should order or wait until he arrived when it suddenly occurred to me that he might not show. We said nine in the morning, and it was one minute past. Maybe he had changed his mind. I stared at my phone, wondering why he didn't text if he was going to be late, and realized that I wasn't even dating him. He really didn't owe me anything. But Cam said he was a good guy. *A good guy wouldn't stand me up without even texting me, right?*

I was reviewing the latest feeds on the social media sites when I heard his voice. "Hey, Charlie." I looked up from my phone and took in the sight of Travis. He was dressed in khaki shorts again, but paired with a T-shirt today, rather than a golf shirt. "I'm sorry I'm a couple of minutes late. I should have probably told you, one of my faults is that I have a hard time getting anywhere on time."

I stood up next to him. "It's probably good that you didn't, because people that are late drive me crazy." I motioned for him to follow me toward the line to order.

His perplexed expression told me he wasn't sure what to say next. "Why don't you sit here, and I'll go place our order. I already know what you like."

I shrugged and sat back down. Our date hadn't even started yet, and I was already texting my brother. **Not going well so far. He showed up four minutes late.**

Give him a chance, okay? Don't write him off already. I was still absorbing what my brother texted me when Travis was back at the table. Apparently, nine o'clock wasn't as busy as earlier in the morning.

"I'm sorry if I gave you the impression that I was upset with you because you were a few minutes late." If Cameron said Travis deserved a chance, then I best make sure he knows he has a clean slate.

"I would really like to apologize again." He took a seat in a chair across from me at the square table and placed a coffee cup in front of me. He dangled the bag containing the muffins in front of me like a peace offering for his tardiness. I accepted the olive branch and pulled one of the miniature blueberry cakes out and sat it on a napkin. "You look really nice."

I looked down at my attire. I knew this was just a casual coffee date, so I chose a scoop neck, fitted T-shirt and paired it with some denim shorts. And of course, I had my brown curls loose around my shoulders instead of the ponytail I usually wore. "That means I looked like a mess the last time you saw me. I'm sure I smell better this time, too."

He shifted uncomfortably in his seat in response to my comment and his dark eyes cast down. "I haven't dated anyone in a really long time, and I guess I'm out of practice. This is not going well at all."

"Lighten up, will ya? I was just messing with you." I tried my best to put him at ease but he still appeared distressed. "Seriously, Travis. Part of the reason I even agreed to this coffee meeting was because you didn't seem to care what I looked like." I offered him a soft smile and covered his hand with mine. It felt weird to touch another man's hand, so I quickly pulled it back.

"You all right?" The deep creases furrowing his brow adequately revealed his concern.

"I guess I should go ahead and tell you." I took a swallow of coffee before continuing—as if the caffeine was going to give me some kind of superpower courage to spit out what I needed to say. "The day before I met you, the man I'm in love with broke my heart. Things ended badly, and I should have told you that before I agreed to meet you again. I'm obviously going to need some time to grieve the end of that relationship before I'll be able to truly move on."

"Is he the reason you and Cameron left the basketball game last week?" If he had witnessed that, I was going to be really humiliated.

"You were there?" I gulped down the lump that had suddenly formed in my throat in anticipation of his recollection of that day.

"I was there waiting to start the game when Cameron's friend left. Then you left, and Cameron followed suit. Is his friend the one that broke your heart?" Damn, he was perceptive.

"Yeah. That's him." I tried to respond nonchalantly, but it ripped at my heart a little just remembering that afternoon.

"Is it wrong for me to say he's a fool?" His attempt at trying to make me feel better pulled a giggle from me.

"How do you know I'm not the fool?" I guess my comment took him off guard. Again, he deflected his gaze down as if he was unsure of how to respond. "I'm only messing with you again." It was going to be hard not to continue to tease him considering how easy it was to get him off-kilter.

"I hope if you're messing with me, it means you like me." His questioning, yet hopeful eyes brought another smile to my face. He was kind and sweet. He was totally—not my type. Which I decided was going to be a good thing.

"Yeah. It does. If I didn't like you, I would just ignore you." I took another sip of my liquid courage. "I have to be honest. I'm really not looking for a relationship. I'm not even looking to date anyone. But hopefully we can be friends?"

"Man, I'm glad you said that. Because you really aren't my type."

I almost spit out my next swallow of coffee as I choked back my laugh. "You probably go for the pretty, blonde, model type."

"Something like that." He was really nervous, I decided as I witnessed his fingers breaking apart his muffin into smaller pieces, without putting any of it into his mouth.

"Hey, what did that muffin ever do to you?" I really tried to put him at ease, but I could tell by his baffled countenance that he was still unable to read me.

"I had a relationship end recently, too." So then it made sense. This would be why Cam had said Travis had a tough year.

"I'm sorry. Recovering from a broken heart is difficult." I felt that compulsion to touch his hand again, so I did. And I didn't pull back this time.

"My fiancée died in a car accident a little over six months

ago." His remark took me so off guard, I pulled my hand back immediately and used it to cover my mouth.

I released the hand concealing my lips only long enough to utter "Holy crap!" My hand quickly found its place back over my mouth, and I instantly wished that comment hadn't slipped out of my mouth. But even if I had thought about it, I wouldn't have known what to say.

My astonishment caused him to reach out and cover my other hand with his. "It sucks, but I'm dealing with it a lot better now than I was."

I felt bad that he felt he needed to comfort me after my blatant outburst. Slowly, I released my fingers and moved my hand back from my face and into my lap. "Why don't you tell me about her?" I ignored my muffin that was still untouched, and I ignored the coffee that was probably getting cold, but was no longer required for my courage.

"Really?" His pathetically hopeful expression was adorable.

"Of course! Tell me all about her." I knew at that moment that he and I were going to be good friends.

He released a sigh of relief in a loud whoosh. "It feels weird to be on a date talking about the last woman I was with."

"So why don't we take the pressure off. Let's not call this a date. It's just two friends hanging out." I was honestly a little relieved that he truly wasn't ready for a relationship. I felt bad about what he had been through, but happy that I could be a friend to him.

So he proceeded to tell me about Mindy. He said she was a beautiful blonde that he described as model worthy. He told me how incredibly kindhearted she was and how they had an amazing connection. His story began when they met their senior year of college and progressed to their engagement on Christmas two years ago. The descriptions from his memories were delivered at warp speed, as if I would lose interest in what he was saying if he didn't get the words out fast enough.

I heard about her favorite color, her favorite food, and their favorite restaurant. I hoped there wasn't going to be a quiz after all the Mindy information being spewed at me. *Maybe I should take notes?* I continued to listen to him for the next twenty minutes. I finished my muffin and my coffee and he was still talking. At some point he realized I hadn't contributed to the conversation for a really long time.

"I'm pathetic, aren't I?" Then there was that adorable puppy dog look again.

"No. Of course not. You're still grieving. It's okay. Really."

"Everyone is afraid to say anything about her around me, which makes me feel uncomfortable talking about her to anyone. I wish people were okay with mentioning her name or sharing memories about her."

"Well, you can talk about her with me whenever you like." Growing up with Cam and Louis, I was unaware there were men like Travis that even existed out there. Neither my brother nor my friend ever committed to one woman for very long, if at all. However, Mindy was obviously Travis's world. He didn't seem like the type to ever have interest in another woman.

"I know it sounds like all I ever do is think about her, but it's not true. I think about her every day, but it's not all day like it was. It will be when something silly happens, or something will come up that reminds me of her. The difference is that now those memories don't make me sad anymore. Those memories make me smile. I guess I just wish I could talk about her without seeing people cringe."

I tried to imagine what he was going through. He would never see the love of his life again. I could see Louis again whenever I wanted. Even though we weren't together, I could still see him and talk with him. I could talk *about* him without anyone getting uncomfortable.

"Seriously, it's better for you to talk to me about Mindy than your next girlfriend." I was joking, and that time he knew I was. His lips turned up slightly into almost a half smile.

"So are you going to tell me about him? The one that broke your heart?" I guess he figured I would share my personal crap with him like he just emotionally vomited all over me.

"Nah. I'd rather hear more about you."

He had a food bolus in his mouth at that moment, and when he opened to speak, a fleck of muffin flew out in my direction. He quickly covered his mouth, and his cheeks turned a shade of crimson. It was a good thing that wasn't a real date. Maybe it could be a practice one for whenever he was ready to go on an actual date.

"Geez, Travis. Say it. Don't spray it." I playfully wiped pretend crumbs off my forearms. "You really need to lighten up. We should go out for beers next time. Coffee and sugar make people too jittery."

"Really. You would consider hanging out with me again?" Wow. His confidence needed some work.

I couldn't help but chuckle at his bewilderment. His awkwardness was refreshing. "I like you, Travis. I would really enjoy hanging out with you again on another non-date."

"I could pick you up next time. Then you won't be annoyed by my showing up late to the bar."

"Thanks for the offer, but if you pick me up, then it would kind of be like a date, right?" He shrugged at my response. "Have you never been friends with a female before?"

"Not that I can recall."

"Me either." He relaxed into a genuine laugh at my comment, and I finally felt better about our coffee excursion.

"So what does that mean? You only have men as friends?" His questioning eyes widened and he placed his forearms on the table leaning in toward me.

"Well, my two best friends are...*were* men." A frustrated, long exhale rushed out of me in response to my reminiscence, and I collapsed back against my chair. "Cameron has always been my best friend, but, well...the other man..."

His voice erupted from his throat before I could even finish translating my thought into words. "The other man was the one that broke your heart." I nodded and he continued. "So you were friends with him for a long time, but when you crossed the line, you got your heart broken?"

"Something like that."

"Maybe a story for next time?" I wasn't sure I'd be sharing that story at our next meeting, but maybe someday.

"I'm meeting Cameron for lunch later. Do you want to come along?" His face lit up like he was just asked to sit at the cool kids' lunch table in high school.

"I don't want to intrude." He made the statement, but his expression implied he only said it to be polite, but he really wanted to go.

"Travis, if your friend invites you to go somewhere, you can either say you can or you can't. You don't need to feel like you have to ask permission for something you've been invited to." After our exchange, I presumed he taught history or economics or some other equally boring social science. He played golf for goodness sake.

"Okay, then I can go. I don't have any plans for lunch." His attempt to conceal a smile still managed to peek through his stoic expression.

"Perfect. We're meeting at Hauston's at twelve thirty." I stood and grabbed the paper liner from my muffin, the balled-up napkins I had used, and my empty paper coffee cup before tossing all the waste products into the trash can.

Travis rose to his feet once I stood. "Am I going to see you play basketball at a pickup game soon?" I guess tossing trash into the receptacle reminded him of the hoops I dodged out of last week.

"Maybe. But I prefer running or biking." Besides, if Cam invited Louis again, I wasn't in an emotional place where I could see him yet.

"Oh sorry. I forgot. The guy." I nodded. He might as well know that much. "Well, maybe I'll take up running." That thought made me smile. I ran alone for so long that I figured things would return to how they always were once Louis abandoned my jogging routine. But I missed the company. I knew it was silent company, but it was so calming to have someone with me during my run. I always had my music to listen to, which I used to think was company enough. But until I had a living, breathing human jogging alongside me, making every turn, climbing every hill, and sprinting at the same stretch every time, I hadn't realized how much I would enjoy it. The sound of Louis's feet slapping the pavement next to mine was soothing, and hearing his quickened breath was sexy. *What the hell?* It wasn't having just anyone with me. It was having Louis with me. Damn him.

CHARLIE

Travis and I went to lunch with Cameron after I had texted him our coffee non-date had ended up okay after all. I let my brother know I was *not* interested in Travis as more than a friend. He actually accused me of trying to replace Louis with Travis in our threesome. After being a little upset that he would even suggest that, I realized he was maybe at least partially right. Travis was already friends with Cam, so once I became friends with him, it was easy for him to tag along on our excursions.

Travis joined me on my runs several times over the last three weeks. The three of us had played pool, gone fishing, and on two long bike rides. We ate fried chicken watching television at my apartment, ate pizza and played cards at Cam's apartment, and ate grilled chicken and vegetables sitting on the deck of Travis's townhouse. He really meshed very nicely with Cam and me. Since I didn't have any romantic feelings toward Travis, things were so easy. That's what I enjoyed the most.

Sure, I missed the hand holding and the hugs and inno-cent kisses with Louis. Of course, I missed the other not-so-innocent things, too. But I knew Cam probably felt like a third wheel when in the presence of the affection that Louis and I shared, whether it was innocent or not. He didn't feel like the third wheel in our newly developed trio. I asked him if he had spoken with Louis, and he assured me he hadn't. I guess my brother was able to avoid letting Louis invade his thoughts. I was not so fortunate. I still thought of him every. Single. Day.

Tonight at work, there was a steady influx of patients. In between triaging patients, I saw my brother strut into the emergency department like he owned the place. I swear the girls I work with continue to swoon over him and he loves every second of it. He proceeded to the nurse's station, I assumed, while I assessed my last patient.

Just as I expected, I found him sandwiched between Tiffany and Cecilia next to the counter. He didn't appear uncomfortable at all. In fact, he seemed to be enjoying himself. I shook my head in disgust but approached the threesome to retrieve my caffeinated beverage that he always brought me. I scanned the counter and the nurse's station in search of my hot drink, but I didn't see the usual cardboard tray that he carried in. I rolled my eyes with abhorrence as I saw another person enter through the ER sliding glass doors. So, I left my brother and my co-workers to return to my triaging post.

However, when I returned to the front of the ER, I saw Travis holding a cardboard tray of coffees. He was my new best friend. "Travis, I hope you brought one of those for me."

"Of course. Cam said I couldn't show up here for a visit without bringing my bestie a large coffee." He pulled a cup out of the tray and held it in my direction.

"You are the very best." I could smell the sweet, yet potent aroma and felt immediate comfort. I motioned for Travis to follow me through the wooden door toward the main part of the ER and he followed closely behind me.

I couldn't exactly figure it out, but Travis seemed slightly uneasy. Maybe I misread his body language. He could just be nervous about being in a new place and meeting new people. I grabbed his empty hand and pulled him in the direction of the nurse's station where Cam seemed to be doing nothing other than inflating his ego.

Cam relieved Travis of the tray and distributed coffees to Tiffany and Cecilia who remained attached to his sides. Once my brother pried himself away from those disgraceful women I had labeled T&C, he approached Alexis, the very shy nurse sitting alone at a computer cart away from the nurse's station.

"Hey, Lex," Cameron said quietly as he walked toward her with soft footsteps. She tossed a glance over her shoulder at him with big blue eyes, and her cheeks instantly flushed. *Maybe she was embarrassed he was speaking to her?* "Here's a coffee." Cam handed it to her gently, like it was a peace offering.

With the innocence of a deer staring into headlights, and holding a frightened expression on her face, she retrieved the cup from Cam's grasp. "Thank you." She shifted her eyes down briefly before turning around to face the computer screen again.

Alexis is a good nurse. She's smart and detail-oriented. But she is extremely quiet and keeps to herself. I think Cam has a sweet spot for her—kind of like the feelings you would have toward a lost puppy. He always looks like he wants to hug her, and she always looks apprehensive and nervous.

All the other females I work with flirt shamelessly with my brother. But Alexis is different. I don't think she has a whole lot of experience with dating, and therefore, she probably presents a challenge for Cameron. She certainly holds his undivided attention when within fifty feet of my twin sibling.

"Thanks, Cam. I appreciate it." Her voice cracked while she continued to look at the computer screen. She didn't even glance in his direction again.

Still a witness to the Cameron show, I observed him lean in toward her attentively. "Alexis, do you want to go to breakfast sometime?" *What the hell is going on?* It must be a full moon. If you asked any emergency room nurse, she'd tell you people behave crazy when there is a full moon. My brother, the guy who had other women literally drooling over his presence and flaunting their assets in his face, just asked out the plain-Jane nurse I worked with.

Alexis was cute in her own way. She had dirty blond hair that she always pulled into a low ponytail at the nape of her neck. Her face was always makeup-free, but when she smiled, it always showed genuine feeling. She never forced a smile or offered one to anyone who didn't deserve it. She was definitely not his type. He liked the blonde, busty type, who had perfect hair and perfect makeup. His type giggled in his presence and flashed a fake smile as if putting on a show in front of a camera. Basically, he enjoyed having a blonde goddess type hanging on him.

"I don't think so, Cameron. I'm not much of a breakfast person." She swiveled in her seat and finally turned back to look at him.

"Okay. Then how about lunch?" He smiled at her encouragingly, as if he could wear her down with his devilish grin. *Is this really happening?* My brother had a girl say no to a date with him, and he was persistently continuing to pursue her.

"Sorry, Cam. I can't." She hopped out of her seat and walked in the direction where I was standing near the counter. Cam reached out and gripped her upper arm, which caused her to freeze in place.

"Why not?" She didn't turn back around. Instead, she stood with her feet planted firmly with pleading eyes that begged for me to intervene.

"Cam, leave Alexis alone." I suddenly felt like I needed to protect her from falling prey to my brother's persistence. She mouthed *thank you* to me while she managed to propel herself forward and away from my shocked brother. "Why are you asking her out?" Of course, I waited for Alexis to be a safe distance away before my inquisition.

"Because I like her." He shot me his arched eyebrow, it-should-be-obvious expression. "The same reason I ask any girl out."

"You don't like her. She just fascinates you because she has absolutely no interest in you." I wagged my index finger at him, which got a laugh from him, as well as from Travis, who I had all but forgotten was still in the nurse's station with me.

I had been paying so much attention to Cam and Alexis, I had completely overlooked Travis's presence. "Sorry, Travis, if it seemed like I was ignoring you."

"I was watching Cameron. It seems like he lost some of his game." Then Travis let out another low chuckle.

"She's different from the other girls I work with," I whispered, not wanting to offend my colleagues. "She's immune to your charm."

He grinned and nodded in the direction of Tiffany and Cecilia, who seemed to need to stay planted with their arms on the counter to keep from falling over. Apparently, the presence of my brother in such close proximity caused them both to lose their footing and almost faint. "No one is immune to my charm." *Has he always been this full of himself? That was a dumb question. Yes. Yes, he has.*

"Have you ever stopped to think that a girl like Alexis isn't going to be interested in someone that flirts with every female in scrubs?" I placed my hand on my hip while my coffee cup remained firmly in the grasp of my other hand.

A perplexed expression crossed his face. His grin transcended into a frown and his eyebrows drew downward. "So you're saying I need to make her feel special?"

"Something like that." Maybe he would get it. "But she is a very nice girl that lacks the experience you have. Please, just leave her alone."

"Challenge accepted." And his smile returned. His bright eyes shone, letting me know that he had just placed a bet for something he was sure he would win.

"What are you talking about?" I realized I raised my voice, so I motioned him to follow me to the front of the department where the triage area was. Cam and Travis followed me and when I reached our destination away from everyone else in the department, I turned around and gave my twin a scowl. "There is no challenge, Cameron Callahan. I have never, ever told you who you could or couldn't pursue, but that is about to change. She is absolutely off-limits to you."

"Like Louis was for you?" Okay, that was a cheap shot. He lifted his eyebrows at me like he was awaiting my response.

"Cam, it's not really fair for you to bring up Louis," Travis offered in an attempt to save me from the embarrassing cry I felt the overwhelming urge to have.

"You get Alexis to go out with me, and I'll get Louis to go out with you." He extended a hand toward me, like I would shake on such ridiculous terms.

"I can get Louis to go out with me on my own." He would eventually go back to being my friend, and I was sure I could convince him to go out for a meal or a movie. I was a little annoyed by my brother's suggestion. It wasn't as if I needed his help.

"Fine. You get Alexis to go out with me, and I'll get Louis to be your boyfriend." I laughed at his suggestion and looked down at his extended hand.

"And what happens if one of us doesn't hold up his end of the deal?" The terms began to get interesting.

"A hundred dollars?" This seemed so weird. Cam was willing to pay a hundred dollars to go out with Alexis? It must be a full moon for sure.

"Make it two hundred." I could easily get Alexis to go out with him. But I didn't think Cam was going to be successful at persuading Louis to be my boyfriend.

"That works." His eyes darted at me and then down at his hand that was still being held midair. I reached over and pumped his hand once with the grasp of my own hand.

"You know, I have to admit, I was extremely uncomfortable coming back to this ER again. I haven't been in here since Mindy…but seeing this crazy thing go down between the two of you has kept my mind off things. You're both nuts." Travis shook his head in disbelief and pulled his keys from his pocket. "I'm going to head home. This has been fun." His voice was dry and humorless.

I fell in step behind Travis and reached out to touch his arm to grab his attention. "Are you upset with us?"

He whisked around to face me and let out a forced sigh. "I just don't know that I agree with you two manipulating people into dating your sibling." So he wasn't going to be my best friend anymore. He didn't understand that Cam and I did this kind of stuff all the time when we were younger. We made silly bets and sometimes I won, and sometimes Cam won.

"I'm pretty sure that Alexis would eventually go out with my brother even if I didn't intervene. He has a way with women." Concern crept into his coal-colored eyes. "What's wrong, Travis?"

"I'm not worried about Cam. I'm worried that you'll get hurt. Is it worth two hundred dollars to have your heart broken all over again?" Yikes. I hadn't considered that. My wound was still fresh. I certainly didn't need my raw emotions to surface again and burn a hole into my soul. I was already aware of the void inside myself. I didn't need that hollow cavity to be further exposed.

I motioned for Cam to join Travis and me near the exit door. He trudged reluctantly toward us as if he was getting ready to be scolded by an upset parent.

"Cam, I'll help you with Alexis, but I want out of the deal with Louis." I darted my glance at Travis and then back at my brother. "If Louis doesn't want to be with me, then I need to just accept that and move on."

He merely shrugged and reached over to give me a hug. "Okay, Lean Bean. Have a good night."

I held up the cup I had been carrying everywhere with me since Travis had arrived. "Thanks for the coffee." I waved to them both and watched them leave through the sliding glass door into the summer night.

19

CHARLIE

A week later Cam told me that he had texted Louis. I guess that was his way of letting me know it was time for me to convince Alexis to go out with him.

Me: What did you say?

I don't know why I fed into the comment my brother made about texting the boy I grew up with.

Cam: I asked him if he was EVER coming home again.

I just couldn't help myself from what I texted next.

Me: And what did he say?

Because clearly, I was a glutton for punishment.

Cam: He said eventually… that he just needed some time to himself for a little bit. He said he wasn't ready to see his parents again yet.

Me: So how did you respond?

Cam: I told him I understood and to let me know when he was in town again. I told him it was good to have my friend back here. Then he just said "will do." I haven't heard anything else since.

Me: Thanks for the update.

I guess. After our back and forth conversation, I figured he would be expecting an update about Alexis.

My phone rang as soon as I finished reading the last text my brother had sent me. His name and number danced across my screen, and I debated momentarily whether to answer or not. But of course, I did. I never ignored my twin.

"Hey, Cam." *What else could we possibly have to say to each other?*

"Are you okay? I mean…should I not talk about Louis anymore with you? I hope I didn't upset you." In all my life, I could honestly say Cam understood me better than anyone. He even understood me better than I understood myself at times. However, he had no idea how to handle this situation, and he definitely didn't understand me regarding Louis.

All I could do was snicker at his comment. "Of course, you can talk about him. He's your best friend."

"No. *You* are my best friend." His reassurance was sweet.

"I know. But I'm still hopeful that someday we'll all be able to get past this whole fiasco and move on…as friends." Although I wanted more than anything for something more to develop between Louis and me, I still wanted the three of us to be friends again. There had to still be a possibility for that. It had only been a couple of weeks, and time heals all wounds…so I've heard.

"I hope we get to that point again, too." His words were

confident at first and then he trailed off as if he was unsure how to say what else was on his mind. I patiently waited. I may not know my brother as well as he knows me, but I know when something is on his mind. I also know that forcing him to tell me never works, so I waited. Once he let out a forced sigh, I knew he was going to speak again. "So… about Alexis."

"Cam…I'm sorry. I haven't had a good opportunity to talk with her privately." I sucked in a deep breath and forced out words that were uncomfortable for a sister to say about her brother. "All the nurses I work with have a crush on you, so I don't want any of them hearing me talk about you to Alexis. If they thought I played matchmaker for my brother, they'd soon all be hitting me up for a chance to go out with you."

Cam's end of the line rumbled with soft laughter. "You have to fight them off me, Lean Bean?"

"As if you don't already know they're all smitten with you?" He knew, and he loved every single second of it.

"They are good for my ego for sure." I could imagine him smiling on the other side of the phone.

"You are a pig. A disgusting pig." I shook my head at his inability to change. He has always been the center of attention and enjoys the limelight. I, on the other hand, would rather blend in with the background. "I don't even understand why you want to go out with her. She is hardly your type."

"And what is my type exactly?" I had no idea why his tone conveyed surprise after my comment.

I stifled a laugh. "You know. Blonde with big boobs." Cam had never dated a girl that didn't fit that profile. He had to know his own pattern.

Silence fell from the other end of the conversation. I wondered if he was thinking back to all the women I had ever seen him with. "I gotta go, Lean Bean. Talk with you again soon."

"Cam…" But before I could even ask him if he was all right, he was gone. *What the hell was that about?*

❧

Cameron remained quiet the next several days. I'd worked three nights in a row, and I didn't see him—any of them—which was odd. Considering that I worked with Alexis two out of the three nights, it was especially weird. It was a very rare occasion when a week passed and my brother hadn't brought coffee to me during one of my shifts.

Are you upset with me? I haven't seen you all week. I finally texted my twin after he dropped off the face of the earth for nearly five days.

Sorry. Just been busy, that's all. The hell if that was true. I wasn't sure why he was lying to me, but I was determined to find out.

I selected his number on my cell phone and waited several rings before voice mail picked up. *How dare he not answer when I call? I always answer when he calls me.*

Either answer your phone, or I'll hunt you down. You're going to speak with me. That prompted a quick response. His name and number flashed across my screen a moment later. I smiled to myself at how quickly I could get a reaction from him. "Hey, Cam," I answered as coolly as I could, given that I was annoyed and worried about my brother's silence for almost an entire week.

"Hey, Charlie." *What? No Lean Bean?* This was more serious than I thought.

"Can you meet for lunch?" I extended the olive branch and could only hope he would accept it.

"Is everything all right?" His voice hitched slightly with

his question. I was worried about him, and he was worried about me because I asked him to go to lunch?

"I just want to have lunch with my brother. Is that okay?" I was fully aware that I hadn't adequately masked my worry given the inflection of my voice.

"Fine. The diner in fifteen?" He huffed a release of air and feigned his own annoyance or worry. Not only couldn't I differentiate my own feelings, I couldn't tell which feeling he had, either.

"I'll be there."

It only took me ten minutes to arrive, so I was already in a booth when my brother walked in. His hair was a frazzled mess, and he was wearing a wrinkled T-shirt and rumpled shorts, as if he had worn the same outfit a few days consecutively.

"What the hell happened to you?" There was no need to beat around the bush. I was always direct when it came to my brother.

His sullen gait caused a shuffle in his step until he finally slid into the booth and across from me. "We probably should have met at my place or yours."

Something wasn't right, and it prickled my nerves. Dark circles marred the skin beneath his eyes and his face wore several days of stubble. I half wondered if he had even showered lately. "Are you okay?"

"I don't know." He let out an exasperated sigh and his lips turned down while his brows drew together. "Is this what life is about for me?" I knew he didn't want me to answer that question. I was wondering where this was going though, so I sat intently listening. His agonized expression gave me the impression many thoughts were weighing heavily on his mind. "We're not kids anymore, you know? I'm twenty-three years old. I graduated college, and I got a job. But where am I going?" Another rhetorical question, so I continued with my exercised patience while he slumped his shoulders forward and broke eye contact with me. "I go out with girls, I flirt, I have fun, but I never commit to anything serious." I wasn't exactly sure when I could ask my own questions. I wanted to know what had caused all these life reflections, but I also wanted to keep him talking, so I held back my prodding. "So that's all I get in return. Girls that like the way I look but aren't looking for anything serious, either." His hazel gaze pulled up slowly, revealing a set of tired eyes. "Are you going to say anything?"

"I was waiting for you to finish." This was a side I wasn't used to seeing. This was my brother humbled, vulnerable, and lacking confidence. I had so many thoughts and questions running through my head, but I really didn't know what to say at that moment.

"I'm finished." His eyes searched mine, begging me to shed some light on his emotional crisis.

"Cameron, you know I'm not the one to come to for relationship advice. I'm obviously lacking in experience myself."

"I've just been feeling on edge lately. Why won't a nice girl go out with me, Lean Bean?" He raked his hands through his dark, unwashed hair as the waitress appeared at our table.

"Just two Cokes please for right now," I said, offering her a reassuring smile as I waved her away. She nodded silently and disappeared quickly, leaving my brother and me some privacy.

"I know you think I have a type that I like to go out with. But I don't. Those just happen to be the *only* girls that will go out with *me.*"

What he said actually made a lot of sense to me. It wasn't his choice to go out with superficial girls. Those were the only girls who were attracted to *him.* He was a good-looking guy, I guess. He had thick, dark hair that he typically kept longer on the top and short on the sides. He always had it styled…well, except for today. He had mysterious, hazel eyes, and of course, he was six feet tall with a body full of muscles from his regular workout routine. I was sure those were the features that attracted many girls to him. But if they only liked him for the surface, they were probably concerned mostly with their own looks and didn't have much depth, either. And of course, there was the attitude that he usually had on display for women. He exuded confidence and flirted blatantly. He would literally smile in a girl's direction, and she would giggle and blush from the attention. I had always found it repulsive, but I loved my brother, so I tried my best to brush it off. He had respected my request and didn't date anyone I worked with, but that didn't stop him from being bald-faced with his affection toward my female colleagues.

And there was no doubt in my mind that any women I worked with would jump at the chance to be Cameron Callahan's next date. That was, until now. Alexis hadn't shown any interest in him whatsoever. "Maybe if you didn't flirt with every female in a fifty-foot radius of where you are, you'd find a nice girl."

"You mentioned that before. Truly, I'm just being friendly." I quirked up my eyebrow at his comment. "Okay. So maybe there is some flirting, but I swear it's harmless. It's just who I am."

"Then you'll continue with the same pattern you've always had." I hoped I hadn't sounded too heartless. But again, I never tiptoed around the issues when it came to my brother. He always appreciated my no-nonsense approach to situations. And he could always count on me to give him honest advice, rather than just tell him what he wanted to hear.

His hand rubbed across his bristly jaw pensively and his facial features softened. "So how do I change?"

I couldn't help but chuckle under my breath. "You really

need to get yourself together. You're acting like a girl and you know Claudette is the sibling you should go to about being a girl." I reached across the table and tousled the unkempt hair on his head with the palm of my hand, just like we used to do when we were kids.

"Thanks, Lean Bean. You really know how to make a guy feel good about himself." His sarcasm was laced with a hint of laughter, so at least I was getting him to loosen up.

"How about I invite Alexis to breakfast with us?" That comment caused the lines on his forehead to raise up. "I would have Travis come, too. Maybe after our shift one morning?"

So we made plans for the following week. Hopefully, that would give me plenty of time to convince Alexis to go to breakfast with us.

I woke up on Cam's uncomfortable couch with a muscle strain in my neck and aching, stiff joints. I would probably have been more comfortable on the floor. I guess *I could consider speaking to my mom and stay at her house in my old bed tonight.* I contemplated that thought for only a moment. Talking with my father last night had been enlightening and disturbing at the same time. *How long had I not known my parents?* Without any siblings, I felt alone on the island of parents with a mistaken identity. I had always thought of Cameron as my brother, but there was no way he would understand what it was like for me to feel as if I'd lived in the middle of a lie my entire childhood. Then the lie continued into my adulthood, and I was completely oblivious to it.

I couldn't believe what an idiot I had been. It was still going to take me a while to get used to the idea of my parents dating other people. It was going to be weird having them live in separate places. I knew I wasn't a kid anymore, but I guess it was hard no matter what age you were when your parents split up. At least they were still friends, I supposed.

I stretched my legs out and pushed myself up into a

sitting position. Although daylight funneled in through the curtains, silence filled his apartment. I clicked on my phone that I had plugged into the outlet next to the couch when I had lain down last night. Seven thirty. It was still early. Cam probably wasn't awake yet. I stood and stretched to my full height, grasping my hands and pulling them up as far as possible. I couldn't lay on that ridiculously uncomfortable couch for any longer, so I decided to go for some coffee. A breakfast sandwich wouldn't hurt, either. I figured I would throw on a clean shirt and a baseball cap, but I definitely wanted to quickly run my toothbrush across my teeth. So I rooted around in my duffel bag to grab a shirt and my toothbrush and then tiptoed across the carpet down the short hallway toward the bathroom.

Cam's door was open, so I felt compelled to peek inside and see if he was still asleep. Only he wasn't in his room. I hadn't seen a text from him when I glanced at my phone only moments ago. I was curious where he could be at such an early hour. Then I shook my head. We were beyond having to report our whereabouts to each other. I was his best friend, but I was acting like his jealous girlfriend. Ironically, he was probably off at some girl's place at that moment having early Saturday morning sex. That was typical Cameron. He enjoyed his one-night stands and booty calls. I wasn't as close to him as I was five years ago, but his behavior hadn't seemed to have changed. He never had a girlfriend in high school, and from what I had heard lately, things weren't any different now.

So after quickly ridding my mouth of morning breath with some minty toothpaste, I slapped on a clean shirt and a cap on my head to hide my serious case of wild bedhead that reflected back at me in the mirror in Cam's bathroom. Coffee and a bacon, egg, and cheese bagel sounded great, so I headed to the diner I used to frequent with my friends years ago.

My intention was to walk in, approach the counter, place an order and leave, keeping a low profile. However, when I walked in, I noticed a familiar braid laying on a perfect shoulder. Even with the Saturday morning crowd filling the restaurant, my eyes immediately found her. In a booth positioned in a corner to the left of the counter, I saw two girls wearing navy blue scrubs. One of them made my heart rate increase. I swallowed a lump in my throat and wiped my perspiring palms on my mesh shorts, while taking in a deep breath. She had her back to me and she was sitting next to a dark-haired man.

My traitorous friend Cam was sitting across from her alongside a girl with dirty blond hair. Pulling my hat down farther on my forehead, I observed their body language. The girl next to Cam appeared shy. He was sitting next to her, but there was distance between the two of them. *They couldn't be on a date, could they?* I only allowed my attention to stay on them for a moment. I was more interested in watching Charlie and the guy she was sitting next to.

With both of their backs to me, I couldn't really make out their situation. They seemed comfortable with each other, but then again, Charlie had a way of putting everyone at ease. However, when she leaned her head on his shoulder while laughing, an intense wave of nausea ran through me, extinguishing my appetite. A squeezing sensation tugged low in my belly, and I thought I would projectile vomit the beer I drank last night. The sour taste traveled up my throat and into my mouth while a burning sensation developed within my chest.

"Sir, can I help you?" A female voice from behind the counter at the cash register broke my trancelike state. I swear I was transported to a place where I was a mere onlooker into the world of my friends—like when the ghosts of Christmas visited scrooge. *I should be sitting at that table with them. Not that ass...or that other girl for that matter. I stayed at my best friend's place last night. He should have invited me to this breakfast outing.* "Sir?"

I shook my head away from those depressing thoughts long enough to order a coffee and breakfast sandwich to go. I have never felt jealousy in my life, but right then I teetered on the edge of near insanity. *How had I let this happen?* Charlie and Cam used to be my closest friends in the world. They were like my family. Now I wasn't even a fleeting thought to them.

This was my fault. I walked away from them. I left five years ago, and I left again five weeks ago. I hadn't truly walked away from Cameron recently, but I guess it was really the same outcome when I left Charlie.

I recalled how sad she was the last time I saw her, and I was the jackass that caused her misery. But today, bright and early, she smiled and laughed with some other guy. *What was wrong with me?* She had wanted to be with me, and I foolishly pushed her away. I was the person that made her laugh and smile. I was the one that she brushed up against. And I was the man she kissed and held.

I stepped to the side of the counter to let others move up in line, but I continued to stare at the life I once had...the life I could have still had. Still in my dumbfounded state, Cameron's gaze caught mine. He waved his hand and motioned me over to the table. My feet remained planted in the same position. I only had flip-flops on, but I felt like my shoes were heavy bricks glued to the floor. My legs held me completely frozen on the tiled surface.

"Louis!" Great. Now he did it. He called me by name.

So what happened? The beautiful brunette that filled my heart with feelings I had never before experienced, turned in her seat and showed me those gorgeous gray eyes of hers. I expected her to give me a scowl, but she actually appeared happy to see me. Those delicate, pink lips were drawn up in a smile I knew was only meant for me. Her contented expression gave me enough courage to propel myself forward and move in their direction. The dark-haired fella that sat next to her glared at me and seemed guarded at my approach. He didn't share in the happiness Charlie had shown me. He seemed downright pissed off.

"Cam told me you crashed at his place last night." My Lord, I had missed the sweet, smooth sound of her voice.

"I figured you would sleep in, so I snuck out this morning without waking you." Cam's voice managed to draw my attention away from his twin. He was wearing his own wide grin.

"You do have a lot of experience sneaking out in the morning without waking anyone." I meant to be jovial, but Cameron's grin transformed to an apprehensive look quickly. Not to mention the girl seated next to him already looked uncomfortable and now visibly blushed.

Charlie, not so subtly, made a slicing gesture with her finger across her throat in an attempt to discontinue the direction of the conversation. *What the hell was going on?* "I'm totally kidding. Cameron has always been a complete gentleman." I offered a smiled to the unfamiliar girl and stuck out my hand. "I'm Louis. And you are?"

"I'm sorry. I don't have any manners this early in the morning, I suppose." Cameron stumbled over his words. *Smooth dude. Real smooth.* "This is Alexis. She works with Charlie."

"I figured as much given the scrubs she's wearing." Charlie's lips turned up once again transforming into one of her amazing smiles as a response to my attempt at humor.

"And this is Travis. He works with Cameron at the high

school." Her words caused my heart to plummet into the pit of my stomach. She might as well have said, "This is Travis. He is the new man in my life because you're a stupid idiot." Having lost the ability to think of actual words to say, I simply nodded.

Alexis grasped my extended hand and pumped it in a dainty handshake. When I turned to Travis, he only furrowed his eyebrows and pursed his lips into a thin line. I was pretty sure he knew something about Charlie and me. He was either jealous or overprotective. I couldn't tell which it was. He either knew that Charlie had feelings for me and was jealous of that fact; or he knew I had broken her heart, and he wanted to protect her from letting me do that all over again.

The cashier yelled my name and startled me; I had completely forgotten about my coffee and breakfast sandwich. "Well, I don't want to interrupt your double date any more than I already have, so I'm going to grab my sandwich and head out." It was crazy that I wanted to get away from my friends, but I really couldn't stomach seeing Charlie on a date with someone else. And I didn't really know what the story with Cam and Alexis was, but it was a little awkward.

The four of them waved to me and said goodbye as I quickly retrieved the items I had ordered and left the diner, heading out to my parked vehicle. I sat in my car thinking about Charlie. Her smile and her laugh was all I needed to feel happy again. I had been miserable and despondent for weeks, but seeing her made everything better. I wasn't sure how to fix what I had broken, but I knew I needed to be able to be around her to fix my fragmented self.

As I started the engine and put the car into gear, I knew I had to be near her again. So I drove to her apartment. Her key was in my glove box. I couldn't bear to see it on my key chain, but now I couldn't wait to dig it out.

It only took a matter of minutes of driving for me to reach her home. It only took a matter of seconds once there for me to unlock the door to her apartment and step inside, closing the door behind me. Memories flooded my brain once I crossed the threshold. I observed the innocent sofa sitting in her living area, and I remembered watching movies with her, cuddling, and falling asleep there. I took a seat on the cushions and thought about how much more comfortable it was than the couch at Cameron's. Then I stood and walked a few strides down the hallway to her bedroom and surveyed her bed. The first memory elicited by her sleeping quarters brought a smile to my face. I loved sleeping with her next to me. Her easy breathing lulled me to sleep and her warm body pressed against me gave me the same security as a child's blankie.

I kicked off my flip-flops and lay on the bed with my head on her pillows, and her fragrance struck my nostrils. I inhaled a long breath and took in the coconut aroma. I missed that damn smell. I missed her, but just as I closed my eyes, the vision of what else happened in the bed waltzed through my happy thoughts.

I had used her when I was hurting, and I couldn't forgive myself. I had needed an outlet for my pain, and I came to her looking for relief. She obliged me willingly, but I couldn't forgive myself for my behavior. She had told me she loved me, and I wasn't in any kind of condition to accept her affection. I was in a dark place, and I didn't allow her to show me the light.

But after several weeks of separation, I felt like I could finally see the light. I know that sounds lame, but it was true. Light illuminates everything around her. Her smile can transport me from any dark place into sunshine-filled happiness. I had definitely screwed up. I needed her. I tried to convince myself that she would be happier without me in the long run, but I hadn't realized that I wouldn't be happy without her. Her presence was key to my happiness. *But how was I going to convince her to give me another chance when she had already moved on with Travis?*

❀

I left Charlie's apartment and pondered possibly speaking to my mother again. I drove to the park and sat in my car drinking my purchased coffee. Alone with my thoughts, I reflected on the relationship I had with my mom. I don't think I had ever gone for over a month without communicating with her. I may have only exchanged texts or brief phone calls at times, but I was always in touch.

We used to have long talks and spend a lot of time together before I left home, and I thought I knew my mom pretty well. Now I really wasn't sure. I guess those brief communication encounters didn't allow me the ability to know her sufficiently anymore. Normally on a Saturday, I could count on my mom being home. Even though the library is open on Saturdays, she has always been a Monday through Friday librarian. There were some part-time employees that kept the library afloat on Saturdays and weekday evenings.

However, given the new development in my mother's relationship status, I was no longer aware of her weekend habits and whereabouts. *Did she and her new boyfriend visit places or stay at home lazily in their pajamas?* I shouldn't have even thought about that. I don't really want to know what it is that my mother does with her new boyfriend. I just needed to know what her availability was for the day. Maybe I should text her instead of calling her.

Mom, I'm in town for a couple of days. I'd like to see you if possible.

I didn't expect to hear back from her right away given my earlier thoughts. She could be busy. Besides, older people don't live with their cell phones attached to them like my generation does. So I was pleasantly surprised when I received a response from her only a few moments after I had hit the send button.

I would love to see you too. I'm available all weekend. Just tell me what works for you.

My father had basically given the same kind of response when I had reached out to him. They really were quite similar, even though I had never recognized it before. **Can I come by the house?**

Of course! This will always be your home. You're welcome whenever you like. I'll be home all day. Stop by whenever. I can't wait to see you.

Rather than respond to her text, I stared at the geese landing on the pond at the city park. There were children and dogs running on the lush green lawns and the sun was shining brightly. I had rolled the windows down in my car due to the August heat, but because I remained in the shade of the large pine trees that lined the edge of the parking area, it was cool enough for me to sit there comfortably.

Flashes of memories danced through my head as I watched the environment in front of me. I remembered playing on the playground swings. I pushed Charlie on the swing and she soared higher and higher. We must have only been seven or eight years old, but I could almost hear her giggling and squealing as I pushed her higher than I could even reach.

Cameron and I threw a football multiple days in the summer on those very lawns when we were small and our parents met friends in the park for barbeques and family get-togethers. There were still paddleboats that circled the river surrounding the park. As I saw a small parade of yellow boats with couples propelling them along the water by the pedaling of their legs, I recalled being in boats similar to those. Sometimes it was just Charlie and me. Sometimes it was the three of us. Cameron and Charlie would take turns trying to push each other off the boat into the river. No one ever fell over, but we had exchanged quite a few laughs trying. Then I saw a couple jog along the paved path, and a dull ache passed through my heart.

I hated jogging. But I loved trotting alongside her. The exercising wasn't the cause of my heart rate increase, it was her presence. For me, the act of running didn't release endorphins, it was running next to her that gave me pleasure. I quickly realized that everything at the park reminded me of Charlie. Really, everything in my life reminded me of Charlie now. She had pretty much consumed my thoughts ever since seeing her in that damn cereal aisle.

I thought I had successfully pushed the memories of her deep down years ago when I moved away. But seeing her again brought back a rush of intense feelings that I couldn't seem to shake so easily this go around. Weeks ago, I hadn't been able to rid myself of the memories. And after seeing her this morning, I knew I never would be able to walk away again. I needed her just as much as I needed oxygen. I wasn't going to be able to live without her. I just wasn't sure if she would be willing to let me in her life again.

I pulled into my mother's driveway behind her car. I didn't see another car, so I assumed she was home alone. As I approached the front door, I felt compelled to knock even though I'd never knocked on the door to this house ever in my life. Probably because the house no longer felt like home to me. I wasn't sure where home was anymore. My apartment in Annapolis was as close to what I would call home these days, I suppose.

My mother pulled the door open and a glowing smile lit up her face. I know it must have been difficult for her to have me give her the silent treatment for the last several weeks. Seeing her sheer happiness at the sight of me standing on the front porch made me feel pretty guilty about ignoring her.

"Hey, Mom." I barely got words out and she tackled me with a tight hug. My mother is not a large woman, but she could embrace me fiercely. I stood over half a foot taller than her, and I easily had sixty or seventy pounds on her, but she could still squeeze me around my waist with enough force to make me feel like I might split in half.

"Louis. I'm so happy to see you." When she released me, I could see a sheen of happy tears over her brown eyes threatening to spill over at any second. I really hoped that wouldn't happen. *What son could stand to see his mother cry?* "Come on in." She pulled me forward and shut the door behind me. "Do you want me to make some coffee?"

The hospitality she tried to offer felt terribly awkward. I just wanted to feel like things were the same. However, the harder she tried to be a good hostess, the more I realized things were different. "No thanks, Mom. I already had some."

"Well, come sit with me in the kitchen while I make some tea." My mother was always a tea drinker. She would make coffee for my dad and for me once I got into high school, but she always stuck to hot tea for herself.

I sat at the kitchen table and my mother sat across from me. I closely observed her light brown hair and her dark brown eyes. She was a contrast to my blond hair and blue eyes. There was no mistaking who my father was, but my mother and I couldn't look any more different in our features.

"I'm sorry I haven't called or come by before now."

"It's okay, Louis. I know I hurt you, and I'm very sorry about that." She hung her head and took in a deep breath before finding my eyes again. "Your father told me that you went to dinner last night."

I found it very weird that they still talked with each other so often. "Yes. We had a good talk."

"That's what he said as well." She stood to fill her teakettle and placed it on the stovetop burner. Rather than sitting back down at the table, she stood with her back to the stove facing me. "He said he thought maybe you had forgiven him. I hope you can somehow find it in your heart to forgive me, too."

"Mom, it's not about forgiveness. I was just shocked. I was hurt and angry that no one had told me what was going on. I was completely caught off guard. I've had some time to digest things over the last several weeks. Although, I'm not completely used to the idea of my parents getting divorced, I'm moving my way toward acceptance. I love you both." Another bear hug around my neck ensued following my spiel.

She released me from the headlock she had me in before busting my windpipe with her crushing embrace. "We love you too, Louis. I promise we won't keep secrets from you again."

CHARLIE

After breakfast, I tried to go back to my apartment and sleep but Louis continued to invade my thoughts. I couldn't stop thinking about him. I stayed up all night at work and then spent over an hour at the diner with Alexis, Travis, and my brother. *Yet here I was lying in my bed staring up at the ceiling unable to shut my brain off long enough to allow sleep to overtake me.*

I picked up my phone from my nightstand, thinking I'd surf my social media sites and relax a little. Two text messages were waiting for me. One from Cam and one from Claudette. I keep my phone on silent when I'm sleeping, so I hadn't heard the ping notification of the messages. I opened Cam's message first.

Tomorrow is my last day of freedom before early morning sports team practices. Wanna hit the beach with me? We can head out in the morning and then grab lunch on the boardwalk? That sounded great to me. I should see if Travis wanted to go, too. His summer vacation would be ending soon as well. Cam's summer was always slightly shorter than the high school teachers'. He returns once the high school sports teams begin practicing for the fall programs.

Sounds great. Should I ask Travis to join us?

Sure and why don't you invite Alexis too? Oh Lord. Was this his ploy all along?

Why don't you give her a little space? You just saw her this morning. We can plan for something next week.

Okay. I'm going to trust your judgment. BTW… you should be asleep. Why are you texting me?

When I didn't immediately respond, as expected, his name and number lit up my phone screen. "Hey, Cam."

"You didn't text me back right away. Are you unable to sleep because you saw Louis this morning?" He really knew me too well. Now I either had to admit the truth to him or deny what he already knew was the truth.

"First of all, I was going to text back. You just didn't wait long enough for my response. And secondly, sometimes I just have trouble sleeping during the day." I hoped I evaded his question enough that he let it go.

"Are you having trouble sleeping during the day because you saw Louis this morning?" Okay. *So maybe he wasn't going to let this go.*

"Cam, I'm really trying not to think about him." I might as well confess. He already knew the truth. No use in denying it. He wouldn't believe me if I refuted his theory anyway. "It doesn't help though when you call asking if I'm thinking about him." A soft chuckle seeped out in my attempt to conceal my true emotions.

"All right. I get it. But if talking about him bothers you, how are you going to be when you see him again?" I didn't know how to respond to his comment, so most likely my silence spoke louder than any words I could formulate.

I sighed noisily and flipped over on my back once again looking up at the ceiling while holding my phone against my ear. "Cam, I want to see Louis. I'm happy when I'm around him. I just wish he felt the same being around me." I couldn't believe I admitted that aloud. My confession put things into perspective, and I was glad that my brother understood I needed to confide in him. "I know he doesn't want to be my boyfriend, but I wish he would at least be comfortable being around me."

"He will be again. I'm sure." His voice was laced with a glimmer of hope, but he didn't share his thoughts with me.

"Cameron Callahan, what are you *not* telling me?"

"Nothing, Lean Bean. Things between you two will be better soon. I just know it." I wish I had half the confidence my twin does.

I decided to wait on answering my sister until after I got some sleep. I love her, but she is a girly girl, which usually involves some kind of drama. I just didn't have the energy for that right now. My eyelids were drooping, so I decided to allow my body the opportunity to relax and let a peaceful daytime slumber wrap around me. As I drifted off to sleep, I imagined Louis's strong arms folding around me as I snuggled up to his warm body and happiness soaked into me.

I woke up six hours later still thinking about Louis. *I guess every time I see him now, this will be what happens.* I'll dream about him and wish I could have him again. I'm not sure what happened to me. I had done pretty well with moving on. I wasn't interested in dating anyone, but I was able to get through my days without thinking about him all the time. I saw him for five minutes earlier this morning, and suddenly I couldn't stop mulling over what we had.

The longing I had for him cauterized a hole in my heart. I wish I could go back to the times when we held hands and cuddled on the couch. Falling asleep next to him was so much better than sleeping alone. Dammit. This was foolish. I picked up my phone to review Claudette's text. Maybe a little girly girl drama would provide a good distraction.

I opened up the text from my sister. **I have exciting news! Call me ASAP**. Yep. Drama, for sure. She answered on the third ring after I punched her number into my phone.

"You're never going to believe what has happened!" Claudette screeched out a high-pitched squeal into the phone when she answered. No saying "hello" calmly from her.

"What's going on, Claudette?" One of us needed to maintain her composure, and obviously, that person needed to be me.

"My boss bought a new location for a coffee shop, and it's in Sandy Cove. And guess who is going to get it up and running?" The excitement in her voice oozed through the phone and buzzed in my ear.

"You?" I played along. Of course, it would be her. She had been the general manager for the store at the beach in Delaware for five years. She was probably his only qualified employee for that large of a task.

"Yes! I'll be coming back home for a while. So we'll get to see each other so much more. You and your friends can come into the coffee shop. It will be amazing!" She continued to speak in exclamation mode.

"That's great, Claudette. When are you moving back?"

"I'll be coming down next week for a few days to look over the place. Take some measurements and such. Then I'll meet with my boss and the interior designer." Her pressured speech continued to spout off more details of setting up a new store. "Maybe we can meet for dinner one night that you're off work?"

"Sure, Claudette. Cam and I would love that." She didn't need to invite our brother. She knew if she invited me, the invitation always included Cam as well. "Maybe I'll invite Travis, too."

"Who's Travis? A new love interest?" The way she sang "LUUUV" unnerved me. It certainly didn't take her long to jump to the wrong conclusion.

"No. He's a friend of Cam's and mine. He's a nice guy. You'll like him."

"Char, you really need to find some girlfriends." Of course she would say that. She had told me that since forever. I never had any female friends when we were growing up, and that suited me just fine, but Claudette thought I needed to spend more time with other girls. I was fairly confident it was because she thought being around women would make me want to do girly things like get manicures or go shopping.

I ended the call with my sister after I assured her that we would get together next week. Then I texted Travis to make plans for the following day at the beach. Travis planned to pick me up at my apartment, and then we would drive to Cam's place to pick him up and head to the ocean. Of course, I texted my brother to confirm the plans with him and inform him of our sister's arrangements for coming home for a few days next week and ultimately moving back to our town for a little while.

I was still a little shocked at how excited Claudette had sounded. She always acted like she couldn't get away from our town fast enough. She loved her cottage at the Delaware beach, and she seemed genuinely happy at her job at the coffee shop. I often wondered why she had found herself in a retail position. Sure, she was a manager of a successful store, but she had an MBA. I figured she would have moved to the Baltimore area and worked in the corporate world. She always seemed like the type to enjoy the hustle and bustle. Sure, the beach is busy during the summer, but in the winter months, life moves at a rather slow pace. Most young people find that pace boring and lonely quite frankly.

However, Claudette seemed to like her life the way it was. Maybe she was just looking forward to the challenge of starting a new business from the ground up. It might be good to have my sister around again.

Cameron had asked me where Claudette would be staying. I knew he wouldn't offer his place to her. He wouldn't even let *me* stay over, and I was his favorite person. The only women who stay at his place—well, actually, I wasn't sure if he let *any* woman stay at his place. He may have someone over, but he pretty much enjoyed his time with her and then drove her home before it was time for him to go to sleep. I know the majority of times, he would go to his date's place, making it easier for him to leave. Besides, luckily for him, Claudette considered me her favorite sibling, not our brother.

Even though I knew my sister enjoyed being with me, she said she would be staying at our parents' house. So I guess my apartment wouldn't be her temporary dwelling, either. I considered that a good thing. I enjoyed the time I spent at her place earlier this summer, but since I frequently slept during the day, our schedules conflicted too often. I really liked my apartment to be quiet when I slept. I could only imagine Claudette blow-drying her hair or knocking over the shampoo bottles in the shower while I tried to sleep. It certainly wouldn't work out. So I was happy to hear that she had already made plans to stay with our mom and dad.

The following morning, Travis was at my apartment at seven minutes past eight. We had agreed on eight o'clock, but he was late. He was always late. We had come to expect his tardiness. Cam and I even joked about being on Travis's time. It was no secret that Travis and I had become close friends over the last several weeks. I had confided in him, and he had confided in me as well.

During one of our heart-to-heart conversations, Travis admitted that he never tried to get anywhere quickly. He just accepted that he would be late and took his time. Apparently, his fiancée was in a hurry to get to wherever she was going on the day that she was killed in that car accident. Even though the accident was not her fault, Travis still felt that had she not been in such a hurry, it may have never happened.

I felt bad about Travis losing his beloved Mindy, so I had spent a lot of time with him in the hopes that he could move on with his life or, at least, not be so lonely. He had other friends. He played golf and basketball. And of course, he spent time with Cam and me. We ate meals together, and even though we went fishing and biking together, he hadn't accompanied me on any more of my runs. That time still didn't feel right to share with anyone other than Louis. But Travis had become a good friend to me, and I'd like to think that I had been a good friend to him, too.

We drove to Cam's apartment, and I texted him that we were pulling into the parking lot outside of his complex. I flipped through my phone mindlessly while waiting for my brother to make his appearance. I was in the front seat next to Travis when I heard the back door open, causing me to peer over my shoulder. Cam slid into the seat easily behind Travis, but when the door behind me opened, I had to hold my breath.

Louis peered inside the car at me. I forced a smile, not because I wasn't happy to see him. It was forced because I was so shocked, I had to make a serious effort to erase the look of panic I must have originally worn.

"Uh, Cam. I think I might just skip the beach today. I have to head back to work tomorrow, so I should probably head back across the bridge early." Louis referred to the Chesapeake Bay Bridge. The suspended crossing links the eastern shore of Maryland to the Annapolis-Baltimore area where Louis now lived. The reminder of that bridge forced me to think about how far apart our hearts and souls were from each other. It was like a large body of water separated us.

"Louis, get in the damn car," my brother huffed out. "It's my last day of freedom, if you're any friend at all, you'll spend time with me today." *Is that a look of anger on my brother's face? And is that a guilt trip he's forcing on his best friend?*

Cam's guilt trip was successful. With a loud sigh, Louis reluctantly slid into the car behind me and slammed the car door. I glanced over at Travis, who appeared rather amused at the scene that had just transpired.

The ride to the beach was a quiet one. All three men sat silently during the thirty-plus-minute drive to the Atlantic coast. I played along in the game of who can be mute the longest. I just increased the volume on the radio and listened intently, not daring to sing along with the words to any of the songs, as that would cause me to lose the battle of reticence.

We finally reached our destination. Travis parked and the rest of us grabbed the items we brought along. Travis unloaded the cooler from the trunk. I grabbed my beach bag, and the guys each grabbed their respective bags and beach towels. With our items in tow, we trudged through the sand to mark our spot on the beach, still not exchanging any words with each other.

"I can help you with that," Travis said as I spread out the blanket.

"Thank goodness you spoke first." I was so relieved that Travis finally broke the deafening silence. "I wasn't about to lose to Cameron and Louis. They would never let me forget it."

"Travis may have been the biggest loser, but Louis and I still held out longer than you, Lean Bean."

I reached into my bag and grabbed a bottle of sunscreen so I could throw it at the face of my twin. He dodged my futile attempt at hitting him and laughed.

"And you throw like a girl." Okay. Now it was game on.

"You won't be saying anything like that when I beat you at volleyball, Cameron Callahan. You'll have to hide your head in the sand when you lose to a girl." I turned my nose up and grabbed the bottle of sunscreen I had tossed, that was now laying in the sand. "Which of you two boys would like to be on the winning team…AKA, Charlie's team?"

Travis and Louis exchanged scowls and grunts. It was very caveman-like. I was used to my brother and Louis fighting over who got to have me on their team. They both had always wanted me on their team, but this showdown between Travis and Louis was uncomfortable. I didn't think either one of them wanted to be on my team.

"Obviously, you should be on Charlie's team since you're her boyfriend." Louis's stern voice held a serious undertone, and I couldn't help but laugh at what sounded like a hostile accusation.

Travis squinted and drew his brows together. "I'm *not* her boyfriend." *Why did all three of these boys seem so indignant?*

The lines on Louis's forehead arched, creating a shocked expression. I guess when I saw him yesterday at the diner, I had been sitting next to Travis. And then again today, we arrived in the same car. I would say it was a safe assumption to make given the appearance of the situation.

"So you're just friends?" Louis no longer looked in Travis's direction. He darted his gaze toward me.

"Yes. We're only friends." I forcefully pulled my sunglasses off my face and peered directly into his big, beautiful blue eyes. I somehow thought I could send him a signal indicating I was not interested in anyone but him.

"Friends like you and I used to be, Charlene?" Obviously, he misinterpreted the signal I was trying to send. His furious demeanor took hold again.

"No, Louis. I have *never* been friends with anyone like I was with you." His allegation stung, and he didn't seem satisfied with my response. He was trying to get under my skin, so I turned my attention to Travis. "Travis, you're on my team. Louis can play with my dumb brother." I was still annoyed with Cam, and now that I was livid with Louis, it made sense to abandon them both for Travis. Still fuming with anger, I yanked off my tank top while I shimmied out of my cotton shorts, revealing my favorite orange bikini. I swear Louis's mouth gaped open as he watched me disrobe. "See something you like, Coleman?"

22

LOUIS

Of course I saw something I liked. She was my kryptonite. I couldn't *not* look. Her beautiful curves were on display for every man on this beach, and I wanted to be the only one that was allowed to appreciate her figure. When she handed the bottle of her sunscreen over to Travis, I forced myself to look away. I couldn't stomach watching another man, friend or not, rubbing lotion over her shoulders and back.

I only caught a quick glimpse after Charlie's comment. I didn't want to appear like I was gawking. As it was, I probably looked like a cartoon character with my mouth hanging open and tongue lolling out as she removed her outer beachwear. The orange pieces of material clung proudly to her bronzed skin. Outdoor running graced her skin with a wonderful, glowing tan. Even though her legs are lean and her stomach is flat, the curves from her breasts and hips reminded me of how much of a woman she is now.

My swim trunks started to feel tight, and I only saw her in that damn bikini for ten seconds. *How am I going to watch her across a volleyball net and not be mesmerized by her body?*

More importantly, how am I going to have my body not *react to the sight of hers?* This was not a good idea, and without my own transportation, I was trapped in this situation. I was stuck with her, my best friend, and some guy I just met stranded on the end of the continent.

"Louis?" Cam calling my name brought me out of the whirling thoughts in my head. "You look like you are a thousand miles away. You okay?"

I shook my head slightly to help draw me back to my current situation. "Yeah, man. I'm fine. Just have a lot on my mind, I guess. Nothing that a day at the beach won't cure."

Cam's lips turned up in a smile. "Well, come on." He rolled a volleyball out of his bag and motioned for me to walk with him toward the nets that were already set up off to the right where we had our belongings set out.

I briefly glanced in Charlie's direction again before following behind my friend. During my brief look, I observed Charlie now applying sunscreen to Travis's back. Part of me wished I hadn't already applied sunscreen to myself prior to leaving Cam's apartment just so I could have her rub her hands on my back. Then the other part was just sad that she was applying sunscreen to another man's back—friend or not. My feet carried me in Cam's direction, but I couldn't look away just yet.

What if things between Charlie and Travis morphed into something like she and I had, although only briefly? I wanted to kick myself or punch something. I really wanted to punch Travis, although I know I'm the one truly at fault here. She wanted me, and I chased her away. I guess I needed to blame someone other than myself, and Travis was the easiest target.

❧

I watched that messy bun of light brown hair bobble around with every serve Charlie made during our volleyball game. When she was up toward the net, I could see the reflection of sun and sand in her aviator glasses. The mirrored lenses prevented me from seeing her eyes, though. I couldn't decipher if she was looking at me or not.

My eyes were on her the entire time. I hoped the dark lenses in my own glasses hid that fact.

I missed their game point because I was caught up in watching her. Cam struck his hand on the back of my head when I missed what would have been an easy spike from my height and position at that moment. "Ow! Sorry, man." I rubbed the back of my head but didn't remove my line of sight away from Charlie—that was until Travis ran toward her and lifted her in a bear hug around her naked waist.

"If you stopped watching my sister and watched the ball, we would have won that game." His sunglasses didn't hide the fact that he was annoyed with me.

"I'm going to grab a water before the next game. It's still two out of three, Cam. Simmer down." The outcome of the game was meaningless to me, which probably only made my old friend more frustrated.

"I'm going for a swim before the next game to cool off." If we weren't on the beach, he would have stomped away. Instead sand just kicked up behind him as he plodded away. He really didn't like to lose. Even worse, he really didn't like to lose to a girl...especially his sister. The two of them are a great team, but they are fiercely competitive when playing against each other.

I reached the blanket where our cooler was and opened the lid. The sound of additional footsteps sifted behind me, prompting me to turn around.

"I'm going to run after Cam and dunk him in the ocean.

Either of you want to join me?" Charlie stood tall and proud next to Travis and me displaying a happy grin on her face.

"Nah. I think I'm going to sit awhile. You go ahead." Of course, Travis responded. I didn't speak. I wasn't about to watch her bikini get wet and barely cling to her skin.

I did watch her run toward the coastline though as I sat down on the blanket with a bottle of water in my hand.

"You know, even though I'm not her boyfriend, it doesn't mean there won't be someone else that will want to be."

I turned toward the man I considered my adversary but remained silent. He knew he was going to aggravate me, so now I felt like I needed to intimidate him. But he didn't budge. In fact, he sat next to me.

"We might as well get out in the open the reason we don't like each other." He sure was full of himself. He leaned back on his arms and crossed his legs out in front of him.

I tossed a brief look at him sitting next to me and then resumed my attention toward the ocean. I watched Charlie and Cameron splashing each other and although I couldn't hear her laugh from where I was sitting, I could see that she was.

"Okay, I'll go first." His deep voice pulled me from the trance Charlie always seemed to put me under. I remained steadfast in my silence, but returned my glare in his direction. I figured I would hear what he was going to say, and if I didn't like it, I'd punch him. "I don't like you because you're the asshole that broke her heart. She's my friend, and you hurt her." Although I couldn't see his eyes through his sunglasses, I was pretty sure his eyes were imagining tearing me limb from limb. "So why don't you like me?"

Was he serious? I thought it was pretty obvious that I despised the closeness of his relationship with Charlie. I also didn't like the fact that he was able to show off his shoulders and chest, and I was forced to cover up with a shirt due to the burns to my back.

I was proud of how mature I was. I was respectful while he spoke. I faced him and listened, and now I was done with that. So I pulled my eyes away from him and back to Charlie and Cam while I continued to sit in silence.

"I'm not interested in her in that way, you know." *Why was he still talking?* "But there will be someone that is someday." That thought caused me to flinch. I couldn't think about her being with anyone else. "If I had another chance to be with the woman I love, I wouldn't be sulking on a beach blanket next to some dude I barely know."

His comment got a chuckle out of me, and I finally spoke. "Another chance to be with the woman I love? What? Did your last girlfriend dump your ass?" He deserved to be dumped as far as I was concerned.

Travis stood and brushed off sand from his legs. "Nah. It wasn't like that. She died in a car accident." He peered down at me from his standing position. "Life is short, man. I know you want to be with her. I'm new to this circle, and I can see how you feel about her from a mile away. Just tell her you love her. Tell her you want to be with her. Appreciate every day you have with her, Louis. Being in my shoes really sucks."

I was relieved he walked away then so I could pull out the foot I had shoved in my mouth. That was some heavy stuff. He was right about so many things. I barely knew the guy, and I had been a total asshole to him. I had no idea what he had been through. I just knew I didn't like him being around Charlie. I wasn't sure how exactly to make things better, but maybe being friends was a good place to start. I figured it was time to splash in the ocean.

After some swimming in the ocean, another game of volleyball, and lunch at a restaurant on the boardwalk, we headed back to our town. We sat in our respective places. Travis and Charlie sat up front, while Cam and I sat in the back seat.

I was confident today helped all of us to move forward. I felt more relaxed than I had in weeks. Of course, that was because of Charlie. She always provided me with a calming presence. When she turned toward the back seat, I was hoping she was about to say something just for me.

"Cam, Claudette is going to be in town in a few days. Can you go out to dinner on Tuesday night?" My hope for a talk between just the two of us blew away since she obviously only had family business to discuss.

I turned toward my friend, and I swear I saw him roll his eyes. I knew that Claudette wasn't his favorite sister, but at least he had siblings. "I don't know, Lean Bean. She usually just ignores me." It was true. Claudette did ignore Cam when Charlie was with them.

"Oh, come on, Cam." She shifted in her seat and lifted her sunglasses from their place perched on her adorable nose to the top of her head, revealing her amazing gray eyes. "I'll invite Alexis."

"That's not fair, and you know it."

Charlie snickered at his comment.

"Then maybe you can be ignored by more than one woman." Then a sweet rumble of laughter from her echoed within the confines of the car. "Louis, you should come, too. I'm sure my sister would love to see you again."

"Sure, I'll go," I replied rather quickly. Even though I had a grueling twenty-four-hour Monday shift upon me tomorrow, I would happily rush back after work on Tuesday to be with them again. Any time I got to spend with Charlie was time I'd gladly accept.

"Fine. Then I'll go, too." Cam sounded reluctant, but we both knew he was going to give in. He never said no to his twin. "Travis, how about you? You want to go with the rest of us to dinner?"

Charlie turned toward the driver's seat then. "That's a great idea. Claudette would love to meet you."

"Sounds like fun. You can count me in." I guess I was going to need to get used to that guy. It seemed Charlie and Cam like him.

After another twenty minutes, Travis dropped Charlie off at her apartment. Each of the three of us offered to walk her to the door, but Cam insisted that he needed to speak to her about something privately, so Travis and I backed down.

The silence was slightly uncomfortable as Travis and I sat in the car alone while the twins walked up to Charlie's apartment. "I'm really sorry I've been acting like such an asshole." I couldn't bring myself to look in his direction. So I stared out the window. "You haven't done anything wrong, and I've been a jerk to you. You have every reason to dislike me. Cam and Charlie think of you as a friend, so I should do the same. I'm ashamed of how I acted earlier."

"Okay." He didn't say anything else. We sat the rest of the time in the car waiting for Cam to return in silence. But even with the silence, I hoped that Travis and I could move beyond this standoff we had with each other. Hopefully my apology was the olive branch needed to insert myself into the new circle my friends had created.

23

CHARLIE

I worked Monday night and slept most of the day on Tuesday, but I woke up in enough time to get ready for my dinner with my siblings and favorite people. I don't know how many outfits I tried on before I decided on khaki-colored capris with a lavender linen sleeveless shirt. I matched the ensemble with some strappy sandals and left my brown waves of hair loose around my shoulders. After applying a coat of shimmery lip gloss, I gave myself one last look in my full-length mirror before grabbing my purse and running out the door.

Travis had texted me that he was driving Cam and Louis and asked if he could pick me up, too. I gently refused, knowing I needed more time to get ready than they did, and I didn't want to keep them waiting. Alexis and Claudette were meeting us at the restaurant, each driving themselves. I hadn't really spoken with Alexis about the situation with my brother, but she must be warming up to the idea since she agreed to come to dinner without any coaxing needed on my part.

The guys pulled into the parking lot at nearly the same time as I did, so we walked in together. Alexis was sitting in the lobby. We exchanged pleasant hellos and the hostess guided us to a six-top table in the middle of the dining room. I followed Cam, and Louis followed behind me to fill the three seats on one side of the table. Then Alexis sat across from Cam and Travis sat next to her, across from me. As I looked to the right at my brother and the left to Louis, I was reminded about how natural that seating arrangement was for us.

During our classes in school, we were seated in alphabetical order. The three of us always sat in this order either next to each other or behind one another depending on the room arrangement. I was always sandwiched between those two boys. And now I was sandwiched between these two men. It still felt the same. I felt secure and protected with these two guys by my side.

Cameron and Alexis began a conversation, which left Travis, Louis, and I to strike up our own discussion. When my brother wanted to speak to me privately the day we returned from the beach, he explained how he strategically mentioned to Louis that I had a new beau. He didn't say the new guy in my life was Travis, but Louis made that assumption. He said he was trying to help, but he was worried he may have caused unnecessary hostility to develop between the two of them. Right now, they seemed to at least be pretending to get along for my benefit, so I wouldn't look that gift horse in the mouth.

Just as we were deep in meaningless conversation about the weather and the new traffic travel pattern due to the construction of a new bypass highway, Claudette flew in like a cyclone of blond hair. Even in the whirlwind state, she was still impeccably dressed. She wore a flowing sundress and high heels on her feet. Her makeup was perfect even though she arrived in such a fury. "I'm so sorry for being late," she said near breathlessly.

She hugged me and then kissed Cam on the cheek. "Hey, Claude," our brother managed to stammer.

Louis stood to hug her, and she kissed his cheek, too. "It's good to see you again, Claude." The boys have always called her Claude, although she always told them she hated it. She didn't mention that now, though.

She made her way to the other side of the table and held out her hand to Alexis. "Hi, I'm Claudette."

"Alexis." She pumped her hand once without standing up from her chair. They nodded to each other and my sister turned toward Travis.

Louis had returned to his seat, but Travis was standing when Claudette reached for his hand. "Hi, Claudette, I'm Travis." But rather than shake her hand as Alexis had done, he grabbed her hand and brought it to his face to plant a soft kiss on the dorsum side.

Claudette blushed as I watched with my mouth gaping open. If I hadn't known better, I would have thought I had seen stars in his eyes. I don't know if I had ever seen Travis look at a woman with such awe before. I guess Claudette was his type. He mentioned his taste in pretty, blonde, very feminine, sweet-smelling, fake smile wearing, stylish woman that resembled my sister. He pulled out her chair for her and after she sat and he pushed the seat in for her, he sat next to her. The two of them began a dialogue, which left just Louis and me to ourselves.

Fortunately, the waitress appeared to take our drink order, and then I was able to be engrossed in looking at my menu. Once the waitress returned with our drinks and took our meal orders, I was left to sit in silence or speak to Louis. The other two couples didn't seem to have any problem with discussion over everything and anything. Yet Louis and

I sat in uncomfortable silence, as if we didn't know each other.

I kindly excused myself from the table to visit the ladies' room. I didn't really need to go, but I needed a break away from sitting next to the man who still owned my heart, but that I couldn't have. After looking at myself in the mirror and reapplying my lip gloss, I pushed open the door to go back to my seat. At least if our food arrived soon, I could fill my mouth with my meal, and not have to talk.

As I released the swinging door behind me, I noticed Louis standing in front of me in the corridor to the restrooms. If he had been walking to the men's room, it would have made sense to run into him in this hallway, but he just stood in the wake of women rushing in and out of the ladies' room.

"Charlie…" The whispered sound of my name on his lips caused a warm feeling deep within my belly.

"What are you doing standing outside the ladies' room?" My hopeful hitch betrayed my desired nonchalant front.

"I wanted to talk with you." He didn't approach me. He continued to stand several feet away, but his desperate eyes lured me toward him.

"Of course. What's up?"

"I apologize if I've made tonight uncomfortable for you. That was not my intention. I've missed you all, and I want to be able to spend time with you and Cam again. However, if that's not something that works for you, let me know, and I'll back off. I swear. I want to be a part of your life, but I don't want to invade your life."

"A lot of stuff has happened between us, Louis." Despair crossed his facial expression as his blond brows slanted down to a frown. "But you'll always be my friend. No matter what." And just like that, relief washed over his face as a smile eased through the mask of his uncertainty. "You'll always be the boy I grew up with. You've been someone Cam and I could always count on, and I want to always be there for you, too." There was so much more I wanted to say, but my heart couldn't provide any translation to my brain.

"So do you think maybe we could go back to the table and talk to each other like things aren't terribly awkward between us?" His eyes searched mine for an answer.

I didn't know how to respond with words, so I merely took two steps toward him and circled my arms around his waist for a hug. He reciprocated by placing his arms around my shoulders and gently traced vertical lines up and down my back with the pads of his fingers.

I pressed the side of my face against his chest and inhaled his scent. I had missed him so much. I missed not just seeing him. I missed his arms around me.

I loved being wrapped up in the cocoon of each other's arms so much, I wasn't ready to let go yet. We definitely held each other longer than was necessary or appropriate, but knowing that the others at our table would suspect something if we didn't return soon, I finally broke our embrace.

"We should get back to the table." I tried to sound sensible, but his silly grin made it difficult. He actually looked… well, happy. I had almost forgotten what happy looked like on him.

"So are we okay?" The hopeful hitch in his tone was affirmed as his brilliant aqua eyes lowered and his smile widened.

"We'll always be okay." Then I slapped him on the shoulder, just like I used to do when we were kids.

We managed to return to our seats at the table and sit next to each other during an entire meal and exchanged conversation like the old friends we were. Travis drove Louis home since Alexis and Cam decided to go out for ice cream after dinner. I would have driven Louis home, but I didn't want to overstep the boundaries that still seemed to be a blur in the sand. I wasn't sure what our friendship would look like once it was reestablished.

It was nine o'clock, and I knew I was only in my early twenties, but lounging on my couch in front of the television in my pajamas sounded so good at that moment. I was nowhere near being tired since I practically slept all day, but I certainly didn't feel like having a night on the town, either. I would contently settle for Netflix and a cup of hot chocolate. Grabbing a blanket from my linen closet, I sat on my comfy couch with the remote in my hand and my hot cocoa steaming in a mug sitting on my end table.

But just as I selected a recently released rom-com movie, I heard a click at my door, and I watched the deadbolt shift its position. My heart rate accelerated as the knob turned and my door opened. *Please let it be my brother. Please let it be my brother.* I said in a silent plea. A tall man entered my door, but he wasn't my twin.

The adrenaline coursing through my veins turned my breathing erratic, and I couldn't seem to swallow the lump in my throat to find my voice. I sat paralyzed on my couch as a breathtaking blond man with amazing cobalt-colored eyes and a tense, hard body approached me. My heart was racing, not just from being scared half to death, but from Louis abruptly stepping into my living room with his brow wrinkled and a determined stride.

"Charlie…"

And then that same feeling overtook my senses. Happiness tugged at my heartstrings, yet caution and worry plummeted into my gut. The last time he was in my apartment, we had made love for the first time. It was over quickly and left my heart shattered, but I still felt a warmth between my legs remembering how it felt for our bodies to meld together.

"What are you doing here Louis?" I knew my voice came out as barely a whisper because my throat continued to be parched so my voice was barely audible.

His tall, lean body swaggered as he approached me on the couch. With a sudden jerk, he stretched his long arms toward me, grabbing my hands with his own, and heaved me up into a standing position. His blue eyes beckoned quietly until his gaze captured me. The intense connection between us crackled in the air.

His churning eyes never left mine, but his hands cupped my face. I subconsciously parted my lips from the smoldering heat spreading throughout my body and the anticipation of an electrifying kiss. When his lips crashed into mine, all the feelings I had tried to cage flew out of me and surrounded us. We kissed each other as if the famine had broken out and our hunger would be cured by devouring each other in passionate kisses.

His tongue was warm and inviting and he efficiently explored the cavern within my mouth. Until he pushed me away, breathlessly causing my heart to plummet into my stomach. My dazed senses turned my legs wobbly and my brain clouded. *What was happening?* I questioned him with only my eyes as my voice had taken refuge deep in my throat and could not be found at that moment.

"I had a whole speech prepared before I drove over here, but once I got here, all I wanted to do was kiss you." His hands had dropped to his sides but now reached up to twirl my loose curls around his fingers. "I can't even remember everything I wanted to say."

I cleared my throat in an effort to conjure up my ability to speak. "Tell me whatever you remember. I promise to listen to whatever you want to say." I had dreamed of the moment that Louis Coleman strutted into my apartment and grabbed me off this couch to profess his undying love for me and tell me how much he missed me while showering me with ardent kisses. I wanted to hear the speech.

He motioned for me to sit on the couch, and he sat next to me, sinking our weight deep into the soft cushions. "I want you to be more than my friend. I want you to be my girlfriend or whatever title you want to call it. I just want to be yours and know you only belong to me. But I still want us to be friends too, though. I know I messed things up last time." A soft tinkle of a laugh escaped my lips as they turned up in delight. "We'll always be friends first, but I don't want any rules. Our relationship can develop into anything we want. I'm totally okay with that. Somehow we did things too slow last time and then fast-forwarded too forcefully. This time, if you give me a chance, I promise to let our relationship progress like it should. We'll go out on dates, and hold hands, and kiss each other. And we can let everyone know we're together. I want the whole world to know that I'm the luckiest man on this continent because you chose to be with me. Please give me a chance to do this the right way." His pleading eyes made my heart swell right before reality slammed into my chest.

"What about the 'L' word? That always seems to terminate our relationship." Tears were stinging the front of my eyes threatening to spill out. I should have happily jumped up and down at the chance Louis was willing to give us, but we still needed to talk about that difficult topic.

His large, strong hands covered my tiny ones and soft light illuminated the depths of his blue eyes, causing a flutter to develop within my stomach. "Charlene Callahan, I've loved you my whole life. No matter what kind of relationship we have, that will never change."

"So if I tell you I love you again, you won't run away?" I felt myself bite my lower lip in anticipation of his response.

"There is no more running away for me. I'm here, with you, as long as you want me to be."

I glanced down at our hands joined together. He broke one of his hands free and placed it under my chin, urging me to look up at him. Several moments ticked by as his cobalt gaze held me captive, forcing me to stare at the man I knew I couldn't live without.

"Well, kick your shoes off and get comfortable. I was just getting ready to watch a good old-fashioned chick flick." I turned away to grab the remote and my blanket while stretching my legs out over his lap.

He took my advice and kicked his shoes off, but then he wedged himself alongside me between my body and the back cushions of the couch. I slid over to accommodate space for him. Then he wrapped his arm around me while I nestled my back up against his chest. It felt natural and wonderful, and warm, and right. Satisfaction pulled a smile from my lips because I sensed Louis was home for good.

24

LOUIS

We fell asleep on that couch again. I didn't feel one bit sleepy when I settled in next to her, but I had no choice except to succumb to my physical and emotional exhaustion before the movie was halfway over. Snuggled up against the warmth of her body was better than any sleeping pill I could have taken. I felt slightly smashed in the tight space, but having her next to me was all I wanted. I did worry that she may not be very comfortable since she shifted her weight several times during sleep.

I slid my hand between our bodies and into the front pocket of my jeans to pull out my cell phone. Just after midnight. She should probably get into her bed. I raked my fingers through her hair to expose her ear. "Hey, sweetheart," I whispered along her lobe.

"Hmmm?" She tried to turn toward me, but almost flipped herself off the couch in the process. I maintained a firm grip around her waist. I wouldn't have let her fall. "Am I dreaming?"

I brushed my lips across hers in her sleepy state. "You aren't dreaming. This is you and me now." I grazed my fingers across her face and watched her eyelashes flutter as she tried to hold her eyes open. "Let me help you get to bed. It'll be more comfortable."

She only nodded in response to my request and sleepily sat up while shoving her feet along the floor beneath her and shuffling them forward toward her bedroom. I followed behind her and watched her climb up into her bed and disappear beneath the covers.

She was facing away from me, so I kissed the back of her head, and turned to walk away. "Aren't you going to stay?" she said while still looking at the wall.

I reapproached the bed. "I can if you want."

She flipped over toward me, still wearing half hooded eyes. "Of course I want you to. Now get in here with me."

She didn't need to tell me twice. I shucked off my jeans and pulled my shirt off over my head. I slid underneath the covers and snuggled up against the warmth of her body. It only felt like a few moments before a peaceful slumber pulled me under its spell.

The next time I woke up, daylight streamed into her room. Her brown hair lay in tumbling waves on her pillow, and her breathing was quiet and rhythmic. I examined every one of her movements, taking in the image of Charlie asleep next to me. I wanted to wake up next to her every day from now on. We've been friends for nearly twenty years. Now we're in love and we're together. I know I said I was going to do things right this time, but I wanted to share not just a bed together. I wanted to share a life together. Hopefully she'd be okay with my staying with her the next couple of days until I needed to go back to work on Friday. I had an overnight bag in my car, having planned to maybe stay at my mom's house or Cam's apartment last night after dinner, but I would probably need more clothes if I stayed until Friday. I guess I'd have to go shopping again.

I had already texted my cousin that I wasn't going to be working any landscaping jobs this week. He had been so great about everything. When I needed to work to get my mind off things, he'd let me work hard. But when I needed a break and time to myself, he'd let me have that, too. Maybe I wasn't blessed in the parent department, but I had at least one family member who I could always count on. And of course, there were the people who weren't related by blood, but they were called family just the same.

Cam had always been like a brother to me. I couldn't believe I stayed away from him for five years. Fortunately, he'd let me back into his life like only a brother would. And then there was Charlie. My feelings for her just couldn't be described sufficiently. I loved her like family, and I loved her unconditionally with all my heart and soul. I know now, without a doubt in my mind, that I absolutely could not live without her. I couldn't stay away from her ever again. I needed to be near her—to touch her and hold her. I had to be able to smell and taste her. I essentially needed her just as much as I needed oxygen to breathe. My world had been so dark until she had brought light to it again. Then, when things turned dark again, I sought refuge in her light. I dove deep into her warmth and sunshine, but I felt a heaviness of guilt in doing so.

When she told me she loved me, I was so consumed by the darkness surrounding me that I refused to believe that I deserved her shining light. I was worried I had used her, and that I would only drag her down in the end rather than what was really true...that she had lifted me up. She made me want to see the light. She made me want to dig out of the hole, come up for air, and see the sun again. And as she lay next to me in her super comfortable bed, I knew I wanted that kind of happiness. There was no other way for me to go forward in life. I no longer had room for resentment, shame, and disappointment. I only had a place for her and the joy she brought me.

She began to stir, and one of her eyes popped open. "Are you watching me sleep?"

Busted. I was still lying down next to her with my elbow propped beneath me, facing her direction. She pulled the covers over her head, but I pulled them back down quickly so I could continue to see her face. Her gray eyes gradually opened fully and brightly gleamed at me, and that intense gaze caused a tightening in my chest.

I gave her a light and flirty smile and she seemed to relax slightly. When I brushed my lips against hers in the lightest of a kiss, I felt her loosen up at my touch. "Good morning, sweetheart."

"Is this really Louis Coleman using the word sweetheart as a term of endearment toward me?" An adorable blush spread through her cheeks which brought my mouth into a half smile.

"Would you rather I call you by another name? Because I think sweetheart fits you perfectly." I leaned over and smacked a quick kiss on her lips again. "You taste as sweet as honey, and you're my heart." Intertwining her fingers with mine, I pulled her hand toward me and placed it on the left upper part of my chest. "I ignored it for much too long. My heart was empty and hollow without you in my life. Now with you back in my life, the heaviness of my heartache has lifted and my heart thunders full of life."

With her fingers pressing harder against my chest, and her eyelashes fluttering, she looked sleepy and sexy. I combed my fingers through her hair and drew her head to me. Her arms wrapped around my neck, bringing our faces only a breath apart. So I reflexively grabbed her firmly around the waist and pulled the rest of her body flush against mine. Then I silenced her whispered gasp as I crashed my lips to her mouth in a hot, sensual kiss.

Her lips parted slightly, inviting my tongue to dance with hers. I wanted to drink every bit of her. Her fingertips skidded along my shirtless back, and I couldn't help but trace my fingers along her bare legs. I had promised myself that I wouldn't move fast, but here I was with no desire to stop until I was embedded in her warmth again.

Dredging up all the strength I could muster, I pulled away from our explosion of feelings and the dancing of our tongues. "What do you want to do today?" I let out near breathlessly.

Charlie let out a soft chuckle. "I thought it was obvious. I like what we're doing right now." Her Cheshire smile caused my boxers to feel suddenly very constricting.

"I'm taking you out on a real date. As your boyfriend, that's what should happen, right?" I was determined to show her how much she meant to me. I wanted a real relationship with her.

Her head flinched back slightly and her steel-gray eyes grew distant. "A date?"

"Yes. A date. That's what boyfriends and girlfriends do, right?"

She released another feminine giggle. That sweet sound of her happiness echoed through to my soul. "You don't have to take me out and win me over. You have me." I leaned into her delicate hand as she caressed the outline of my bristly jaw. "I love you, Louis. I'll go anywhere, anytime with you. We don't have to call it 'dates.' I just want to spend time with you."

Well damn. I wasn't sure how I could possibly deserve this. "Okay. Then let's go out and spend time together." My mind raced with ideas. "Breakfast? A run? A trip to the beach? Paddle boarding? Kayaking? Biking? Fishing?"

"That's going to be a full day." Her lips curled up and revealed her perfect white teeth in the most cunning of smiles.

"I just mean, we could do whatever you want." The thought was interrupted when a very non-sexy rumble emitted from my stomach. "Although breakfast is probably a top priority for me."

"Then let's go to breakfast." After a quick kiss on my lips, she pulled back the covers and left her comfortable bed and walked toward the bathroom. I had to remind myself that I wanted to do things right because having her leave the warmth of her bed was torture. I could ignore my grumbling belly and stay curled up in bed with her all day if she let me.

We each showered separately and changed before going to breakfast. We held hands and slid into the same side of the booth at the Pancake Cabin. We talked and ate like old times, but I could feel the new layer of our relationship that had developed.

"So what changed your mind about us?" Charlie asked very nonchalantly in between bites of her pancakes.

I was a little taken aback by her question. I guess I wasn't really prepared for her to ask me outright. "A friend told me I needed to stop acting like a jackass and tell you how I feel."

She coughed and nearly sputtered out tiny pieces of pancake from her mouth. "Who? Cameron?"

"No. It was Travis." I couldn't believe I even admitted that out loud. I was slightly surprised how I not only admitted I considered him my friend, but that he also had given me the single best piece of advice I had ever received in my twenty-three years of life.

"I wouldn't have seen that coming from him." She put her fork down and turned toward me, even though I was seated right up next to her in the cozy booth. "I was pretty sure he didn't like you." Gliding her hand across the vinyl of the bench, she found mine and gave it a gentle squeeze. "I didn't exactly paint a pretty picture of you to him. In fact, I probably made it seem like you were kind of a jackass."

I located her other hand so that I was holding both of her soft hands in mine, and I gently kissed her on her forehead, admiring her angelic face. "It's okay. I was a jackass. I hope that someday you can manage to forgive me for hurting you like I did. And I promise if you let me, I'll spend every day showing you how much I love you."

A pink glow illuminated her cheeks before she turned away. I embarrassed her. It was pretty thrilling to see. The girl I grew up with didn't embarrass easily. She was bold and strong, and stood by her convictions. She could be absolutely intimidating if she wanted to be. Seeing her vulnerable side was something I hadn't expected or even knew I wanted. There was still so much to learn about her, and I was going to enjoy every minute of it.

25

CHARLIE

We sat on my couch watching nothing in particular after returning from a bike ride at the beach. Today had been so wonderful, I truly didn't believe I could be any happier. We ate breakfast at my favorite place. We drove to the beach talking about everything and anything like we used to, all while holding hands. Louis occasionally glanced over at me and smiled while he drove. I love that I am, at least part of, the reason he is so happy.

We parked at the visitor center and took our bikes for a ten-mile ride. We rode along the coastline so the breeze kept us protected from the typical scorching August day. We rode side by side so we could continue our easy conversation. I knew at that point that he was meant to always be by my side. No wonder I had missed his presence next to me during my solitary runs. Once I had him at my side, there was a large void when he was no longer there.

We decided to go back to my apartment after our ride to change before heading out to enjoy our day together, but somehow we made it as far as the couch where we both collapsed from exhaustion. Since I wasn't going to work

230

again until tomorrow night, I was happy to spend every second with him next to me. There was knocking at my door while we lay next to each other on the sofa.

Since Louis was lying behind me, I figured it was easier for me to get up and see who was knocking. I stood on tiptoe to peer out the peephole and discovered the only other man that knew my heart better than I did. "It's Cam." I opened the door while Louis fumbled to straighten into a seated position. I hadn't shared with him that I had already texted my brother about the change in our relationship.

"You have a key, you know." I swatted at my twin as he entered my apartment.

"No way. I won't be opening this door without warning now." Cam shook his head and stepped toward the couch where Louis was wearing a perplexed expression. I followed behind my brother and stood next to where Louis was still seated.

"I told him." Louis leered at me, seeking an answer to a question he only asked with his eyes. "I told him about us... that you and I are in a relationship." Confusion continued to crease his brow even after my attempt at explanation.

"And how does he feel about that?" Although Louis responded to my comment, he looked in Cam's direction, while raising to a standing position.

"Are you kidding me?" Cam's smile broadened in approval and the lines across his forehead raised with excitement. "My best friend and my sister? It's about time!" He fist-bumped Louis and then turned to give me a quick hug.

Louis let out an exaggerated sigh of relief. "I should have told you." His guilt-reddened face reminded me of a little boy caught with his hand in the cookie jar before dinner.

"Tell me? I knew even when you didn't admit it to yourself." Cam snickered. "I knew before you admitted it out loud five years ago. And although I feel bad that you both went through the stuff you did, I'm glad that you didn't let it stand in your way. I couldn't be happier that you ended up finding your way back to each other. You two are truly meant to be together."

"That was really deep coming from you, Cam." I inched toward Louis and wrapped my arms around his waist.

A deep, gruff sound surfaced from my brother as he cleared his throat. "But I don't want to see all the PDA…and I don't want to hear about it, either."

Louis kissed the top of my head. "We aren't going to put rules on our relationship again. So if I feel like kissing my girlfriend, and you happen to be around, then you will just have to ignore us if you don't want to see it."

The sight of Cam cringing made me laugh. I knew he was happy for us. The fact that he was giving us a hard time with the PDA was proof of that. He had seen me kiss boyfriends before and never seemed to care. He only teased us because he likes us being together. He approves of our relationship. I know he was secretly always cheering for the Charlie-Louis connection from the sidelines, and for some undetermined reason, he has become quite a softie when it comes to romance.

"So I guess Louis will be going with me tomorrow night for the coffee run?" Cam examined me as if I already knew the response to his question.

"I guess that means Alexis is working with me?" I raised an eyebrow, questioning my brother's motivation.

"That's a good assumption." His matter-of-fact tone caused me to shake my head in denial.

"I wasn't sure I'd ever see the day that my brother would look for a serious relationship with a girl."

Louis and I exchanged laughs, and my brother didn't flinch at my implication. "Oh, grow up, you two."

"I'm just surprised that *you* grew up." I grabbed ahold of

my brother and pulled him into the embrace I still held with Louis, so I could hug my two best friends. My brother had always been more than a sibling. He was my best friend. And Louis had always been more than a friend. He was the man who owned my heart. Now, here in my small living room, I had both larger-than-life men next to me. I couldn't think of anywhere else I would rather be at that moment.

We'd picked up Chinese food on our way back to my apartment after canoeing in the lake. Cameron and Alexis joined us. I definitely approved of their relationship. I hadn't ever seen Alexis smile so much. I knew it was my brother who did that for her. I loved my brother no matter what, but saying that I was delighted that he finally found a girl of substance to date was an understatement.

The fact that I could even have a conversation with a girl my brother was dating was quite an accomplishment as far as I was concerned. Alexis was smart, and I obviously had a lot in common with her, given that we worked together. She was quiet and humble, and pretty in a subtle way. I was thrilled to see someone like her with Cam.

She also wasn't afraid to get her hands dirty. But given that she was an ER nurse, that really wasn't a surprise. We paddled around the lake in the canoe as a foursome. The boys splashed at each other, and soon, Alexis and I joined in. Her hair became a soggy mess, but she didn't seem to care. I remembered the comment my brother made not so long ago. *You don't care if you mess up your hair or get dirt under your fingernails. You are every guy's dream.* I was certainly happy that he was able to find his dream girl. I didn't know how long their relationship would last, but I hoped it existed for a while. Alexis was the first girl who I could really see myself having as a close girlfriend. It had always been easier for me to develop friendships with boys than girls because I always seemed to have more common interests with men than women. But Alexis was so much like me, I could see why my brother got along with her so well. After all, he and I had been best friends since the womb.

Feeling quietly contented, Louis and I sat at my small table in my small kitchen and ate sesame chicken and egg rolls. All my surroundings felt small with Louis's larger-than-life presence in it. Small wasn't the right word, I guess. Cozy would be a better description. My apartment felt like home with him sitting at the kitchen table sharing a meal or stretched out on the couch watching television. Everything just felt comfy and right with him near me. With these comforting thoughts anchoring in my head, I found myself ridiculously grinning while sitting with Louis.

"What? Do I have something in my teeth?" He was obviously confused by my goofy smile. He didn't have anything stuck in his teeth. He was perfect, and he was mine.

"I'm just happy to be with you." My senses became overwrought as my feelings bubbled to the surface. I had been having these crazy feelings all day. It was surreal, yet wonderful, and overwhelming all at the same time. Joyful tears pricked at my eyes as I soaked up the intense elation overfilling my heart.

"Sweetheart, are you okay?" Evidently, Louis didn't recognize my tears as happy ones. His tenderness was so endearing. I have never felt so loved and cared for by anyone. He has always looked after me, but things between us were at such a different level now, I thought my chest would explode if I kept my emotions shoved down inside much longer.

I pushed my chair out from the table, and I approached his side, determined to show him that everything was okay. Everything was more than okay. Standing next to him, I leaned in and grabbed his face, bringing my lips to his for a brief kiss. He pushed himself away from the table but remained sitting and pulled me into his lap.

His compelling, cobalt eyes glazed with animated emotion. I brought my mouth to his again and caressed him softly with my lips. That only lasted a few moments because my lustful state intensified. While I nibbled on his lower lip, he obliged me by partially opening his mouth for me to explore. I snaked my arms around his neck to pull him closer.

Louis lifted me up from his lap as if I weighed nothing and carried me out of the kitchen while I continued to kiss him. He walked the short distance from my kitchen to my bedroom and pushed the door open with his foot. Then he gently placed me down on the bed and even though the beginning of darkness developed outside and there wasn't a light on in my bedroom, the smoldering lust in his eyes was discernable.

"I planned to take things slow this time." Confliction swirled in his heated stare with heartrending tenderness and eager affection. "But my God, I want you."

I pulled at his cotton T-shirt and tugged it up over his head. With his naked torso in front of me, I couldn't help but run my fingers across the hard muscles of his chest and pepper kisses along his pecs. He moaned when I let my tongue graze his nipple.

In response to my initiation of clothing removal, he forcefully ripped my T-shirt from my body when he yanked it over my head and threw it on the floor next to the bed. I slipped my finger along the waistband of his shorts as I felt his growing erection straining against my core. Wanting to free him from his constricting outerwear, I snatched his shorts and boxers and pulled them down simultaneously. He finished removing them from his legs quickly by kicking the garments onto the floor.

His impressive body hovered over me, propped up by the corded muscles of his arms. I broke away from our heated kisses just so I could admire his nakedness. Staring boldly, I raked my eyes over his body. Sure, I had seen him naked that one time right from the shower, and the first time we had sex, but I didn't have the opportunity either of those times to truly appreciate his magnificent body. Once he reached for the button on my denim shorts, I arched toward him as a warmth spread throughout my body and a moistness developed between my legs.

He pushed my shorts down and then it was his turn to stare at me. I watched as his gaze dropped from my eyes to my neck, to my breasts. I was thankful I opted for the matching lacy, lavender bra and panty set today, rather than the often mismatched undergarment choices I usually made. He continued to scan my body critically, but beamed with approval.

"You weren't wearing any more than this on that day at the beach," he said in a sultry voice. "You drove me crazy then, and you're driving me crazy now." His breathing became erratic, and I felt my own breathing increase while we continued to explore each other with our mouths and hands.

"That orange bikini is one of my favorites," I said, nearly breathlessly. "I was hoping you'd like it, too."

"Oh, you knew I'd like it. Seeing you in that bikini gave me a hard-on, which is the reason I couldn't even look in your direction during that volleyball game. No wonder Cam and I lost."

I let out a small laugh. I liked knowing that I had caused his undoing. Brazenly grabbing ahold of his shaft, I stroked it up and down with my hand. He released a groan and started a trail of kisses along my collarbone and across the top of my breasts.

I wiggled out from beneath him and pushed him down onto his back. Reaching for his silky shaft again, I placed my mouth at the crown and licked the sensitive tip. Louis reached around my back and released the clasp of my bra. I pushed the undergarment out of the way to free my breasts from the restrictive hold of the brassiere.

As I remained hunched over him with his erection again in my mouth, he teased my nipples with the tips of his fingers. Brushing his thumbs over the sensitive buds caused them to pearl and harden at his touch. I began to lose concentration at my task with his teasing strokes of my nipples. I released my hold of his extraordinary shaft and he pulled at my underwear. I shimmied them down my legs and tossed them off. They went airborne, and I wasn't sure where they landed, but I didn't care.

Louis tossed me onto my back and placed my breast into his mouth. I arched toward him and felt moisture intensify between my legs. He parted the sensitive folds between my legs with his fingers and exposed the sensitive nub that he eagerly began to stroke with his thumb. Once he inserted his finger into me, I screamed his name, and he tightened the sucking hold he had on my nipple with his mouth.

I felt myself trembling from the inside, and I knew I needed to have Louis in me at that moment. "I have condoms in my nightstand," I blurted out with my eyes shut tight.

So with the swiftness of a jungle cat, he jumped off me, to my nightstand next to my bed, and then back to me. Tearing the foil wrapper with his teeth, he removed the latex covering and placed it along his full length. He hovered over me while teasing his covered shaft against my opening, I switched positions with him and pushed him onto his back again.

As I straddled him, I guided him into the place I wanted him to be, but as he began to push into me, a quick thrust caused forced entry, but I didn't feel any pain. I was swept up by the ripples of pleasure. The heat and fullness of him completely filled me. We fit each other perfectly. He was the only one for me, and I was the only one for him.

I slid up and down him with increasing speed and friction. He matched my movements with his thrusts until I felt my channel tighten around him. Placing his firm hold on my hips kept him deeply seated inside me. He continued to pound into me at the same time as I was so desperately trying to ride him vigorously. As hot waves began pulsating around him from within me, I inched closer and closer to the ocean ecstasy roaring inside the depths of my soul. With an earsplitting grunt, he let out his release only a moment after my inner core squeezed around him. A white flash of light ignited behind my clenched eyelids, and I fell against his chest after the waves of pleasure brought me back to shore.

Exhausted from our lovemaking, we lay naked in each other's arms with me still collapsed on top of him for several moments. His thudding heartbeat pulsed against my ear resting on his chest as we remained fused together as one. Quiet peacefulness surrounded us, and I finally felt like I was in the right place in my life. I knew what love was now, and I would never want to be anywhere else ever again.

I knew Louis got off work from a twenty-four-hour shift Saturday morning, but I couldn't wait to be with him again. I knew I still needed to wait a little while before seeing him, but I couldn't wait before hearing his voice again, so I punched his number into my phone. I knew he would be home.

"What are you doing?" I asked in an unintentional singsong voice when he answered with a hello.

"I'm packing." A rustling sound bounced around in the background.

"Oh really? To go where?" Maybe he was planning a getaway for us.

"I think I'm moving." I gulped for air. He hadn't mentioned anything about moving. Annapolis was already far enough away from Sandy Cove. I certainly didn't want him any further away.

"Where are you moving?" I barely managed to squeak out.

"Back to Sandy Cove. You see, there's this girl there that I want to see every day, and living all the way here makes that difficult." I pressed my palm to my heart and gasped as relief washed over me. "I hope she lets me stay with her until we can find a bigger place together." His end of the line grew quiet except for a knocking sound. "Hey, Charlie, there's someone at my door. Hang on a second."

I held my breath as he opened the door. "What are you doing here?" I heard him say.

"I couldn't wait to see you again." He pulled the phone away from his ear and grabbed me by the waist to pull me into his apartment.

"This is the best after-work surprise I've ever had." He looked sexy as hell in his firefighter uniform, while I stood before him in my frumpy pajamas. "I hope you're here to cuddle with me under the covers while I catch a nap before going back to my girlfriend's apartment."

"I think I'm dressed for that." I missed his arms around me last night. I hadn't slept much, but I knew the moment I was lying next to him, I would once again enjoy a peaceful slumber. I wanted to sleep next to him every night and wake up in his arms every day for the rest of my life.

He locked the door behind me and pulled me toward his

bedroom. "Get comfortable under the covers, and I'll join you right after I shower."

I simply nodded and smiled. I knew I wouldn't fall asleep until he returned from his shower, but I figured I'd warm up the bed for him.

I stripped off my clothes once he shut the door of the adjoining bathroom, but instead of scooting beneath the covers of his bed as I originally planned, I pulled open the bathroom door. Without hesitation, I slid open the shower curtain and stepped into the steaming spray of water.

Louis offered me an approving grin. "Charlene Callahan, you don't have any clothes on."

We stayed in the shower until the water ran cold and then moved back to the bedroom where we continued our love-making. Once our bodies were depleted of all energy, we let ourselves recuperate with a restful slumber. Before Louis fell asleep, he mumbled how much he loved me while simultaneously wrapping his arms around me. I whispered that I loved him too before closing my own eyes. No longer being afraid of our feelings of love for one another has really allowed us the opportunity to connect with each other on a new level. I guess love was exactly what we both needed all along.

26

EPILOGUE

LOUIS

One year later...

As I reflected on this past year, my heartbeat quickened and a warm sensation formed in my throat. There had definitely been a lot of changes. Charlie was in the shower right now in the townhouse we bought six months ago. I'm not sure how we lived in her tiny apartment together for six months, but we managed somehow. I let the lease on my apartment in Annapolis go September first—only days after we had our first date. I knew I wouldn't live anywhere ever again but with her.

My phone vibrated on my dresser, and I quickly turned it over to see a text from Cam. **Text me when you're headed over.**

Alright, wing nut. But no more texting me. The last thing I needed was Charlie questioning the cryptic messages from her brother.

Thankfully, I still heard her humming in the shower. She does that. She doesn't sing, but merely hums. I find the sound incredibly sexy, which is why more times than not, that sound is a precursor to me stripping down and joining her.

So right now, even as tempted as I was to jump under the hot spray of water with her, I refrained from doing so because I didn't want to be late.

She quickly changed into a sundress and sandals. I told her we were going for a walk on the beach and out to dinner. So we dressed casually. I chose a pair of khaki shorts and a gray golf shirt which I paired with sandals as well. After a quick kiss, we climbed into my car and left our driveway to head to the ocean and sand.

We rode with the air conditioning on, rather than having the windows down. It was an exceptionally hot August day. I hoped the breeze coming from the ocean would cool things off. The last thing I wanted was to have armpit sweat stains during our walk on the beach. Fortunately with the sun descending toward the horizon, the temperature dropped by the time we reached the coast a half-hour drive later.

We left our car and walked hand in hand toward the boardwalk and kicked off our shoes once our feet hit the sand. The sand kicked up behind us and hit our bare legs as we walked along the shoreline. There was still an abundance of people at the beach. It was summertime after all, and the Junebugs don't leave until after Labor Day. There were still umbrellas dug into the sand, towels thrown askew, and people in the water, as well as on the beach. *Maybe this wasn't a good idea.*

I had researched what time sunset would be. I reviewed the weather conditions for precipitation. And I made plans with friends and family. I really wanted this to be perfect, but it definitely wouldn't be private. There would be an audience wide and long with easily hundreds of people. Maybe all of them would be so involved with themselves that they wouldn't pay us any attention.

Charlie and I continued to walk along the beach close to the waterline. The waves were lapping around our feet and receding back toward the ocean. The water was warm. It is usually pretty heated by this time of year. May and June yielded cold ocean water, but August and September gave way to the perfect temperature for swimming in the oceanic waters of the Atlantic.

The sun moved down farther toward the horizon and the sky began to change from the brilliant blue to shades of orange, pink, and purple. The colors painted a perfect picture for this moment for us.

Heart palpitations pounded within my chest, an empty feeling developed in the pit of my stomach, and the muscles of my body quivered. I felt more nervous than I ever had in Charlie's presence. I was usually at ease around her. Being with her had always been natural. She was my childhood friend. I know everything about her, and she knows everything about me. But right now the hand that was holding hers perspired heavily as I thought of what was about to happen. I hope I know her well enough to anticipate she'll be happy about my surprise, but I also know what her rejection feels like unfortunately.

I pushed that horrible memory away during this last year, convincing myself that ultimately we ended up together and she loves me. But I have questioned a time or two if she and I are on the same page about life and our future. I don't know if my heart could withstand being shattered like it did when I was eighteen. *No more negative thoughts, Louis. This is going to be a wonderfully happy occasion.*

I glimpsed over to Charlie. We hadn't spoken a word to each other since walking along the beach, but we don't always have to say anything. We truly just enjoy being together. As I watched her brown hair flying in the breeze, I decided we had walked far enough. We approached an area with very few people, and I decided that brief strip of sand was going to be the place for us.

So I stopped walking and Charlie stood beside me. A glint of wonder shone in her storm-cloud eyes. I pulled her toward me and gently kissed the sensitive skin on the side of her neck while still holding her hand. Realizing I still had my sandals in my other hand, I tossed them into the sand as I kneeled down on one knee.

Charlie tossed her sandals to the side and covered her mouth with a hand, never breaking the grasp I still had on her other hand. I reached into the pocket of my shorts with my free hand trying not to disrupt our magnetic gaze. But of course, I fumbled a little and had to look down to my pocket to retrieve the box wedged in there. That damn velvet box was determined to be as difficult as possible being extricated from the confinement of the lining of my shorts.

She laughed at my blunder, and I relaxed a little. After all, I lived for that laughter of hers. I always have. My favorite is when we laugh together. I'm sure one day we'll both laugh about this, but today is not going to be that day.

I finally managed to free the damn felt box but before I opened it, I kissed the hand of hers that I was still holding and broke our grasp. When I opened the box to face her, she gasped with her hand still covering her mouth. I hoped that was a happy gasp.

"Charlene Callahan. I've loved you for as long as I can remember. I loved you with pigtails catching fireflies, and with a mouthful of braces, and when you hit a grand slam home run in high school playing softball. I love fishing with you and biking with you. I even love running with you. I want to chase sunsets with you and go on adventures with you. You're the most amazing woman I know, and nothing would make me happier than to spend the rest of my life married to you and raising a family with you. You're the reason I know what love is. You're the reason I believe love is good and kind. I didn't know where home was for a long time, but now I know home is wherever you are. Please make me the happiest man alive and agree to be my wife. If you say yes, I promise I'll spend the rest of my days trying to make you as happy as you make me. So will you marry me, please?"

A moment passed as I held out that velvet box containing the solitaire princess cut diamond ring I intended for Charlie to wear. Tears ran down her cheeks. *I hope those are happy tears.* Time seemed to tick by for several long moments before she finally nodded.

"I'm going to need to hear you say the word."

"Yes!" My heart almost exploded from my chest right then. I quickly stood and slipped the ring on her finger. Then I lifted her up, encircling my arms around her waist, and spun her around before letting her down to land on her feet. Clapping broke out, and I turned toward the beach to see onlookers giving us a standing ovation. It felt awkward having a bunch of random Junebugs witness my heartfelt testament of love and proposal.

But I only cared for like half a second. My favorite person agreed to be my wife. Nothing could bring me down from the cloud I was floating on. I figured we might as well give the vacationers a show, so I pulled Charlie in close to me and crashed my lips against hers. Although I refrained from displaying a distasteful open mouth tongue tangling kiss with my fiancée, the kiss still showed passion.

We grabbed our sandals we had thrown along the sand and retreated back to our car. I had dinner reservations after all. We drove to the Solar Sea restaurant along the Coastal Highway and managed to find the last spot available in the parking lot. They were busy. Thank goodness I called for a reservation several days ago.

We walked into the restaurant hand in hand and we were quickly ushered to our table in the back room where we were greeted with a loud shout of "Surprise!" by our closest friends and family. I had managed to text Cam **"On my way"** when Charlie brushed the sand off her legs before she hopped back into the car.

Charlie's eyes sparkled and her light golden skin was glowing with radiance. I had wanted a private proposal, but I wanted to tell everyone immediately afterward. So it made sense to invite everyone out to celebrate with us.

Cam, of course, greeted us first. "I always knew you two would end up together." He clapped me on the back and gave Charlie a quick hug.

"Oh, you did not," she quipped back at him. "You only recently became a gooey romantic since dating Alexis."

Cam shrugged and pulled Alexis from the group walking close by. He smacked a loud kiss on her mouth and she giggled. "Congratulations. We're very happy for you." We thanked Alexis before Cam pulled her away, probably to go make out somewhere. They've been together for nearly a year, much to the dismay of Charlie's female colleagues. There was quite a ruckus when Cameron Callahan was suddenly off the market. I was sure many girls had broken hearts over that announcement. Alexis is a good friend to Charlie, and she fits in with our little circle, so I'm happy Cam found her.

Travis and Claudette moved toward us next. They were part of our circle of friends, too. They had both said their relationship was completely platonic, but I felt like something else may have been developing there. They seemed to complement each other nicely. They both gave their congratulations to us and then advanced toward the seafood buffet the restaurant was famous for. Maybe once Travis was ready to move on, their relationship would evolve into something more, I thought to myself as I watched them walk away together side by side.

The Callahans gave bear hug embraces to both of us. John

and Rita Callahan stood before us as the physician-attorney power couple that raised Claudette and the twins. They were a true testament to a good marriage and family. I want to be just like them when I grow up. John stood the same height as Cam with the same hazel eyes. Rita has the same wavy dirty blond hair Claudette does and the same gray eyes Charlie inherited. They have always been like a second set of parents to me, and my heart is full of gratitude that someday my kids will get to have them as grandparents.

My mom and dad approached us afterward and hugged both Charlie and me. They remain good friends, and I can't say that isn't still weird. But they both seem happy, so I guess that is all that's important.

"I told him when he found someone that was his friend *and* made his heart skip a beat, he should marry her," my dad said and glanced in Charlie's direction. She blushed, and it was adorable.

"I just hope I can make Louis as happy as he makes me Mr. Coleman." She put her arm around my waist, and I felt as big as the world. Even though my parents' marriage didn't last, I had no worry about us. Charlie and I would be together always. Our love is so powerful, it could conquer the world if necessary. I couldn't wait to show her all the ways I would love and cherish her, but I figured it could wait until our engagement party was over. After all, we have forever.

THE END

GRATITUDES

Brian: You are the love of my life. My childhood friend, and my favorite firefighter. Thank you for the support you have given me with all of my ambitious endeavors!

To my beta readers Christy and Tania: Thank you for taking the time to read my ideas as soon as I put the words on paper and solely looking at the story, while overlooking the grammar and spelling errors. You two are the best!

To my sister Anna: Thank you for reading this book even though you had to close your eyes during the sex scenes!

To Robin: Thank you for working with a rookie like me and creating a book cover that was exactly what I was looking for!

To ellie: Thank you for being my editor. You are a gem! I am extremely appreciative that you held my hand when I needed it, and ultimately convinced me that I could really do this.

To Leddy: I owe you everything! Thank you for being my mentor, my sounding board, and my friend. I know you came into my life randomly, but I feel deep in my heart and soul that you were meant to show up and be a big part of my life. You are the reason I can check this off my bucket list. You inspire me every time I put words on paper. I will always be your biggest cheerleader, and I will forever be grateful for you. You truly have made a dream of mine come true.

To my readers: Thank you for taking a chance on me. I have always believed that stories are written for other people to read, so I am extremely grateful to each of you that decided to read this one. I hope you enjoyed it! I really enjoyed writing about the Callahans. I couldn't seem to get Cameron out of my head, so I decided to write down his story also. I hope to release it summer of 2021, so keep an eye out for it!

ABOUT THE AUTHOR

Greenleigh lives on the Eastern Shore of Maryland with her husband and four children. Being an ER nurse for two decades and married to a firefighter, she write stories about what she knows. Coffee and chocolate are everyday must haves in her life, but fishing and relaxing at the beach are her favorite pastimes.

After a pancreatic cancer diagnosis in 2019, Greenleigh began to check things off her bucket list—one of those things being "write a novel." Today she is healthy and continues to write whenever she can, so she can get the stories in her head down on paper. She is inspired by people that chase their dreams and is a firm believer in happily ever afters, so you will find her characters and their stories mirror these ideals.